Green

Keith C. Clark

ISBN: 1493783130
ISBN 13: 9781493783137

Dedicated to my father, Keith Clark

Early morning, the coolest and quietest part of the day, was his favorite time. The dew that blanketed the tee boxes, fairways, and greens had a magical, virginal quality to it. The ground was cushiony, the air clean, the colors of the flower beds crisp, bright, and cheerful.

His friends, still asleep for a few more hours, would never understand this feeling.

A little later in the morning, when the work began, he loved to see the tracks the putts had left in the dew. He appreciated the elegant curves of the perfectly manicured fairways, the subtle nuances of the rises and falls in each green, the graceful arc of a well-struck shot, the skill required to succeed at the game.

As the day wore on, the other guys often privately grumbled, muttering obscenities about the heat, the weight of the bags, and the irritating habits of the members. But invariably, he was happy to be there, in that place, at that time, doing what he was doing. It was so much better than the alternative.

It was green.

Chapter 1

1969

The bus ride always seemed to take forever. It was especially difficult for Wish to grab any sleep, what with the trip between South Norwalk and neighboring Darien, Connecticut, requiring two transfers. As the crow flies, the distance between home and work was just a few miles. In reality, the trip was more difficult.

But it was worth it. The money Aloysius "Wish" Fitzgerald made as a caddie at Wee Burn Country Club was far better than anything he could make in South Norwalk, especially for a seventeen-year-old Negro. Six feet tall, solidly built, handsome, and gregarious, the work was relatively easy for him. His eager nature and reserved charm helped him to achieve his goal—generous tips.

Some of the club members were nice, even asking him about school and his plans for the future. Most of the others pretty much ignored him, which was also fine. But when it came to his customers, Wish had become adept at his job, which earned him excellent tips on a daily basis.

A handful of members even asked for Wish to be on their bag on a regular basis. They knew that the young man would always hand them the right club for the distance and conditions and give them great reads on their putts. Amazingly, Wish could even tell these wealthy, high-powered men something they seldom heard—the word "no." As in, "No, not the seven. Won't get you there. With this wind, I'm giving you the six iron."

Sometimes there was even the briefest tug-of-war between caddie and member. Wish almost always won, and the member got his money's worth.

It was like Pete, the caddie master, often advised his charges: "This is a service business, boys. You wanna make more money? Serve!"

"You're late, son. We tee off in ten minutes, and now you haven't left enough time to warm up."

"Yes, sir. Sorry," Jackson responded.

"We've talked about this before. If you don't approach this game properly, you'll have no chance of winning the junior championship," his father admonished. "None."

Bingo. Jackson kept a stone face. *I have absolutely no chance, even if you hound me about it for the entire summer.*

"Well, go get your shoes on and meet us on the tee. And even if you haven't warmed up, that's no excuse. Just try not to disappoint me, son. I keep telling you to believe in your ability. Let's see some of it!"

Seventeen-year-old Jackson Spears, a chubby five-foot, two-inches tall and hunched over as if perpetually hiding from the world, traipsed off in the direction of the men's locker room at Wee Burn Country Club.

"Posture, Jackson, posture," the elder Spears commanded. A tall, balding fifty-year-old with the cocky air of the über-successful, Yale-educated executive he was, Howard Spears frowned after his only child. Who knew? If it hadn't been for the damn knee injuries that ended his career as an all-star college tight end, he might have been able to add the title of "NFL player" to his impressive list of accomplishments.

Wish had caddied for Mr. Spears a handful of times during the spring and had found him to be a talented but often volatile golfer. Of course, this wasn't unusual to see among these high-powered, driven men in Madras slacks. The betting stakes could get pretty crazy as the testosterone levels rose over the course of a match. By the 18th hole, you'd think that they were playing for the US Open championship the way they stressed over routine putts.

While today's foursome didn't feature any big-dollar wagers, the air was still filled with the ozone of male competition. The two men in the match, Mr. Spears and Mr. Livingston, had pitted their respective sons, Jackson and Tommy, against each other as if the boys were gladiators and the fathers, emperors. The two younger contestants knew each other and talked a little. Only Tommy, however, was having a good time.

No wonder, Wish thought. *That Spears kid is as tense as all get out. Mr. Spears needs to get off his back.*

Howard advised his son on the nuances of every shot. Suffering in silence, Jackson struck a few beautiful shots. Just as frequently, he'd slice a drive into the woods or stub a delicate chip shot. On the sixth green, Jackson had a five-foot putt that would have given him a tie for the match. Although his putt followed the line recommended by his father perfectly, it stopped on the lip and failed to drop into the cup. Howard shook his head in disgust.

Wish easily lugged the two heavy Spears bags, leading the way into the woods on their right to find Jackson's errant ball. Alone for the first time with Jackson, Wish debated a few moments before speaking.

"This isn't supposed to be torture, you know," the caddie said.

About to address his ball, Jackson turned his head and quizzically eyed Wish. "Yeah, I've heard."

Jackson stepped away from his ball, regained his concentration, and got back into position to swing. Precisely as he was about to swing, his father's voice bellowed from the fairway.

"Don't go for the home run, son! Play it safe and just chip it out sideways!"

"Just what I was about to do," Jackson muttered, shaking his head as he backed away from the shot. He looked at Wish as the caddie stifled a chuckle. They shared a sardonic smile.

"Your father's right," Wish commented. "You probably shouldn't try to hit a home run here. Wrong sport."

Jackson smiled at Wish's humor, and Wish made note of the fact that it was the first time he was seeing the kid do that. Relaxing a bit, Jackson negotiated a chip shot through the trees and onto the fairway. He followed this up with a long, high-arcing iron that landed on the green and stopped just a few feet from the pin.

When Jackson rejoined his father during the walk to the green, he was greeted by an arm around his shoulder. The gesture caused the son to lift his chin off his chest an inch or two. A few steps behind the pair, Wish overheard what was said next.

"A great shot, son," the unsmiling Howard said. "A great shot. Where was that on the tee?"

Howard gave his son a hearty pat on the shoulder before walking over to his own ball in the nearby greenside bunker. Wish saw Jackson's chin drop and his shoulders slump down to their previous posture.

———

Two hours later the foursome and their caddies arrived at the sixteenth hole, located as far
from the clubhouse as possible. Since his son
was already clearly not in a position to win his
match, Howard's incessant advice and criticism
had finally begun to subside. Instead, he had
begun to focus his ire on the tiniest of flaws
in his own game. An earlier series of grumbles
had by now turned into curses, at first under
his breath but eventually very vocal. Finding
this highly entertaining, his opponent peppered
Howard with a variety of imaginative jibes.

Both Livingstons struck excellent tee
shots that traversed the long pond that
began thirty yards from the front of the tee
box and landed on the green. After his son's
tee shot also landed on the other side of the
pond (albeit well off the green), Howard was
next up. He shifted his stance three times
and waggled his club several times before
finally swinging too fast and too hard. The
result was a bad topping of the ball, sending
it ignominiously fifty yards into the center of
the pond. Enraged, Howard took the iron in
both hands, raised it over his head and then
behind his back, and, with a mighty effort,
launched the offending club high into the air.

It landed with a loud splash well short of where the golf ball had descended.

Glowering, Howard marched quickly ahead of the others, who remained silent. Wish hustled to catch up and caught Howard as he passed the driver's watery grave.

"I think it's pretty shallow here, Mr. Spears," Wish reported. "I might be able to get your club for you."

Steaming ahead, Howard replied, "Leave it. I never want to see the fucking thing again."

As he kept pace, Wish turned to take a surreptitious look back at where the club had helicoptered into the pond.

———

Walking up the long slope of the 18th fairway that lead back to the clubhouse, the bag-toting Wish displayed an abundance of energy relative to his dejected pair of golfers. Discourse between father and son had been scant for the past few holes; Wish wondered how badly the mood would affect the size of his tip.

Jackson slowed his pace to join the caddie. "You play?"

"Here? Not allowed to," Wish responded after a moment's hesitation.

"Well, there's a public course around here."

"Yeah, in Norwalk, where I live. I hear it's nothing like this, though. Doesn't matter, because I'm here just about every day. If the weather's OK, I'm working."

Jackson grunted in response, and the conversation was over, as was the round.

———

All the lessons with the club pro and the best equipment money could buy had given Jackson what was, at least from a technical standpoint, a decent golf swing. Here and there, he even scored reasonably well. So why in the world did he not enjoy the game?

God knows he wanted to please his father. In his seventeen years, he had never so much as gotten a detention. Honor roll, close to becoming an Eagle Scout, active in several clubs at Choate— he was an overachiever who received little to no recognition for his efforts from anyone but his teachers and his mother. He appreciated his mother's constant praise and support, but his father was a far tougher nut to crack. With him, it all boiled down to sports, sports, sports.

Sadly, this is where Jackson let his father down. What else could be expected from a short, pudgy, slow, and decidedly uncoordinated non-athlete? Starting at the age of eight, Jackson had eagerly learned how to play each of the "big three" sports of baseball, basketball, and football. At first, it was fun; after all, everyone started out on the same page. But by the time he was eleven or twelve, it was growing increasingly obvious that enthusiasm alone couldn't help the young man jump as high, run as fast, or hit as hard as his peers. Soon, it was a matter of not being picked for the teams—first by the other kids, and then by the adult coaches.

By his early teens, Jackson had regressed from a late-in-the-game substitute to riding the bench to flat-out not making the team. Worst of all, he was never one of the popular kids in school. If anything, he was a classic loner. Experience had taught him that avoiding most relationships automatically negated the probability of rejection.

At each step, Howard did his best to manipulate his son onto the court or playing field. Unable (or unwilling) to spare the time during the week to coach, the father endeavored to control the various leagues in which his son participated by virtue of being an officer and big-time financial contributor. This strategy worked for a short while, at bare minimum ensuring Jackson a roster spot. Eventually, however, nothing could compensate for the boy's lack of size, strength, and talent.

Finally, relief for both father and son appeared in the form of a Spears family tradition. At the age of fourteen, Jackson was dispatched to attend Choate, one of the nation's top prep schools for the scions of blue-blooded families. Having escaped the pressure to excel as an athlete, the young man was surprised to find that he actually loved sports—just not as a participant. Instead, he gravitated to the role of manager for the football, basketball, and baseball teams. Many an athlete looked down his nose at the towel-collecting, laundry-cleaning, and equipment-carrying managers. Jackson understood his lowly position and made the best of it, happy to be even tangentially related to the competition. Eventually, however, he discovered exactly how he could best contribute to each team's success—with statistics.

Jackson found that by mining the great wealth of stats created by each team, he could show the coaches innovative ways to better evaluate who should be in the game from moment to moment and more importantly, why. By the end of his sophomore year, this talent for figures had already garnered him letters in all three sports. In addition, he received grudging praise from the coaches, if not from the players. It was a solitary pursuit of excellence that at minimum gave him some measure of self-satisfaction.

His father made it clear that he did not consider Jackson's letters to be legitimate. "On the playing field, son. That's where letters are earned."

With this emphasis on success in sports being the be-all and end-all, Jackson's lack of athletic prowess, coupled with his lack of popularity, bred a pronounced absence of confidence in the young man. He was quiet, shy, and yes, he even sat, stood, and walked with a posture that betrayed how he felt about himself.

There was a different side to the young man, although few found out about it. Jackson was actually a funny guy. He had a wonderful knack for impersonating the television and movie stars of the time, albeit with a decidedly teenaged timbre. Barney Fife, Bob Hope, Gomer Pyle, Captain Kirk, Ed Sullivan—even JFK and Alvin and the Chipmunks—Jackson had them all down pat. As lame as his jokes were, his tiny coterie of friends still marveled at his talent, garnering him the slightest measure—his own version—of popularity.

But now that he was home for the summer, the sports campaign was back on. Howard had discovered the one sport that Jackson could do reasonably well despite his physical shortcomings, and that was golf. At this point, all bragging rights were focused on one event, the club's junior championship, scheduled for August. Jackson knew full well that the pursuit was pointless, but there was no way to avoid it.

As nighttime fell on the pond on the sixteenth hole, the silence was broken only by the loud croaking of bullfrogs. Fireflies floated lazily in the still, humid air as the placid surface of the water was suddenly broken by an emerging body. His dark skin glistening in the moonlight, Wish took a gulp of air and dove back underwater. He reemerged thirty seconds later, clutching Mr. Spears's iron over his head. Half wading and half paddling with his free hand, he made his way over to the shoreline.

Lying in the rough alongside his clothing was a ragged canvas golf bag with a few clubs. And next to the bag were two shoes, which were connected, as Wish quickly saw as he raised his eyes, to the body of one Jackson Spears.

Jackson reached a hand down to help Wish clamber out of the water until the two boys faced each other. Wish, dripping in nothing but his white briefs, held the club by his side. Jackson was still outfitted in the polo shirt, Madras shorts, and never-scuffed golf shoes he had worn during the match earlier that day. Neither spoke for several moments. In fact, neither knew what to say.

"Your father didn't want this," Wish said in an attempt to take the higher ground. "I asked him."

"I know."

Surprised at this response, Wish deliberated on where to go from there. "So?" was the best he could muster.

Jackson was equally confused as to how to best begin the dialogue.

"So, you're right. He didn't want it. I don't need it. You found it; it's yours."

Now Wish was thoroughly confused. Before he could think of something intelligent to say, Jackson jumped in.

"I thought you said you didn't play golf," he said, nodding his head toward the golf bag.

"I didn't say that. I said I wasn't allowed to play…here, that is," Wish said, defensively.

"But…"

"Look, I'm not hurting anyone."

"Didn't say you were. So, you do play golf. I thought so…I mean, I could tell."

"You gonna rat on me? Is that it?"

"No. Why would I want to do that?"

Once again the boys were at a standstill. Suddenly realizing that he must look pretty silly standing as he was in nothing but his wet shorts, Wish reached down for his clothing and began to get dressed.

"It's just that, if you do, I'll lose my job, and I need this job. We need this money, Mom and me—"

"Hey, Wish…It's Wish, right?" Jackson interjected. As Wish nodded, Jackson continued. "Get this straight. I don't care about the stupid golf club, and I don't care if you're out here playing golf." He held out his hand, and after a moment's surprise and hesitation, Wish solemnly shook it.

"I don't get it," Wish remarked. "Why did you come out here at this time of the night?"

"To say hi, I guess."

"That's it?"

"Yeah…I…"

Suddenly remembering the time, Wish panicked. "Geez, I gotta get going! I can't miss the last bus…My mom's on it. If I miss it, oh, man…"

"Well, let's go, maybe you can still make it!"

Wish gathered his bag, and the two boys high-tailed it through the dark toward the clubhouse, brightly lit from within, up on the distant hill.

Minutes later, out of breath, they approached the exit of the club's grand driveway. Far down the tree-lined road that flanked the grounds, they could see Wish's city bus approaching. Wish was still in a panic.

"Geez, what do I do with these?" he asked himself, indicating his bag of clubs.

Jackson held out his hands to take the bag. "Where do they go?"

Sprinting for the bus, Wish yelled over his shoulder, "In the storage shed! Up in the rafters! There's a ladder behind the carts!"

"Storage shed…ladder…OK!"

"But don't get caught!" Wish yelled, right before the bus door opened and he disappeared.

"Don't get caught…right," Jackson said to himself. "OK," he repeated, turning back toward the club, smiling.

———

Early the next evening, the boys met near the caddie shack and decided it would be best to rendezvous again with their respective golf bags at the second tee box, out of sight of the clubhouse.

The first tee shot hit by Wish was eighty yards longer than Jackson's best ever, with a perfect fade around the dogleg. Jackson was stunned, realizing the shot had been far better than any he'd ever witnessed.

"Never seen a Negro play golf before, huh?" Wish kidded.

Jackson could only shake his head.

"That's OK," Wish said with a chuckle. "Come to think of it, neither have I."

———

Thus began an improbable friendship between the two boys, played out only under the cover of dusk and only on the golf course. Each relished playing golf, hanging out, and just plain "hacking around" with the other.

Each evening, the boys met before dusk on the second hole. Wish learned to take his clubs out of his canvas bag and put them in Jackson's big leather bag. With Wish pretending to be

Jackson's caddie, the boys were able to pass muster if they ran into the occasional member out on the course that late in the day. The key, of course, was that no one but Jackson was allowed to see Wish swing a club.

To Jackson's mind, that was a real shame. *Man, this guy can play golf,* Jackson thought nearly every time his friend struck a shot. Wish not only hit the ball a country mile, but he seemed to be able to bend shots around doglegs, right or left, at will. He could even make his wedge shots spin back toward the hole once they landed on the green, just like on TV!

One thing puzzled Jackson, and after a few days, he just had to comment. One evening, he spoke up. "I saw you throwing a ball with the other caddies, and when you signed that paper the other day…Both times you were a leftie."

"I *am* a leftie," Wish responded.

"But you play golf right-handed!"

"Oh, yeah." Wish smiled. "Well, look at these clubs."

There was no need; Wish's collection of clubs, too, had already greatly confused Jackson.

"Yes, I noticed. They don't match—all different brands."

Wish took a five iron out of the bag, took a practice swing, and then struck a high arcing shot that settled onto the green about fifteen feet from the pin.

"Nice clubs, though, right?"

"Yeah, but like I said, they're right-handed and you're not!"

Having thoroughly enjoyed this little game, Wish decided it was time to stop torturing Jackson.

"Where do you think I got these clubs, Jack? I sure as heck can't afford them!"

As Jackson pondered the question, Wish studied his face. Not appreciating the conclusion he thought the other boy was reaching, his joviality quickly disappeared.

"And no, I didn't steal them!"

"I…I…I…," Jackson stuttered. "I wasn't…I wasn't thinking that."

Of course, the thought certainly had crossed Jackson's mind, and both boys knew that. Wish decided not to pursue the matter.

"Well, I didn't," Wish said. "I got every one of these out of a pond, or a stream, or a tree, right here on the course. Every one of them, thrown away."

"OK."

"They didn't want them. Just like your father."

"I get it, Wish." Jackson paused, hoping the bad moment had passed. After a few moments, he continued. "But they're all right-handed."

"Yeah, I never found a left-handed one. Guess lefties don't throw clubs."

Jackson pondered this seriously.

"Or maybe we throw them, but we're too cheap to leave them."

Realizing that the moment of tension had passed and that his leg had just been pulled, Jackson allowed himself a smile.

———

The boys reached the seventeenth green as the darkness rapidly closed in. They quickly pretended to study their respective putts, a waste of effort considering the lack of light.

"Gotta hurry if we're gonna finish," Jackson said.

"We're done," Wish replied.

"But the 18th…"

"Can't play the 18th. You can, but I can't."

"Oh, yeah."

"Nope," Wish repeated, as much to himself as to his friend. "I'd be sure to get caught if I tried to play the 18th. Can't ever play the 18th."

Jackson bent over to pick the balls out of the cup as Wish picked up the golf bag and slung it over his shoulder. The boys proceeded toward the clubhouse, each lost in thought. Eventually, Jackson broke the silence.

"Isn't that frustrating?"

Wish pretended not to hear the question, but Jackson was insistent.

"Wish?"

"Not a member, Jack. Remember? Not a member."

"That's not an answer, Wish."

"No, Jack, that's what they call a non sequitur."

———

As the summer progressed, the strangest thing happened to Jackson. For the first time, he actually started to enjoy the game of golf. Removed from his father's pressure, he was able to see how good he could be when he simply relaxed.

More importantly, he saw how much fun the game was supposed to be.

Not that there wasn't *any* pressure. The boys loved to compete with each other; both tried hard to win each and every hole.

"Here in the thirteenth fairway, Wish Fitzgerald faces the tough decision that has confronted all the greats at Augusta National," Wish said in his best baritone, television commentator voice, his golf club held in front of his face like a microphone. "Does he go for the green, taking the chance of leaving his ball in Rae's Creek, or does he take the safe route and lay up?"

Ignoring the fact that the thirteenth hole at Wee Burn Country Club looked nothing like any hole at Augusta National, home of the Masters, Wish and Jackson proceeded with the fantasy color commentary. After all, there *was* a creek in front of the green ahead of them, and Wish would have to go for it to reach the green in two.

Changing hats from commentator to teenage golfer, Wish stepped up to the ball, waggled his three wood a few times, and took his swing. The ball barely cleared the creek, landed on the opposite bank, and spun back into the water. Wish groaned in agony as Jackson smirked, picking up his own imaginary microphone.

"Another gamble and another poor decision by Fitzgerald," Jackson reported in his best deep voice. "That error puts him in a hole, and not the hole he was hoping for."

Wish advanced on his friend, pretending to be ready to swing his club at Jackson's body rather than a ball. Laughing, Jackson danced away. Wish picked up the golf bag and followed him.

"No guts, no glory," Wish shouted after his friend.

"Yeah, Wish, no glory. At least not on this hole!"

They arrived at Jackson's ball. Wish resumed his role as broadcaster.

"Spears chose to lay up and now must put his approach shot close to the hole in order to stay in the running for the Masters Championship and the coveted green jacket. He's ready now…"

Jackson's wedge shot lofted toward the pin and stopped dead within six inches of the hole.

"Holy cow!" Wish exclaimed, momentarily forgetting his broadcasting role in his amazement at Jackson's display of prowess. He quickly recovered and resumed speaking in his squeaky baritone, teenage announcer voice.

"Well folks, there you have it. Miracles do happen, even here at Augusta National. Even this observer is dumbstruck at the sudden display of talent on the part of Jackson Spears."

"Dumbstruck?" Jackson chided.

"And most importantly, that gives Spears the win!" Wish announced. "This is a tremendous upset for the young man, beating the ten-time green jacket winner. A great accomplishment. One for the history books."

Dropping the announcer act, Wish patted his friend on the back. "Man, you sure got better!"

"Well, you did spot me eight strokes."

"Doesn't matter. Lately, you're a different guy."

"I'll never beat you."

"But can you beat the other guys here at the club? That's the question. And by the end of the summer, I bet you will."

"They always kick my butt, Wish."

"Past tense, Jack. I know, because I caddy for those kids. You could beat most of them right now."

They had reached the green, and Wish walked down to the edge of the creek to retrieve his ball. He waved at his friend to concede the tap-in putt.

"But every time I've played against anyone but you, I suck," Jackson lamented.

"And who else was with you?"

Jackson considered this for a moment until he suddenly realized what Wish meant.

"You mean my dad."

"Yep. It's a game," Wish said. "A game is supposed to be fun."

"Not to him it isn't."

"Well, you're not your dad."

———

Once again, in the gathering darkness, the boys trudged up the hill toward the clubhouse, sticking to the woods and bypassing the 18th hole.

"Dumbstruck, huh?" Jackson asked.

"Yeah, dumbstruck."

The boys continued to weave through the trees for a while until Jackson suddenly stopped. Wish continued on as Jackson shouted after him.

"What does 'dumbstruck' mean?"

The boys had created their own, unique world, a world that was perfectly suited to nurture their improbable friendship: the tees, fairways, and greens of the second through seventeenth holes of the bucolic Wee Burn

Country Club, available to them for only an hour or two each summer evening. Although both were in constant fear of being caught by Pete or another adult, in reality, this was the ultimate cocoon. There was no interaction whatsoever with others—with the outside world. No one could interfere, interject, or influence their friendship.

As their friendship grew, the boys became less and less guarded with each other. They confided in and trusted one another—to an extent.

Wish remained puzzled by the fact that the rich white boy had befriended him in the first place. To the young man from the projects, this was a surprising and flattering present, in addition to another glimpse into a privileged world he had never known. However, his pride would not allow him to display or even feel jealousy about the life his new friend had.

"Hey, Wish, what do you want to be when you grow up?" The boys were standing under a shelter next to the sixth green, passing the time as they waited out a torrential thunderstorm.

"I don't talk about that, Jack."

"Why not?"

"Just because, that's all. How about you?"

"I don't know, exactly. Some kind of business, maybe an executive, I guess. Sure wish I could be in sports, but..."

"I hear ya, buddy. Executive, that's boss, right?"

Jackson chuckled. "Yeah, it's boss to be the boss, right?"

"Good one," Wish said with a laugh.

After another half hour of trying to wait out the storm, the boys gave up and trudged back toward the clubhouse in the still-strong deluge.

"Golf pro," Wish suddenly said.

"What?"

"Golf pro."

"Boss. At a club?"

"Nope, on the PGA Tour. The players call it 'The Show.' Read that in a magazine."

They continued down a sodden fairway, Wish carrying Jackson's bag as always, Jackson empty-handed.

"Is that possible, Wish? I mean—"

"Mr. Charlie Sifford is on the tour. He even won the Greater Hartford Open a couple of years ago."

"Who's Charlie Sifford?"

"A great golfer, Jack. A great *Negro* golfer."

"Oh. Sorry."

"Yeah, well. I guess there's no reason for you to know that."

"You're gonna be a really good pro, Wish. You're already an unbelievable golfer. Everyone knows that."

Wish laughed.

"They do!" Jackson exclaimed.

"Exactly three people know that I even play golf, Jack. My mom, me, and you. That's it. And you're the only one who's actually seen me play."

"How come?"

"Well, here, it's obvious, right?" Wish nodded toward the clubhouse a few hundred yards in the distance.

"What about your friends?"

"No time for friends. The kids at school call me Whitey, Caucasian, Cracker, junk like that. They don't get the golf thing, and they *really* don't like the way I talk."

The boys fell silent as they walked up the 18th fairway, climbing the hill toward the clubhouse. By now, both boys were drenched.

Jackson asked, "Is that why we always pretend we're playing the Masters? Because you're gonna be a pro?" Jackson said, hoping to end the evening on a higher note.

Wish suddenly stopped in the middle of the fairway. "Don't tell anyone, ever, that I said this, Jack. Got it?"

"Yeah, sure, I got it! What's up?"

Wish stared intently at his friend, water dripping off his golf cap.

"This is just between you and me. Swear."

"OK, I swear!"

"Someday, I'm playing Augusta National, Jack. Don't know when, but I'm gonna win the Masters. Gonna wear the green jacket. Like Jack Nicklaus and Arnold Palmer."

"Wish Fitzgerald, Masters Champion," Jack said. "Yeah, I like the sound of that."

Chapter 2

Not surprisingly, Jackson had a tendency to go on and on about his father. Howard's demanding and critical attitude toward his only child was clashing on a daily basis with the teenager's growing but still stifled desire for independence. This was becoming such a focus for Jackson that it came up in conversation with Wish nearly every day.

"Bet your dad is better than mine," Jackson said one evening.

"My dad's dead. Vietnam."

"Oh, sorry."

"Yeah, he was killed in a firefight with the Cong. Saved a bunch of other guys by jumping on a grenade to protect them."

"Holy shit!"

"Yep. He was awarded the Medal of Honor for bravery. Posthumously, of course."

"Of course." Jackson nodded, trying to remember what "posthumously" meant.

"What was he like?"

"I don't remember much about him. He was away mostly, at war, and junk like that. He hugged me a lot when he was home. He smelled like Aqua Velva, and boy, was he big and strong. He read to me before I went to sleep, and we used to go out for ice cream. He was really nice. And he loved me. A lot."

"You're lucky," Jackson muttered before he quickly realized how unfortunate the thought was.

Lost in his own thoughts, Wish failed to notice his friend's faux pas. But that conversation put an end to any further references to Wish's father.

What didn't end, however, were Jackson's nearly obsessive complaints about his own dad. Weeks later, Wish had had enough. One night he decided to interrupt Jackson's umpteenth soliloquy about Howard.

"At least you *have* a father, Jack."

———

Wish's mother, Annie, an already worn-out thirty-five, also worked in Darien as a maid for the Johnsons (of Johnson Aerospace fame) in one of the ubiquitous mansions perched in the middle of acres of immaculate lawns. Had worked for them for thirteen years, as a matter of fact.

Sometimes Annie would share anecdotes about life in the Johnson household, tales of wealth that amazed and greatly entertained her son. Multiple servants, multiple large, new luxury cars and smaller, brand-new sports cars, acres of lawn for the gardeners to mow in the summer and rake in the fall, many extra bedrooms and bathrooms with closets bigger than any room in the Fitzgerald apartment. Descriptions of the food, while not necessarily appealing to Wish's own palate, sure *sounded* pretty darned delicious. Annie assured him that it was, amplifying Wish's disappointment that his mother wasn't allowed to bring home any of the usually abundant leftovers.

Annie refused to run down the Johnson family to her son, no matter how spoiled she perceived them to be, especially the children. Instead, she endeavored to instill in Wish the desire to attain a higher standard of living for himself and, someday, for his family.

"Mr. Johnson works hard, Wish. He gets on that train to Grand Central early every morning and gets home late. He's a smart man, and he knows how to get things done—make things happen. That's how money is made, son. Hard work, brains, and who you know, don't forget that. I hear him talking: 'Forge the right relationships. Make the right friends. You never know from where the next deal will come!'"

"But Mom," Wish would say. "Mr. Johnson, he's a white man. We're—"

"Yes, son, I'm well aware of all that."

"So how am I supposed to—"

"By not making excuses. By studying instead of watching television."

Pretty hard to watch television when you don't have one, Wish thought.

"By speaking like an educated person instead of a juvenile delinquent or a servant. That means caring about your grammar and your vocabulary, Wish. That means knowing more than those around you and not being embarrassed to show it. Remember, your environment doesn't have to dictate your future. Your past—my past—doesn't have to dictate your future. *You* need to dictate your future.

"Times are changing, son. We've got a long way to go still, but we need to be ready to take advantage of our moment when it comes."

In her lowest moments, Annie thought of herself as a disappointment and a cliché. A disappointment because she was an unwed mother. A cliché because she was "just another" black, unwed mother. She hated this so much. She couldn't even share her feelings with someone, because there was no one in her life with whom she could do that.

Twenty-year-old sharecropper Leon Rogers had smooth-talked seventeen-year-old Annie into bed at his cousin's shack in Anniston, Alabama, on her prom night. Something about loving her forever, Annie recalled often, feeling disgust toward Leon both for him and for her own poor judgment.

"Oh, Lord, oh, Lord, oh Lord!" were the first words out of Annie's mouth when the county doctor, a white man, had confirmed the pregnancy.

"No way" were the first words out of Leon's mouth. "That ain't mine. You been sleepin' around, I knowed it. Don't look for nothin' outta me."

"That's OK," her mother had reassured her. "They all like that, from you grandfather on down. We take care of the baby, jes like I take care a you and the others."

Annie left town the next morning, with $210.35 to her name and a small valise containing three threadbare dresses.

Aloysius Gonzaga Fitzgerald was born on December 10, 1950, in a Catholic hospital in Atlanta, Georgia. Annie had been taken in by some Jesuit priests and given accommodations in a home for unwed mothers and a housekeeping job at the rectory. Saint Aloysius Gonzaga was a Jesuit priest in the 1500s who had been canonized and named patron saint of young students in the early 1700s.

The Jesuits took the young woman into their hearts, tutoring her each evening in the hope that she might obtain a college scholarship. However, the stress of juggling work, a baby, and lessons, coupled with no money, proved to be too high a mountain to climb, even for someone who aspired to greater success. When a young suitor began to apply the full-court press for sex, Annie began another odyssey that eventually landed her in South Norwalk, Connecticut, at age twenty-three.

Her vow was to sacrifice everything for her son. He would not turn out like Leon. "Wish" would be different.

———

Wish and Annie lived in a one-bedroom, fourth-floor walk-up apartment in the projects of South Norwalk. Wish slept on the sofa in the immaculately neat and clean living room. Annie felt both disappointment and disgust at the fact that the community had "flat-out given up," ignoring decades of disrepair and neglect. Why continue to accept the graffiti on the buildings, both inside and out? Why not pick up the ubiquitous garbage in the alleyways? Why tolerate the constant noise after midnight? These were questions that Annie asked herself—and Wish—over and over.

Annie refused to give in to what she called "that kind of mentality." The Fitzgerald apartment was sparsely furnished, but it was furnished in good taste. And each morning, the first thing Wish did was put away his bedding and police the room.

"You never know who might stop by," Annie was fond of warning. "It's important to make a good impression, the first time and every time."

"We may be poor, Wish, but we don't have to act like it," was another of Annie's maxims.

Annie's relationship with her employers, the Johnsons, was full of contradictions. On the surface, she was dedicated to the family. Fourteen-hour workdays were not uncommon. In fact, when Wish was working at the country club from dusk to dawn each summer, Annie took advantage of that to work as many hours as possible in order to pay bills and even save a few dollars.

The Johnsons were under the impression that Annie viewed them as family. They often told Annie and others that Annie was "a part of our family" and sincerely believed that she was treated as such. After all, to young and old, she was "their Annie." Annie saw things a little differently.

Certainly she had affection for Horace and Betty Johnson and especially their children, Jimmy and Susan. After all, she had practically raised the kids, what with their father spending so much time in Manhattan, on the road, and at the club and their mom preoccupied with tennis lessons, bridge, and multiple charity committees. No doubt Jimmy and Susan were spoiled, but not overly so, compared to the many other Darien kids who had come through the Johnson house over the years. To Annie's mind, it would be hard to not be spoiled, given the silver spoons that were so firmly implanted in each Johnson mouth.

But when it came to the Johnsons' oft-used term "family," Annie wasn't buying it. By her definition, "family" also meant "respect." With compensation that was barely minimum wage and included no overtime and no paid vacation, respect was sorely lacking. No wonder the Johnsons wanted her to consider them "family"—she did most of their work without any of the requisite benefits. It was a great deal for the family.

In the end, however, Annie realized that it was always her choice to stay or leave, and she stayed, year after year. Despite the exhausting commute and the lower-than-desirable compensation, the environment was comfortable, the work was always there, and Mr. and Mrs. Johnson had never treated her rudely. She had heard the opposite from other maids in Darien, so, to a certain extent, she counted her blessings. The "bottom line" (a phrase she had heard Mr. Johnson use many a time) was that she and Wish lived paycheck to paycheck.

There was no backup plan whatsoever, not even an extended family. Her number-one responsibility was to take care of her son. *Wish* was "family"—her only family.

———

As always, the next Monday was a day off for Annie and Wish. As usual, their dinner together fostered the kind of conversation that was rare, even during their morning and evening commutes.

Although Wish's mouth was still full of meatloaf as he gabbed away, Annie resisted the urge to once again comment on his manners. The subject was his newfound "friendship" with Mr. and Mrs. Spears' son, Jackson.

"So, Jackson, he's gonna ask his dad about letting me play in the junior championship," Wish garbled enthusiastically. "You know, Mr. Spears is on the tournament committee."

"So I've heard," Annie replied.

"Jackson thinks I could win it, Mom."

"Yes, dear."

"I've seen all the club kids play. Pretty sure I'm better'n all of 'em."

"Watch your diction, son," Annie reprimanded gently.

"Yes'm."

Annie let out the slightest sigh of resignation. This, of course, went right by her son. *When he's excited about something, there's no stopping him,* she thought.

Wish plunged on. "Course, no caddies have been allowed to play in the tournament before…"

And certainly no Negroes, Annie thought.

"But, Mr. Spears *is* on the committee. And Jackson *is* his son. And I *am* Jackson's best friend…"

Oh Lord, please help me with this, Annie silently prayed.

"Anyway, I'm hoping. It'd be cool."

"Don't," Annie said.

"Don't what?"

Annie reached across the table to grasp her son's hand.

"Don't what, Mom? I don't understand."

"Sweetie pie, that's the problem. You *don't* understand."

Wish pulled his hands away and sat straighter in his chair. Annie winced as she searched for the right words to let her son down as easily as possible. Realizing that such a goal was impossible to achieve, she proceeded more directly.

"Honey, this isn't going to happen. It just isn't. And I don't want you to get your hopes up."

"But…" Wish sputtered.

"There is no way on God's green earth that those folks are going to let a caddie, let alone a Negro caddie, play at that club. And you're an employee, not a member. I'm sorry, but that's the truth, son."

"But, Jackson said—"

"Honey, Jackson is white. His father is white. Every single member of that country club is white! They have their rules, Wish, and the biggest one is 'whites only.'"

"Jackson is *not* prejudiced, Mom!"

"Maybe he's not, Wish. But Jackson does not make the decisions."

A moment of silence gave Annie the false hope that her son was finally accepting what she had said.

"You'll see," Wish soon responded, defensively. "I hear what you're saying, Mom. I know you love me and you want what's best for me, to protect me. I get that, and I love you for that."

This touched Annie to the core.

"But," Wish continued, patting his mother's wringing hands with a soft, enveloping touch of his own. "I'm gonna prove you wrong on this."

Annie shook her head. Her son, who was still grasping her hands, had one more thing to say.

"And wouldn't that be a good thing?"

———

"But Dad," Jackson protested.

Father and son were seated across from each other in leather wingback chairs in the family's library. Built-in mahogany bookshelves rose to a fourteen-foot-high vaulted ceiling. Mr. Spears calmly swirled the brandy in his crystal snifter.

"I have absolutely nothing against that young man, son," Howard explained. "It's just that he is a caddie, after all. He's not a member of the club or a family member. He has no *standing*, Jackson."

"But you could make an exception—"

"I'm afraid not, son. We have our rules, called bylaws. And I'm only one member of one committee. I'd love to be able to help you with this. I'm sure he's a fine young man, but it's simply out of the question."

"He's a good golfer, Dad."

"That may be, but it's beside the point." Howard studied his son's face. "And just exactly how would you know that this young man is a good golfer, Jackson?"

Jackson suddenly recognized the trap he had accidentally laid for himself. *Geez, I can't let him know that Wish has been playing the course and that I've been joining him,* he thought.

"Well, he's been caddying for me, see, and he gives great advice. I've been getting better."

"I see. Well, that doesn't make him a good golfer, son."

Inadvertently, Jackson was digging himself an ever-deeper hole. Over the last few weeks, his father had complained repeatedly about the fact that Jackson was not joining him for his weekend games. His son's preparation for the junior championship was paramount to Howard, and now he knew why Jackson had wriggled out of almost every invitation. He was not happy.

"And the question remains, son. What leads you to believe that this 'Wish' character even owns a golf club, let alone can play the game?"

"He…He *says* he's pretty good," Jackson responded. He hoped that the evasive answer would suffice. As much as he had wanted Wish to be able to play in the championship, his highest priority now was for this conversation to be over.

Howard pondered the situation. He was used to being in command of all situations he faced, and anything involving his son certainly topped the list. This conversation, however, was uncomfortable. Clearly, letting the Negro boy play in the tournament wasn't even remotely possible. Fortunately, club rules really did forbid such a scenario. Even if one wanted to pursue the matter with the committee (and one didn't), the very idea of having someone who amounted to being a servant—and a Negro to boot— play was clearly unthinkable. The dilemma was whether to get into this any further with his son.

As important was this mysterious relationship between Jackson and the Negro caddie. Yes, times were changing, but not, he hoped, in Darien. What in the hell was going on here? And as far as his son's golf education, that was a matter for a father and the club pro. What in the world could a Negro caddie impart about golf (or anything else, for that matter) to Jackson, and when and how was this happening?

Too many questions to be posited and answered right now. Best to take his time with this and get back to that fine brandy.

"I'm sorry, but the answer is no, Jackson," Mr. Spears said, trying his best to add a sympathetic smile.

"I understand, Dad." Relief outweighed disappointment. Jackson had dodged a bullet.

Chapter 3

The afternoon of Saturday, August 15, 1969, the day of the junior club championship tournament for Wee Burn Country Club, turned out to be hot and very humid. Wish had arrived nice and early in order to reconfirm with Pete that he was still going to carry Jackson's bag.

A wizened seventy years old, the caddie master was short and bent over, with a potbelly and a single tuft of snow-white hair at the very front of his scalp. Originally from West Virginia, he had long forgotten what the hell brought him to Connecticut in the first place.

Four years earlier, Pete had lobbied the club membership to allow him to hire Negro caddies to help populate his staff. "These days there ain't no rich white kids willin' to carry your bags no more," Pete had explained. "And you damn sure ain't gonna carry 'em yourselves. Only other choice is for those bags to magically follow you around on they own. Course, those bags ain't gonna find your lost balls for ya—ya'll know there ain't a one of ya that could deal with that, neither." He had gone on and on until he got his way.

The members put up with Pete's coarse and often disrespectful manner because, after all, he was what they considered a "character." "Colorful" was another word commonly bandied about. In reality, he had served them for decades, didn't cost an arm and a leg, and was almost always right.

Nothing, but nothing, got by Pete. Wish and Jackson were certain that they had covered their tracks throughout the summer and therefore believed that no one was aware of their illicit evening matches. Pete was not only aware of them, but he was a big fan of the young caddie's astounding ability with a golf club. He himself had wondered what might happen if Wish was ever allowed to challenge the best of these strapping, blond, blue-eyed young golfers. In fact, he was convinced that Wish could probably whip all their fathers. However, Pete also knew full well that such a match would

Green

never take place, not even for fun. First of all, Wish needed to keep his secret, and secondly, the club had its rules. Yeah, sure, rules.

Pete ran his fiefdom the way he wished, well aware of the "wink and a nod" he got from the relevant members of the golf committee. Today was a perfect example. The rules for all club championships clearly read that caddies must be assigned by lottery. Who conducted the lottery? Pete, of course.

Who would be young Jackson Spears's caddie today? Wish Fitzgerald, of course.

———

The day started poorly for Jackson. His nerves got the better of him on the very first tee, where he shanked his drive forty yards offline, through the trees, and onto the middle of the ninth fairway. He told himself not to look over at his father, but that was no help.

"Come on, son," the elder Spears practically shouted. "You're better than that! Calm down! Concentrate!"

Although it was only early afternoon, Howard and some of his friends who constituted Jackson's gallery were already enjoying the liquid refreshments available from their gleaming silver flasks. As his friends tsked away after each of Jackson's inaccurate iron shots and missed putts, Howard's ire with his errant son grew and grew. This was embarrassing.

Wish held his tongue until the fourth tee, a long and especially narrow par five. He handed Jackson his three wood for the tee shot.

"No!" Howard exploded. "It's a par five, for Chrissake! Give him the driver, boy!" The Spears sycophants nodded their agreement.

Wish calmly whispered to Jackson, "Tees are back today, buddy. Gonna take three shots to get to the green no matter how we slice it." He smiled at his inadvertent pun. "Sorry about that. Forget that I said 'slice.' Let's just take it one shot at a time, play conservatively. Put it in the fairway, and I know you'll get right back in this thing."

As he prepared to address the ball with the three wood, Jackson allowed himself the slightest of smiles in reaction to his caddie's verbal gaffe. He wasn't surprised by the resultant explosion from a few feet behind him.

"Dammit, Jackson, come over here!"

His complexion turning redder by the moment, the boy turned and walked the few steps over to an even more florid father.

"Yes, Dad?"

"I told you to use the driver!" Howard whispered as loudly as it was possible to whisper. "It's a par five!"

"My caddie thinks it's better to play this conservatively," Jackson retorted. "And I agree with him."

Now, this was something of a watershed moment for Jackson. Never in his life had he stood up to his father in such a manner. While it felt oddly liberating, the young man still cringed as he awaited the expected tongue lashing.

Stunned by his son's display of independence, Howard was momentarily at a loss for words. Interestingly, what was paramount in his mind at this moment was not losing face in front of his friends. That simply wouldn't do. Despite his growing fury, he managed to collect himself and somehow lowered his voice.

"I want to understand this, Jackson. You're actually going to take the advice of a Negro boy over that of your father?"

There was a lengthy pause as Jackson contemplated his response. He was acutely aware that several sets of eyes and ears were waiting and that he was also holding up the entire tournament. In fact, out of the corner of his eye, he spied a member of the golf committee who was headed his way.

Finally, he steeled himself enough to speak, albeit in a far less than steady voice.

"Yes, Father, I am. And besides, during the match we're not supposed to take instructions or assistance from anyone *but* our caddie. You don't want me to be disqualified, do you?"

It was all Howard could do to hold his rage in check. Quickly settling upon a course of action that would best allow him to preserve his dignity, he replied in a voice loud enough for his friends to hear.

"Well, son, rules are rules."

With a nod to his coterie, he turned and headed away from Jackson and Wish, in the direction of the clubhouse.

"Holy shit," Wish and Jackson quietly mouthed to each other. They could not believe that Howard and his followers had left, let alone that Jackson had finally stood up to his dad. They turned around to find the tournament committee member, a distinguished-looking gentleman of about sixty, directly in front of them.

"Is there a problem, young man?" the scowling official asked Jackson.

"No...no, sir."

"Then perhaps you would entertain the idea of teeing off."

"Aaa...absolutely, sir."

Taking nary a moment to gather himself, Jackson stepped up to his ball and promptly proceeded to hit a dead pull to the left that ricocheted off two trees and lofted lazily high into the air to settle in the left rough about thirty yards in front of the group. Having already witnessed Jackson's mortifying few minutes on the tee, the opponent, his family, and his caddie all reacted with wonderful nonchalance.

"I can't believe I did that," Jackson whispered as the boys walked the short distance to where his ignominious tee shot lay buried in the rough.

"Yeah, that was weird."

Wish pulled a four iron out of the huge leather bag and handed it to his friend.

"Now, take your—" he began.

Jackson had already rushed his way to another terrible shot—this time a shank across the fairway, off another tree, and into some more deep rough.

"—time," Wish said, irritated.

Jackson quickly handed him the iron and rushed away. Grabbing the heavy bag, Wish hustled to follow. As soon as he caught up, he realized that Jackson was trying his best to hide the fact that he was crying. Wish sized up the situation.

"You know how in the movies, they slap people?" he asked.

"What? What are you talking about?"

"You know, when someone's upset, or they fainted, they slap 'em. To wake them up. They yell 'Snap out of it!' Like that!"

Jackson momentarily switched his focus to deal with this crazy conversation.

"Yeah, I guess. So?"

"So, do I need to slap you?"

Instinctively taking a step away from Wish, Jackson repeated, incredulously, "What are you talking about?"

"Look, Jackson, we've only played four holes so far. It's not too late to fix this. But you have to wake up, buddy."

Jackson sniffed, but the tears had stopped.

"You can worry about this other stuff later," Wish continued. "But right now, we're here to play golf."

Jackson nodded as he accepted an iron from Wish. "OK," he muttered.

Fortunately, the small group that accompanied Jackson's opponent was many yards down the fairway and had not been privy to their conversation. However, the gray-haired tournament official was again headed their way, his scowl now further deepening the many furrows on his face.

"Oh, geez," Jackson whimpered.

"Forget about him. Just take your time and line up the shot."

Ignoring the counsel, a still-tense Jackson rushed to hit his shot, with predictably bad results.

Wish winced. "Okay, we're going to concede this hole."

"Good idea."

As they trudged down the fairway, Wish playfully bumped into his friend. Jackson responded by giving his caddie a behind-the-back kick in the butt.

———

As they approached the tee box on the next hole, a par three, the two were laughing.

After watching his opponent successfully reach the green with his tee shot, Jackson accepted a club from Wish and planted his ball and tee into the ground. Instead of striking the ball too quickly, he froze, and the stress returned to his face. Finally, just as he began his backswing, Wish stepped up to his friend and grabbed the club. Wish whispered into the startled boy's ear.

"Jack, this isn't work. It's not torture. It's not even a test. It's a game. It's *supposed* to be fun. Ya know, like when *we* play?"

The opponent and the other observers stood by, some mouths agape at what they were seeing.

Wish continued. "Now, let's have some fun, buddy. If you can't do that, I'm gonna throw you in the pond."

"No, you're not."

"Yeah, you're right. I'm not."

Jackson laughed.

"Not now, at least," Wish said. "Maybe later, though."

Wish stepped back toward the bag. "It's a game, Jack...fun."

This time, Jackson took his time, and his relaxed swing resulted in a tee shot that landed on the green, coming to a rest within ten feet of the pin.

Surprised, the boys looked at each other and laughed.

The Men's Grill at the club featured more mahogany than one could find in most Fortune 500 boardrooms. Gray heads predominated at the busy tables. Aged whiskey and imported beers were being freely imbibed. After all, the five o'clock hour was drawing near, and it *was* a Saturday.

Howard Spears and his coterie of buddies were loudly enjoying a card game. Well, at least the buddies seemed to be enjoying the game. Several drinks had helped Howard to settle lower and lower into a rather sullen quietude.

Suddenly, a three-foot-tall trophy with four faux-marble Roman columns, a loving cup, and a golden golfer swinging a tiny golf club was plunked onto the table in front of Howard. Startled from his reverie, he looked up to find that his chubby son had been the one to deposit the prize. It took Howard a moment to understand what had just happened.

"You *won*?" he asked, incredulous.

"Yes, Father, I won. I'm the junior champion. I imagine you're pretty surprised by that."

Howard's followers, at first unabashedly shocked by the news, began recovering enough to offer their buddy a series of rousing congratulations. They began to compete among themselves for the honor of offering the first and then the loudest toast to the great accomplishment. Howard ignored them all, his attention instead focused on Jackson. He managed to fumble his way to a standing position.

"This deserves a celebration, son! I'll call your mother so we can have dinner together."

"No thanks," Jackson responded.

"Excuse me?"

"I already have plans."

"Plans?" Howard said. "What plans could you possibly have?" None of this made any sense.

"I already have plans for dinner. Don't worry; I'll be home before curfew."

With that, Jackson turned and left the room.

Desperate to regain control of the situation, his inclination was to chase his son and put a stop to this behavior. But he considered how this might look to his colleagues. *Appearances,* he reminded himself. *Best to deal with this tomorrow.*

By now Jackson had disappeared anyway. Howard turned back to his friends.

"Cause for celebration, gentlemen. This round is on me!"

———

It was early evening when the boys arrived at Wish's apartment building in South Norwalk. At Wish's suggestion, they had driven around the block a couple of times in order to find just the right well-lit (and thus a bit more secure) parking spot for Jackson's shiny red Mustang. Wish laughed when he realized that Jackson had not locked the car.

"You planning to just give that away?" Wish asked.

"What?"

"The car, numbskull. Take a look around. Does this look like Darien to you? You need to lock the car."

"Oh…oh, yeah."

As a matter of fact, Jackson had been doing nothing but "taking a look around" since driving into South Norwalk. Although the drive from the club had taken only about fifteen minutes, it was if he had arrived on the moon.

It wasn't merely the contrast between suburban and urban; Jackson had been in the ultimate urban environment—Manhattan, only an hour away—many times. It also couldn't be completely chalked up to the change from a white environment to one populated predominately by Negroes and Puerto Ricans. Although Jackson couldn't quite put a name to it, it was the stark contrast in what his parents might call "class." He had now left his upperclass cocoon of Darien, and, try as he might to hide it, he was really nervous.

The early evening was still hot and very humid. The languid air had driven many of the area's residents to the street to catch just a breath of breeze, or at least air that was a degree or two cooler than in the apartments. Most wore as little as possible, stripped right down to sweaty undershirts for the guys and the flimsiest of cheap shifts or slips for the women. Children played in the street while their parents conversed on the stoops, some with a can of Schlitz or Rheingold in hand. Jackson was curious as to why the kids weren't using a vacant lot across the street for their games until he noted that the nearly grassless ground was covered in many spots by broken bottles, discarded tires, and other trash. *Yeah, I'd probably be in the street too,* he thought.

And what *really* ratcheted Jackson's discomfort level up was his perception that each and every eye on this street was on the white guy. Recalling the inner-city racial riots of the summer before, he suddenly realized that maybe this wasn't such a great idea after all.

The two boys approached the entrance to the apartment building. One of the men sitting on the steps abruptly addressed Wish, nearly causing Jackson's heart to jump out of his body.

"Who's your friend, Wish?"

"This is Jackson Spears, Mr. Hazel," Wish answered.

"Where you from, young man?"

Jackson very nearly stuttered but managed to salvage his dignity. "Darien, sir."

"Oh yeah, this is Wish's little golfing buddy!" Mr. Johnson loudly announced as some bystanders edged closer to check out the action. Suddenly, a cacophony of comments came from nearly every direction.

"Darien? You crazy?"

"I done told you, Wish, you need to forget that silly game!"

"Darien!"

"What in the world you doin' in this here neighborhood, boy? You *must* be nuts!"

Startled and caught off guard, Jackson began to respond just as Wish also tumbled into the conversation.

"He's—" Jackson began.

"Mr. Hazel's right—" Wish interrupted.

"—a great golfer!" Jackson finished.

"—Jackson's my friend!"

This news quieted the small crowd for the briefest of moments.

"Great golfer? Who you kiddin', boy!"

"C'mon, now!"

"This boy's you friend, Wish?"

"No way. No way in hell!"

"Yo' momma know about this crazy nonsense, Wish?"

"Does the white boy's momma know about it?"

Everyone erupted in laughter at this last comment. Even the boys had to smile. Realizing that the ribbing had all been in good fun, Jackson tried to relax.

"Go on, get your butts on inside," Mr. Hazel ordered. "You stayin' for dinner, young man?"

Jackson nodded.

Mr. Hazel turned his attention to Wish. "It's Saturday. Bet your momma got somethin' really special on the stove. Don't pay any attention to these knuckleheads. You boys go on and have fun."

As hot as it was outside, the temperature in the stairwell was sweltering. By the time they reached the landing for the third floor, Jackson was not only sweating profusely but also huffing and puffing.

"Coulda sworn I saw an elevator down there," Jackson said, just about out of breath.

"Oh, yeah, it worked for a little while, I think, sometime last year. It's a real gas to get stuck in it."

"So you do this every day?"

"I do it, and my mom does it," Wish answered. His breathing was fine. "Every day."

They finally reached the fifth floor and emerged into a dimly lit hallway. Wish used his key to unlock the apartment door, and the boys stepped into a different world.

The living room was small by Jackson's standards, but he was surprised by how neat, clean, and bright it was. Two cushy armchairs and a large sofa framed an attractive Oriental rug that covered a portion of a gleaming hardwood floor. Magazines, all unfamiliar to Jackson, were arranged neatly on the oak coffee table.

What struck Jackson most was the fact that all of the upholstery was covered by clear plastic.

A wonderful aroma led the boys across the room to the kitchen, where Wish's mother,

Annie, stood in front of a modest white enameled stove, frying chicken. Smiling at the boys, she wiped her hands on a gingham apron prior to giving her son an affectionate hug. She then turned to greet Jackson, who was visibly surprised.

"Hello, Master Jackson Spears," Annie said, barely suppressing a smile at the young man's astonishment. Wish, who had been all set to make the introductions, was puzzled by the demeanor of his mother and friend.

"Aaa…Annie! You're Wish's mom?"

"I see you didn't put two and two together, Jackson." Annie chuckled.

"Mom, you already know Jackson?" Wish blurted, trying to understand.

"Oh, yes, son. Since he was a little one. Right, young man?"

"Yes, ma'am," Jackson said. "Holy cow, Wish—Annie, I mean your mom, she's Jimmy Johnson's…I mean, she works for the Johnsons!"

"So?"

"So, Jimmy and I used to be best friends, before he went off to Hotchkiss," Jackson said. "I was always over at his house, and Annie…I mean, your mom, she watched us."

"And cooked for you, if memory serves," Annie added. "Seems to me you liked my fried chicken, so I've whipped some up for you in honor of your visit tonight."

"Holy cow, holy cow" was all Jackson could say. He caught himself before he actually rubbed his hands together in anticipation.

"You boys go and wash up now. And do a thorough job of it, after a day at that club. Dinner will be on the table by the time you're cleaned up."

———

As Jackson expected, dinner was fantastic. As he worked through a second and then a third helping of the chicken, Wish and Annie carried the conversation. Eventually, they ran out of variations on the "congratulations on your victory, Jackson" theme.

"You're a little quiet, Jackson," Annie eventually commented. "Is everything OK?"

"Oh, yes, ma'am."

"The meal is obviously to your liking."

"Oh, yes, ma'am."

Annie stared at Jackson, waiting for him to be more forthcoming. His discomfort growing, Jackson realized that he couldn't stonewall any longer.

"Well, you see…"

"Actually, I'm not sure I do see. Why don't you enlighten us?"

"Well...well," Jackson stammered. "You see, all this time, I knew you, and you were Annie."

"Yes..."

"And now...And now, all of a sudden, here you are, and you're Wish's mom."

"And not just Annie?" Annie smiled.

"Yeah. Yes, ma'am, something like that."

"So, if I am to understand what you're trying to say, you're confused as to how to address me."

"Yes, ma'am," Jackson answered, relieved to have Annie's assistance.

Annie contemplated her answer for a moment before answering.

"Well, young man, what you call me is entirely up to you. As with many things in life, I'd merely recommend that you do what you feel is proper. It's hard to go wrong when you follow that rule."

Jackson let that advice percolate.

"So, I think, 'Mrs. Fitzgerald,'" he responded. "Is that OK?"

Annie allowed herself the tiniest of smiles.

"Yes, Jackson. That would be fine."

And that was the end of that discussion.

After Jackson had headed home, Wish helped his mother with the dishes. Annie scrubbed and then handed each dish to her son, who perfunctorily made a swipe or two with an already sodden dishtowel and placed it in a countertop rack. Normally, Annie would have corrected this halfhearted performance, but tonight she was more concerned with what Wish was saying as they stood side by side.

"You should have seen it, Mom," Wish enthusiastically reported. "Jack started out lousy—"

"I'm certain you meant to say 'poorly,'" Annie gently corrected.

"Oh. Yeah…yes, right. 'Poorly.'"

"Go on."

"Well, in the beginning, he didn't have a chance. He was so tense, he coulda lost the match by the time we reached the tenth hole. But as soon as his father left, we had a good time, ya know? And when Jack calmed down, he started playing good—I mean well—and he won!"

More interested in where this narrative was headed, Annie made a conscious decision not to continue correcting her son's grammar and diction.

"And why did Mr. Spears leave? Was there some kind of emergency?"

"Oh, no, that wasn't it. He was bugged."

"Bugged? Bugged with what?"

"Well, at first he was mad that Jack wasn't doing better. But Jack never does well when his father is yelling at him. I mean, how could he?"

"So…" Annie said, urging her son to get to the point.

"So, I guess, in the end, Mr. Spears was mad because Jack finally stood up to him. Told him that only his caddie could give him advice during the round."

"Is that true, Wish?"

This question gave the boy pause. "You know, I don't know, Mom."

"Was it wise?"

"Well, Mr. Spears left, and Jackson won."

"So, in your opinion, that was sufficient to make it a wise decision."

Wish's earlier, boyish enthusiasm was rapidly waning, replaced by teenage irritation with parental authority. His voice rose as his words came out rapid-fire.

"His dad split; Jack was happier. He had a good time, and he played better. *Much* better.

He won the *junior championship*! And Jack gave his father the trophy, and Mr. Spears was proud of him, right?"

Mother and son now faced each other, the dishwashing temporarily suspended. Although sorely tempted to respond in kind to Wish's escalating challenge to her parenting, Annie held off.

"And OK, yes, I know what you're thinking. Maybe Jack was being rude, leaving his father like that. But he had a great time here tonight, didn't he? Better than even at his house, or the club. He said so, Mom."

"I'm glad he enjoyed his visit, Aloysius. But—"

"And he invited me for dinner at his house."

"Wish—"

"I know what you're gonna say, Mom, and you're wrong! Jack invited me!"

"If memory serves, you were also excited about playing in that club championship."

"Jack and I talked about that. The club has these rules."

"But you were disappointed, sweetheart."

"Yes, I guess, but this is different, Mom."

"Honey, please," Annie pleaded. "You need to understand."

"No, Mom. *You* need to understand! He invited me, and I'm going to go. Jack goes back to school in a couple of weeks, so he's telling his parents tonight or maybe tomorrow."

"Wish, that's simply not going to happen."

"Yes it will, Mom. I know what you think, but I keep telling you, Jack's not like that. He isn't! Yeah, you were right about them not letting me play in the tournament. But that was because of the rules, right? I'm not a member; I just work there."

Annie struggled with how to get through to her son. Her hesitation gave Wish another opening to repeat his case.

"This is different!" Wish's voice rose with every word, as if that would change things. "Jack and I, we're best friends, Mom, and I *am* going."

Now, it was Annie's turn to raise her voice.

"You need to listen to me, son. I know how much you'd like that to be true, but it *isn't about your friend.* Jackson is a fine young man, Wish, but it isn't *about* him. It isn't his home. It is his parents' home, son.

"And it is Darien. *It's Darien.*"

"There you go again!" Wish exploded. "It's always prejudice with you, isn't it? Why can't you see the good in people? Not everyone is like that, Mom. Jackson isn't prejudiced!"

"Jackson isn't my concern here, son. I tried to warn you when you first started spending time with that boy…"

"Maybe you're the one who's prejudiced, Mom!" Wish continued shouting as he rose from his seat. "Did you ever think of it that way? I can't stand this!" Furious, he stormed out of the apartment, slamming the door behind him.

At first Annie started to follow, but she quickly realized there was no point. She returned to her seat at the table, head in hand, a single tear dropping onto the Formica surface.

———

When Jackson returned at about nine o'clock, Howard and Barbara Spears were waiting in the living room. Barbara made a show of hardly looking up from her fashion magazine, but it was apparent that Howard had been doing much more than his fair share of pacing. He pounced on his son immediately.

"Where have you been, son?" His volume was just short of shouting.

"I had dinner at Wish's house…well, apartment. I thought I told you that."

"As a matter of fact, you didn't," Howard retorted. "Who is this 'Wish' person?"

"My caddie." He paused for a moment. "No, my friend."

"That Negro boy?" Howard's tone was incredulous with a tinge of contempt.

"Yes, Dad, that *Negro* boy."

Not at all happy that a battle was brewing, Barbara interjected, "Jackson, why don't you sit down. You, too, Howard. No reason to be unpleasant."

Both males did as they were told. Jackson sat on the floral loveseat across from his mother, who was on the matching sofa. Howard sat at the opposite end of the sofa from his wife. Both males had their arms folded rigidly across their chests.

"Where was this apartment, Jackson?" Howard asked.

"In South Norwalk."

"Oh my God." Both parents exhaled together.

"Are you out of your mind?" Howard shouted. Before Jackson could answer, the father answered his own rhetorical question.

"Never mind, it's abundantly clear that you are. Out of your mind! Our son has lost his mind, going to such a dangerous neighborhood," Howard said, turning to his wife.

More reserved than her demonstrative husband, Barbara nevertheless was also clearly disturbed by the news.

Still desiring to be respectful, Jackson worded his response carefully.

"I'm still here, Dad, in one piece. No one mugged me, see?"

"That's not the point, son. The mere fact that you were fortunate to survive a monumental case of bad judgment this one time in no way erases the fact that you made a very serious mistake!"

"I don't look at it that way, Dad. Wish is my friend, and I had dinner at his house. It was a very nice dinner. His mother is a great cook."

Howard struggled to keep his temper in check.

"Yes, you mentioned that, that this 'Wish' *boy* is somehow suddenly your friend—"

"Not *suddenly* my friend."

Howard studied his son's face before responding to this new attitude emanating from Jackson.

"Semantics aside, I'm curious, Jackson. Just exactly how and when did a Negro caddie from South Norwalk become your friend?"

"He just is, Dad, and he had me over for dinner, and now I want to have him over for dinner. Here. In my house."

This was greeted by what seemed to be an eternity of stunned silence, finally broken when Barbara quietly spoke.

"It's just not done."

"It's just not done? What does that mean?"

Howard intervened. "Watch your tone, young man."

As badly as the entire discussion had already gone, Jackson was nevertheless surprised by his parents' immediate intransigence and perplexed by this answer.

"Dad, I honestly don't know what that means."

The elder Spears looked at each other, each hoping that the other would take the lead from here. Howard nodded to Barbara.

"Well, honey, we just can't have those folks as guests in our home. It's just not done."

"*Those* folks? *Those* folks!" Jackson erupted, surprising his parents. "Do *those folks* include Elberta, who practically raised me? She lived here, Mom! And Joshua—what would our life be without him? Isn't he a 'member of our family?' He's here every day, isn't he? Correct me if I'm wrong, but aren't they Negroes too?"

"It's just not the same, son," Barbara answered, still calm, at least on the out-side. "I suppose we shouldn't expect you to understand—"

"You're right, Mother, I don't; I really don't," Jackson responded, his manner sud-denly subdued, his voice pleading. "Please explain this, because I really *don't* understand."

Howard had seen and heard enough of this new Jackson.

"Jackson, your mother and I don't have to explain anything to you. This is our house, and we will invite only those whom we wish to invite into our home. You are our son, and we love you, but we will not tolerate another word of disrespect."

"But—"

"No, son, no 'buts' whatsoever. That's the way it is, and you're going to have to live with it. End of discussion."

And that truly was the end of the discus-sion. Tired from his long day of ups and downs, Jackson felt nothing but defeat. He said his good nights and trudged up the grand staircase to his very large bedroom on the second floor. With each step he thought about how he was going to explain this to Wish.

Chapter 4

Shortly after dawn the next day, Wish was in his customary spot at the club, already reading which members had what tee times for the upcoming day. Noting that Pete didn't have him scheduled to caddie for a while, he grabbed the brown bag containing the bacon and egg sandwich that his mother had prepared and climbed the deserted fire stairs on the side of the clubhouse to a seldom-used landing where there was a great view of the first and 18th fairways and the massive 18th green.

From this perch he had whiled away many an hour daydreaming about tournament-winning chips and putts, most often turning Wee Burn Country Club's 18th green into the 18th at Augusta National.

Today, however, his thoughts quickly turned back to the events of the previous day. He smiled with pride at how Jackson had turned things around in the middle of the tournament in order to come from behind for the win. He chuckled at the memory of how stunned and quiet the opponents and the gallery had gradually become as the tide turned.

Virtually no one had expected it, least of all Jackson. Certainly, Mr. Spears fervently *wanted* it to happen, but Wish was certain that deep down, Jackson's dad had had no confidence that his son could actually pull it off. Only the caddie—the friend—had actually believed.

The fact that the caddie, the friend, Wish himself would have lapped the field had he been allowed to play in the tournament never crossed his mind as his reverie moved on to the usual fantasy scenarios, back to thoughts of last night's dinner, and finally to simple enjoyment of the panorama before him. At the appointed time, he descended the stairs and walked over to the caddie shack.

There, a surprise confronted the young man. His name on the schedule had been crossed off, replaced by "Wilson," one of the few white caddies. Curious, he stepped inside to find Pete. The crusty caddie master was not happy, but then again he rarely was.

"Fitzgerald, yeah, I've been lookin' for ya," Pete rasped. "Close the door and take a seat. We need to talk."

This was a first for Wish, more a cause for heightened curiosity than concern. That changed immediately as Pete started to talk.

"Got bad news for ya, son."

Wish was accustomed to sitting with proper posture, on the edge of his seat, when being addressed by any adult. Now, his shoulders slumped. He searched his mind for any reason why Pete, or worse yet, one of the members would be upset with him. Only one thought came to the fore.

"If this is about Mr. and Mrs. Rogers, I know I lost two balls. But honest to God, Pete, I'd be looking for her shot in the woods and then he'd hit his before I could even turn around. They're so old, and you know they can't see—"

Pete shook his head, holding a hand up to stop Wish.

"That's not it, Wish. I'm really sorry to say this, but I gotta let ya go, son."

"Let me go?"

"You can't work here no more, Wish."

"I don't get it. I know I screwed up, but what if I apologized?"

Pete sighed, looking both sad and angry.

"This wasn't my decision, son. I know it doesn't help to hear it, but this came from a member of the golf committee. As far as I'm concerned, you haven't done a damn thing wrong. But this is out of my hands."

"That's it? No reason?"

"Not that I'm allowed to tell you." It pained the older man to see his young protégé suffering like this.

"Ya gotta get off the property now, Wish."

"But my bus—"

"Yeah, I know. It's Sunday. No more buses for a few hours. Sorry, but I got my orders. I'm afraid you'll have to wait at the stop across the street."

With that, Pete stood up, indicating it was time for Wish to vacate the premises. Close to being in a state of shock, Wish rose himself. Pete offered his hand, which Wish shook weakly. He left the small shack, and Pete watched as the young man slowly walked through the tree-shaded parking lot and crossed the street to the bus stop on the corner.

Wish sat on his usual place on the stone wall close to the bus stop, searching his memory for any legitimate reason why this could possibly happen. Failing to come up with an answer after half an hour, disappointment was beginning to turn to anger. Still, shock remained the strongest emotion. Thoughts rushed through his mind. *This just doesn't make any sense. They've taken my favorite thing from me! How can I help Mom now? I'm not gonna find another job with only two weeks left in the summer! Damn! Labor Day weekend meant three solid days of good tips!*

His thoughts were interrupted by the sudden sound of a car horn. He looked up to see Pete stopped at the corner in a beat-up 1958 Chevy, gesturing for him to come over. Puzzled, Wish complied.

"Get in," Pete said. "I'm gonna give ya a ride home."

Grateful, Wish opened the passenger-side door. As he did so, he saw his canvas bag of golf clubs lying on the back seat. At last, the answer.

"I shouldn't a done it, I know," Wish said as he settled into the car and Pete turned right on the route toward South Norwalk.

"Done what?"

"Played the course, stolen the clubs, I guess. I'm sorry, Pete."

"First of all, ya didn't steal no clubs. Those jackasses wanna throw 'em away, screw 'em. I got no problem with you retrievin' those clubs, Wish. You make better use of them than mosta them members."

"So you knew?"

"Hell, yeah."

"Why didn't you yell at me?"

"Because all you was doin' was havin' some fun, not hurtin' a soul. And besides, you're one hell of a golfer. I'm proud of ya, son, bein' self-taught and all. I'd say ya have a future, but…"

Confusion poured over the young man. What had happened to get him fired?

"Look," Pete continued. "It wasn't the golf that fucked ya, son. It was your friendship with the Spears boy."

Completely perplexed, Wish waited for this to be explained.

"Jackson's dad called first thing this morning. He had already called a majority of the golf committee and gotten approval to fire you."

"But I didn't do anything! Ask Jackson, he'll tell you!"

"My guess is that Jackson don't even know what his dad done."

"Well, let's call him," Wish suggested. "He can explain. He can fix this."

"'Fraid not, son. The Spears are on their way to the airport. They up and took Jackson to Europe for the rest of the summer. Then I imagine he's off to that private school of his."

Wish searched his mind for answers, logic, explanations, sense. He found none.

"So I'm screwed," he said at last, despondent.

"Yep," Pete responded. "You're screwed."

Chapter 5

1979

It felt strange, dressed as he was in this golf getup in early March. If he was back in Manhattan, he'd be wearing a suit and a topcoat. It had been freezing when he left, but it sure was nice here.

The directions lying on the passenger seat of the rental car (a maroon Buick sedan, as nondescript as he could order) were simple to follow. Take Route 402 east from Atlanta, hang a right on Route 21 once he hit Augusta, and about a half hour later, he should be in Waynesboro. "Shouldn't be hard to find a driving range in that burg," he said out loud. "How the hell big could it be?"

He had that right. Only one range in the town, and it was kind of amazing that such a town could even support a driving range. He pulled into the small parking lot. The first impression—pretty much the only impression to be had—was one of dust.

Man, I'm really in the South now, he thought. *Hope the guy is actually here. If not, what a waste of my time and the client's money.*

He popped the trunk and emerged from the car, a swarthy, almost six-foot-tall Italian American man. He still felt out of place in the golf togs, but then again, he felt out of place in Waynesboro, Georgia, period. He pulled a huge leather golf bag with a full set of the latest, most expensive clubs from the trunk and slung the strap over his shoulder.

Walking to the range, he took stock of his surroundings and chuckled to see that golfers in the South were like golfers everywhere. Three people occupied the stalls on the range—a teenager and two older men. All three were black. Even so, like everyone at every driving range everywhere, all three were attempting to hit the poor guy operating the little vehicle that was out picking up the range balls. *Yep, none of us can resist that urge,* he mused.

At that moment he saw and heard a ball ricochet off the vehicle's cage.

He placed his bag in a rack and opened the squeaky screen door to the office/shop, which slammed behind him. The tiny shop— if you could call it that—was stocked with a few sets of clean, yet probably used, Wilson and Spalding golf clubs and other equipment, neatly displayed. There was even some polyester golf clothing.

At the far end of the room, next to a door leading to the golf tees, stood a tall, middle-aged, dark-skinned man with a weather-beaten countenance. The man stood behind a counter with beat-up putters, used drivers and irons, and wire baskets of truly abused range balls arranged on top. Shelves packed with more buckets of range balls were behind him.

"Welcome," the gentleman said in a high-pitched southern drawl. "What can I do for you?"

"Well," the visitor replied, "I need a lesson."

"Don't we all," the black man replied, phrasing it as a statement rather than a question.

The visitor chuckled. "You got that right."

"Well, you've come to the right place. If you want to take a bucket of balls out to one of the tees—there's plenty of 'em, this time of the week—and warm up, I'll be right with you. Gotta wait for my son-in-law to man the office."

The black man turned to look through the window behind him. "He's just about finished pickin' up the balls. Should be just a coupla minutes."

"Actually, with all due respect, I'm looking for a pro nicknamed 'Wish.' Heard he's the man around here, and I need some major tuning-up. Just finished a business trip in Atlanta, and I'm on my way to St. Simon's Island to play with an important client. Don't wanna look too bad tomorrow, you know?"

"Sure, sure," the black man answered, a bit quizzical. "This is a little off the beaten path from Atlanta."

"Yeah, but like I said, I've heard that this guy Wish really knows his stuff."

"I see."

"Would you be Wish?" The New Yorker knew full well the man in front of him didn't match the description he had been given, especially when it came to age.

"No, my name is Albert" came the unusually high-pitched reply, along with an offered hand that the visitor shook firmly. "Wish would be my son-in-law. I can see if he's available. And you're right, he's pretty damn good. Course that means he gets pretty booked up. But we'll see when he finishes up." Albert noticed that a name wasn't forthcoming from the stranger, but he figured that was OK.

It was mid-afternoon on a Tuesday, and there were three other customers on the range. Thus, the proprietor's reticence to book a lesson for this Wish fellow seemed odd to the man.

"Well, if it'll help, I'm perfectly willing to pay double for his services," he said. "Like I said, I heard he's pretty good, and I'm rusty as all get-out."

"Yeah, well, that could run as high as, well…fifty bucks."

"No problem," the visitor said, removing a one-hundred-dollar bill from his wallet and laying it on the counter. "I'll take you up on your suggestion and warm up a little while I'm waiting."

As soon as Albert saw that the customer was heading to the far right end of the tees, with his back turned to him, he stepped out of the office and gesticulated wildly to catch Wish's attention. Eventually succeeding, he then tried to wave

Wish in. Wish held up five fingers, indicating that he'd be finished in five minutes, but Albert would have none of that. He shook his head emphatically and waved his arms even harder. Finally, Wish got the message and headed in, parking the little vehicle next to a shed at the left end of the range. Albert was waiting for him.

"C'mon, c'mon, I've got a lesson for you."

Wish uncoiled himself from the cab of the tiny vehicle. He was now a muscular six-foot-three with no fat detectable anywhere on his frame, outfitted in the latest pastel blue golf shirt and white Bermuda shorts. He smiled at Albert's excitement, which always made his father-in-law's voice go up a notch or two in volume and intensity, from tenor to alto.

"There's nothing on my schedule, Pop. What're you so excited about?"

"One hundred dollars, that's what I'm excited about. The fella demanded you, Wish. Says he heard about you somewhere."

"A hundred dollars? Where is the guy?" Wish gazed down the line of tees.

"Down at the end. Now, I know what you're gonna say..."

Wish frowned. "The white guy? Are you kidding me?" Wish's voice had risen and was suddenly strained. He wasn't happy.

"I know, I know, but—"

"No whites, Pop. You know that."

Albert turned serious.

"I'm well aware of that, son, and you know that normally I'd accommodate you there. Don't like it; don't like it a bit, but I figure that's you. But right now I have one hundred dollars from this fuckin' guy, and who knows how much he'll be willing to tip you on top of that. It's a Tuesday in March, and this is a business, and I don't have to tell you how much we can use this money, so get your damn butt over there and be nice to the damn white man."

Wish considered his dilemma. On the one hand, there was his hard-and-fast rule—no lessons for whites. Of course, this was not normally a concern, given the fact that few whites patronized the range. If one happened to come into the shop, Wish was civil, but reserved. If one asked for a lesson, he turned them over to Albert.

On the other hand, this was his boss, and much more importantly, his father-in-law, his "Pop." He loved and respected this man more than any other.

Sour-faced, Wish peered down the tee line, studying the white man hitting balls.

"The guy stinks," he said.

"Could be why he's lookin' for a damn lesson," Albert retorted.

"Could be," Wish said to himself, his mental wrestling match over. He slowly began to traipse in the direction of the man, shoulders slumped and still visibly disgusted.

"Try smiling," Albert shouted after him. "Even if it kills ya!"

———

To say that Wish's choice of colleges had been "his" would have been inaccurate. Annie had made that choice, after a protracted and heated debate between mother and son. Entering his senior year, Wish had suddenly decided to apply only to historically black colleges. Annie would have nothing of that idea, even if she sympathized with her son's motivation.

"Life—*real* life—is not 'black,' son," she lectured. "It's white, whether we like it or not. Not gray, not striped, not polka dot. White. I am *not* going to let you learn, let alone live, in a black cocoon. You've got brains, Wish. On top of that, you've got a wonderful personality and good looks too. God gave you all the right tools. Use them well, make the right decisions, and you *will* be a success."

A great part of making the right decisions was choosing the right college. Capitalizing on the recent trend of many institutions to finally integrate, Annie played the race card for all it was worth. Fortunately, she was right about the fact that Wish was just the right candidate to seize this opportunity.

Despite his outstanding record, however, Wish failed to gain acceptance to any of the Ivy League schools. He did get accepted to Amherst, Lafayette, and Lehigh, but with only a partial scholarship from each institution. Only Emory University in Atlanta offered him a full scholarship. As much as Annie grieved at the thought of sending her son so far away, money sealed the deal.

The transition in the fall of 1970 from high school to college and from Connecticut to Georgia was tough. Black kids at Emory were still a tiny minority, and as such, tended to band together. Wish encountered little overt racism. To the contrary, his cynical mind found the many friendly and usually sincere overtures from the white kids to be patronizing and insulting. White acquaintances, including his roommate, soon gave up and kept their distance.

School was the least of Wish's challenges. His hard work as a teenager, both in high school and at home, had prepared him well for this task. Making the dean's list his first semester didn't surprise him in the least. Unfortunately, that's where the good news ended. He was lonely and homesick. He hated everything about Atlanta—the southern accents, the food, and especially the heat. He begged to come home; Annie repeatedly assured him that things would work out.

One day in February of his sophomore year, everything changed. Wish was seated at a table in the college library, his head buried in a biology textbook, when he first heard the voice from heaven.

"Is this seat taken?"

Wish looked up to see the most beautiful girl he had ever laid eyes on. Her skin was a flawless mocha, her teeth white and perfect, and her raven hair long and shiny, held back with a white headband. Her eyes were an amazing, improbable green. In short, she was perfect.

Smiling up at her like a fool, Wish was incapable of even responding to her question.

"Should I take that as a no or a yes?" the angel asked.

"Yes" was all Wish could manage, still grinning.

Hearing this, the angel began to look for another seat in the crowded library. Suddenly realizing his mistake, Wish leaped to his feet and offered the angel the chair across from him.

"I'm sorry, I meant to say 'no.' I mean yes, the seat is available. Which means, of course, that no, it is not taken."

The angel smiled. "OK, OK, I think I've got it now. Thanks."

She placed her armload of books on the table, removed her coat and placed it on the back of the chair, and sat. Wish spent the next ten minutes trying to look at her as much as possible without her knowing it, an impossible feat. Finally, she laughed and introduced herself.

Donna Jameson was a sophomore at nearby Spelman College, one of the most prestigious historically black colleges in the country. Finding the library at Spelman lacking, she spent much of her time in the library at Emory. Interestingly, she told Wish she was also escaping the all-black environment at Spelman for what she perceived to be the more "real world" environment at Emory.

The magic began from the moment they met (years later, Donna admitted that there had been a number of other open seats in the library that first day, some at completely empty tables). The two left the library a few minutes later and didn't stop talking until late that evening. By the time the night ended, they were already a couple.

Wish quickly learned that Donna was someone who had plans for her future. She believed that she would be a success in life, despite the fact that she was both black *and* a woman. She was an intelligent, attractive, well-dressed, and well-spoken young woman, a corporate recruiter's dream at the dawn of the age where corporate recruiters cared about those things. She was well aware that she was a very marketable package, but more than that, she simply understood (as did everyone with whom she came in contact) that her future burned bright.

Of course, most of that was pretty much irrelevant to Wish. In addition to her beauty, Donna's effervescent intelligence had Wish thinking about her day and night. "I can talk to her," he would tell his friends, and talk they did, for hours on the phone and in person. If it wasn't for his mother's constant reminders that he stick to business, Wish might have failed that semester. As it was, his average dropped

Green

a full grade, albeit temporarily. It turned out
that Donna cared about his grades as much as
Annie did. She wasn't about to accept medioc-
rity from her guy.

Given that, Donna's girlfriends wondered
what it was about Wish that had her so enamored. Sure he was great-looking, with a smile
that melted the female heart. Some of the
few black girls at Emory—those with whom
he had not yet gone out—described him as
charming. Those who had already experienced the Wish charm chose less-flattering
adjectives, yet still retained a place in his circle. They continued to aspire to join him at
the center of the circle.

What puzzled Donna's friends most about
Wish was his relative lack of ambition, a stark
contrast to Donna's drive. They liked that
he was intelligent, attended class, got decent
grades, and wasn't a big partier. In short, other
than the fact that he was a bit of a hound
dog, he would have been acceptable boyfriend
material to most of their parents.

But was this boy shooting for a career on
Wall Street, or in academia? Was he a budding
entrepreneur or (God forbid, in those days of
anti-Vietnam War furor) looking to the mili-
tary? No, he wanted to be a golfer!

For the girls of Spelman, this was preposterous. And in the predominately white crowd at Emory, no one believed that this black kid from Connecticut could possibly pull that off. Forget that not a one of them had ever seen Wish even touch a golf club. He was black! Basketball? Sure. Baseball or football? Maybe. But golf? Not a chance.

Surprisingly, the hidden link in this attraction mystery was exactly that—golf. What few knew about was the serendipity that Donna herself was an excellent golfer, and so was her father, Albert Jameson. Crazier still, Albert owned and operated a driving range in eastern Georgia, just south of Augusta.

And both Donna and her dad *had* seen Wish play golf.

———

Like any young lovers, the couple found every opportunity to be with each other.

Their relationship opened the overwhelmingly black social world of Spelman College to Wish. Weekend after weekend, Wish could be found at Donna's dorm and around the Spelman campus, "hangin'" with the students he called his "brothas." Donna often tried to steer them to events at Emory, but Wish made his disdain for what he labeled "that white world" quite evident. He was a black man, and that was that.

The trouble with that stance (at least in Donna's mind) was that Wish didn't really fit in at Spelman. Wish's background—his mother's protective nature, the way he spoke, his love of golf, and his years at Wee Burn Country Club—had produced a young man who didn't quite fit in either world, black or white. He was from the 'hood, but he wasn't a *product* of the 'hood.

Donna, on the other hand, was a product of the rural black South. Like Wish, she was the first in her family to attend college. Unlike Wish, she had no desire or need to immerse herself in Atlanta's black culture. Instead, she had a laser-like focus on her single-minded goal—success. To Donna, success would be found in what she labeled the "real" world— the white world.

Donna used the historically black college that she attended merely as a base for her game plan. When she could use the better college libraries, such as the one at Emory, she did. When she could add classes at such schools to her schedule, she did. When she could qualify for minority scholarships and internships from major corporations, she did. She knew that when it came to race, the national attitude was finally changing. Opportunities were there for the taking by someone such as herself. With her 4.0 GPA and stellar resume, she was on her way.

Wish's strident antipathy for everything white was both puzzling and a distinct turn-off to the love of his life. Finally, as was her practice, Donna decided to confront the issue head on. It happened one rainy Sunday a few months after they met, as the two whiled away the morning in Donna's tiny dorm room at Spelman.

As was the case in thousands of dorm rooms in those days, the conversation had centered on the war in Vietnam. Wish was repeating a well-worn complaint, that this was a "white man's war" being waged "on the backs of us niggers." Donna had heard this all too often. Although she was as against the war as anyone else on campus, she objected to the use of the term "niggers."

"Are you a 'nigger,' Wish?" she asked.

"According to the white man, I am," he responded.

"Who?"

"What?"

"Which white man, exactly?"

"Huh?"

"Which white man, Wish? What's his name? Where is this 'white man'?" She used her fingers to indicate air quotes.

"You know what I mean."

"No, Wish, I know what you *think* you mean."

"What I 'think' I mean? What the…?" One of the many things that Wish loved about this girl was the way she challenged him. But at times this could also be plenty aggravating. Apparently this conversation was headed in that direction.

"First of all, save the clichés for everyone else, Wish," Donna said. "The man. There is no 'man', sweetie. You know that as well as I do. That's just *downtrodden* black man talk, and Wish, you are not a *downtrodden* anything." She was using those darn air quotes again.

"I'm black, baby, and us blacks gotta stick together." He held up his right fist. Donna wanted to laugh out loud but managed to hold things to a chuckle, which, fortunately, the very serious Wish failed to notice.

"'Us blacks?' We 'gotta?' Exactly where does that come from?"

"What are you talking about, woman?"

"Wish, you only talk like that to impress people, and let me tell you, you're trying to impress the wrong kind of people. It sure doesn't impress me."

"That's the way I talk."

"No, it isn't," Donna replied sternly. "You were taught better than that. We both were."

"Maybe we were taught wrong."

Donna paused, giving herself time to consider what she was about to reveal to her misguided boyfriend.

"Am I a nigger, Wish?"

This caught Wish off guard. Where was she going with this?

"Not to me, baby. But to the white man—"

"Even if I'm half white?"

Momentarily stunned, Wish offered no response.

"I told you my mother died."

Wish nodded.

"My mother was white, Wish. Does that make me white or a 'nigger'?"

Again, no response.

"Come on! What's with your attitude toward whites, Wish?"

"My *attitude*?" *What in the hell was going on here?*

Memories of how things had ended at Wee Burn flooded Wish's mind, for the moment replacing his confusion over Donna's stunning news. He had never shared those memories with Donna.

"This is the seventies, Donna. I'm a black man. A proud black man. We're not the white man's niggers anymore, baby. You need to get with the program."

"Again, I ask you. Who's been treating you like a nigger, Wish?"

Wish chose not to answer. Donna took that as confirmation of her point. She sighed.

"You are no one's nigger, Wish. You won't answer me because no one has treated you like a nigger."

"I stand in solidarity with my brothers."

This only elicited another sigh from Donna. "I've got a news flash for you, darling." She carefully enunciated her next statement. "Please don't take this the wrong way, but *you* are not a 'black' man."

"I'm not a black man?" Wish repeated, incredulous. He gestured with both hands indicating his skin, making a great show that it was quite obviously dark.

"No. Based on your definition of a 'black man,'" Donna answered, again with the air quotes, "you, Wish Fitzgerald, qualify only as a wannabe black man."

With this insult, Wish fought harder to dampen his growing anger. What was going on here?

"I'm a wannabe black man," he repeated, mimicking and greatly exaggerating his girl-friend's use of air quotes. "Not a real black man, evidently. So what does that make me?" His tone was saturated with sarcasm.

"It makes you Wish—Aloysius Fitzgerald. An individual...a man. Not a black man, a white man, a striped man, or a polka-dot man. A good man, who doesn't have to pretend to be someone he isn't."

Angry and out of answers, Wish left in a huff, convinced that this would be the last contact he would have with Donna.

Wish's boycott lasted all of three days. He waited in vain for any sort of apology from Donna. When none came, he actually started to think about what she had said, although he was not sure how to process the news about her mother.

Perhaps he had not been the most pleasant person to be around for someone who didn't share his animosity toward the white man. Still, he didn't want to share what had happened in Darien. That episode spoke volumes about his naïveté—his stupidity. It was not a mistake he was going to make again.

On the other hand, he really didn't quite fit in with his new black friends in his new, all-black world. Upon reflection, he felt completely comfortable these days in only one place—wherever Donna was.

So he swallowed his pride and returned to her arms. He agreed to not place any preconditions on where they spent their time. No black world, no white world, just Wish and Donna's world.

And somehow, that worked. He still felt the same about whites but did his best to keep that to himself when he was in her presence. Donna, of course, knew exactly what was going on.

———

The wedding took place in June 1974, shortly after Wish graduated with a degree in history and literature. Annie took the train down from Connecticut for the festivities, thrilled with her new daughter-in-law but worried that the kids were rushing into things. Donna had graduated Phi Beta Kappa the year before and was already a budding star in the marketing department at IBM in the Atlanta suburbs. Wish joined Albert at his sleepy little driving range in Waynesboro, another decision that Annie questioned. The young couple found a comfortable "fixer-upper" home with a big, wraparound porch in Greensboro, Georgia, which was closer to Atlanta and thus a nice geographic compromise between their two workplaces.

———

Business at the range always picked up in April. The most obvious reason for this was the warm spring weather in Georgia, but the biggest impetus probably came from the enthusiasm generated by the annual telecast of the Masters from neighboring Augusta. Although golf held no interest for the vast majority of blacks, many local folks worked at Augusta National. Add to that the ability of Albert and Wish to promote the driving range experience, and as sure as the azaleas bloomed each spring, attendance at Jameson's Golf Center soared.

In April 1975, there was a whole new enthusiasm in the air. For the very first time, a black man—*a black man!*—had actually played in the Masters. Lee Elder had teed it up on the first hole and every hole this week. Sure, he hadn't made the cut to play on Saturday and Sunday, but he had played. That's what really mattered to the crowd at Jameson's.

On both mornings of Masters Weekend, the range was packed with young and old belting balls out onto the patchy, dusty grass of the range. By the time the tournament coverage began on CBS, a crowd had developed around the thirteen-inch black-and-white Zenith in what passed for a pro shop. Albert was over at Augusta, caddying. That left Wish, Donna, and a couple of local teenagers hustling to sell, pick up balls, empty trash cans, and just keep up with the welcome rush of business. This was one weekend when there was no time for Wish to teach lessons.

Such was the crush around the television and the press of business that Wish could barely take in the drama of the tournament, especially the excitement that was inevitable late every Sunday afternoon. He greatly enjoyed kibitzing with his friends and customers as they enjoyed the telecast, but not being able to see much of the action pained him.

Fortunately, the stories that Albert brought home from Augusta each evening were good for weeks of workplace conversations. Not only did he share with his son-in-law/partner tales of the top pros like Arnold Palmer, Jack Nicklaus, Gary Player, and Tom Watson, but he could describe in detail each shot he had observed and every nuance of all eighteen legendary holes.

And of course, he spoke about Lee Elder. Albert had been out on the course when Elder teed off, so he hadn't actually witnessed the historic first swing. But he knew every black employee at Augusta National, and many had snuck away from their posts in order to be a witness. According to them, the tee shot had been beautiful—right down the middle of the fairway. Elder had followed with a shot that found the green in regulation and two-putted for a par.

Later in the day, Albert had had the opportunity to speak to Elder himself, if only for a moment.

"Mr. Elder, it's an honor, sir. We're proud of you."

"Lee. Call me Lee. Been a long time comin', right?"

"Amen to that. Sure wish I'd seen ya play, but I was on a bag. Heard you were cool as a cucumber on that first tee shot, though."

"Don't you believe that for a second," Elder demurred. "I was shakin' like a damn leaf."

Wish celebrated the historic occasion but did so privately. The Masters had remained a singular icon for the young man from Connecticut. He longed to see Augusta National for himself, but then again, so did every avid golfer in America. For Wish, however, it was tantalizingly close, both in terms of physical proximity and the fact that his father-in-law worked there.

And yet, this entire attraction was a conundrum. He had a difficult time coming to terms with his love for one of the whitest traditions in American culture—the Masters Golf Tournament at lily-white Augusta National.

He remembered an earlier conversation with Albert.

"Don't get you, young man," Albert had commented. "You got this thing against the white man, but you dig Augusta. Augusta don't let us in, never will, but you can't wait to get there. Bugs me every damn day to see it."

"It sure looks to me like the most beautiful place on earth, Pop."

"Well, it's not like I've been to too many places, but I'd have to agree with you there. Still, doesn't change the facts. That's one white place there, Augusta National."

"You win the Masters, you're the best."

"Damn straight about that!"

"I aim to be the best, Pop."

"Well, you sure got some potential, son," Albert responded. He had stifled the rest of his comments on the matter.

Don't know how the hell you're gonna manage that as a damn driving range pro, Albert thought. *And a* black *driving range pro, at that.*

Wish did his best to keep this dream of his from Donna, but of course, she was well aware of what she labeled his "secret passion." Although she was still very disappointed by her husband's prejudice toward whites, the intelligent, fun, and loving Wish who inhabited her life more than compensated for that weakness. He had long ago ceased trying to be Super-Bad Black Guy.

Chapter 6

1979

The late-model Cadillac kicked up a cloud of dust as it pulled into the parking lot of the driving range on a sunny, hot, and humid Saturday morning that July. The driver who emerged was a tan, twenty-something white man, short and overweight, yet sharp-looking in his tailored golf shirt, linen slacks, and slightly long and expensively styled haircut. He paused to observe from a distance the small crowd gathered at one of the stalls about forty yards down the line of tees, wondering what the commotion was about.

Donna was manning the front counter when the gentleman approached. She smiled as she greeted him, hoping that she had sufficiently disguised her curiosity.

"I'm hoping you can help me," the gentleman said.

"Well, if it involves golf, I would imagine we just might be able to," Donna responded.

"I'm looking for Aloysius Fitzgerald."

That sentence was more than enough to push Donna's curiosity meter into the red zone. What could this white man possibly want with Wish? And what was up with the "Aloysius"? No one but his mother and Donna ever used that name.

"I'm his wife, Donna. And you are?"

"Oh, my apologies," the man said. "Forgot my manners there. My name is Jackson Spears."

He stuck his hand out, and Donna cautiously shook it. The name didn't register with her. "What can we do for you?"

"Wish...Your husband and I are, well, we *used* to be friends."

That's odd. Wish was friends with a white guy?

"Well, it's nice to meet you, Mr. Spears."

"Jackson, please."

"Okay, Jackson. To answer your question, that would be Wish, down there, in the middle of that group." She pointed down the tee line to the crowd that Jackson had observed upon his arrival. "He does these tricks, you know, golf tricks. The folks ask him for a demonstration all the time. Usually, he manages to put them off. Every once in awhile, they won't take no for an answer. I guess this is one of those days."

They both smiled, and Jackson nodded his head knowingly. He wasn't surprised to hear this.

"Yes, he's a pretty good golfer, isn't he?"

"Oh, he's better than good, Mr. Spears," Donna said proudly. "He's great."

Again, Jackson nodded. "Mind if I watch?"

"No charge for that, Mr. Spears."

"Jackson."

"Yes…Jackson. Please, help yourself."

Jackson ambled over to the edge of the crowd of about thirty that was observing Wish. He noticed that the group ranged from teens to senior citizens and that there wasn't a single white person. Other than himself, of course. Several of the customers gave him sidelong glances before returning their attention to the show.

Wish turned out to be quite the entertainer. At first he laid five balls out in a line in front of him on the well-worn plastic mat. Without hesitating a moment between shots, he used a seven iron to hit all of the balls to a two-foot circle 180 yards away. The demonstration took about ten seconds, and not a single one of the balls ended up outside the circle.

Next, he set up the same format of five balls and again quickly hit each ball. This time, however, he took a lob wedge and, with a mighty swing, hit each ball almost straight up in the air. Each landed less than ten yards away, but with the tremendous backspin Wish had applied, each ball zipped backward to end up near Wish's feet.

The atmosphere was festive. With each trick, Wish received multiple "oohs" and "aahs" along with loud applause. Members of the audience shouted out their suggestions for tricks that they had seen Wish perform before. There was often crowd noise in the middle of Wish's backswing, which didn't affect him in the least. In fact, he kept up his often-humorous repartee during each effortless swing. Throughout the show, he engaged individuals in the crowd in conversation.

"Jerome, you can do this, right? You've got the skills, I know, I taught you, boy!"

"Now, Lily, you are looking mighty fine over there. You know darn well you can't hide from me, darling. Step right up so the folks can see how beautiful you are looking in that polka-dot outfit today!"

"Charles, if I remember correctly, you told everyone I couldn't possibly do that again. I believe you were wrong, now, weren't you? And I believe you put some money on that, big guy. Let's see the cash, man. Let's see that cash! I know you have that cash, Charles…"

"And who is this fine young man right here? Are you a golfer, young fellow?" When the little boy answered with an "ain't," Wish gently chided him.

"No such word as 'ain't,' little guy. No such word as 'ain't.' But you come see Mr. Wish, and we'll make you a fine golfer some day. OK?"

Just as Wish was preparing one last trick to satisfy their craving—something about hitting a teed-up ball out of a teenager's mouth with a driver—he was startled to see the white man at the edge of the crowd. With a visible double take, Wish realized who the man was. His mood changed in an instant; the smile transformed to a glare.

To the great disappointment of the audience and despite vociferous objections, Wish abruptly cut the show short. Confused and a little dejected by the sudden turn of events, the group dispersed and headed back to their various tees. Many cast a curious eye at Jackson as they passed him.

Finally alone with Wish, Jackson smiled nervously and stuck out his hand.

"Hello, Wish," he said. "Good to see you."

Wish stared at the outstretched hand with disdain and made no effort to shake it.

"Can't say the same," he said, responding to Jackson's smile with a glare.

Patrons in the nearby stalls were whispering and pointing at the uncomfortable conversation.

"I guess I shouldn't be surprised by that," Jackson said. "Anyway, I came here to—"

"Not interested."

Wish now noticed that he and Jackson were the center of attention along the tee line. Without a warning or sign to Jackson, he suddenly began to walk toward the shop. A disappointed Jackson followed, searching for a way to break through to his old friend.

"I wanted to apologize for what happened, Wish."

Almost back to the shop, Wish stopped and turned to face Jackson.

"Great. Hope that made you feel better, but I'm not interested."

"I sure wish you'd let me explain—"

"Not interested. Now, please leave."

Clearly rushed, perspiring profusely, and now keenly aware of being in the proverbial spotlight, Jackson struggled to come up with something—anything—that would help him break through this wall. Failing to do so, he reached into his pocket and produced a business card that he offered to Wish.

"Well, if by any chance you ever change your mind…"

Once again, his outstretched hand was ignored. He paused for a moment to look around, seeing the curious frowns of the nearby patrons. Dejected and embarrassed, he nodded at his former friend and headed to his car. Before he had reached it, however, he heard Wish.

"There is one thing I'd like to know."

"Sure."

"How did you find me? My mother?"

"I tried that, but she wouldn't take my calls or answer my letters. I even tried reaching her through the Johnsons, where I understand she still works, but they weren't very helpful."

"So?"

Jackson considered for a moment whether he wished to reply.

"I hired a private detective."

Wish nodded as he remembered the lesson he had given to the businessman with a New York accent a few weeks earlier.

"Must have been expensive, hiring someone to drive all the way down here."

"Yes, as a matter of fact, it was. But—"

"Too bad it turned out to be such a waste of your money."

Wish turned and went into the shop, leaving Jackson staring after him. After a moment had passed, the solitary figure got into the Cadillac and drove out of the parking lot, kicking up a trail of dust.

———

For the rest of that busy afternoon and early evening at the range, Wish was able to deflect Donna's incessant inquiries as to "What in God's name was that about?" His time had run out, however, as they sat down for a late dinner of leftovers in the kitchen at home.

"Who was that guy, Wish? And stop trying to slough this off," Donna said.

"Just a guy I knew a long time ago."

Donna just stared at him. Wish concentrated on his dinner, doing his best to avoid her intensity. Within a couple of minutes, the pressure was too much to bear.

"I made a mistake, when I was a teenager…"

This rather ominous start caused her to hold her breath. She waited patiently for further clarification.

"I trusted the guy, let him be my friend. My mother warned me not to, but like an idiot, I didn't listen."

Donna's countenance softened. Reaching across the table to lightly squeeze his hand, she encouraged him to continue.

And he did. His eyes downcast, slowly the words began to flow. His voice was almost wistful as he described the kinship and good times that summer. She even detected the notes of pride when he described Jackson's victory in the club championship. But shortly thereafter he came to the end of the story, and the tone of the tale descended to disappointment and eventually hardened into bitterness. Wish practically spat the words as he described his last morning at the club and the fact that he had never heard from Jackson again.

Several times during Wish's monologue, Donna surreptitiously wiped away tears in order to not add to Wish's self-consciousness. Finally, Donna understood the reason for her husband's unusual antipathy toward all things Caucasian. This explained so much!

She felt the friendship—the love—that Wish must have had for Jackson. Donna had often wondered why Wish had never even tried to form a friendship with any male, black or white, in the years since. Now she knew.

The temptation to get into a deeper discussion in order to offer her thoughts and assistance was strong. But wisely, she decided that now was not the time. There would be plenty of time for that later.

And as to why Wish had not opened up to her about this earlier, what difference did it make now?

It was late, and they went upstairs to bed. There was an extraordinary sweetness to their lovemaking that night. Just about nine months later, they celebrated the birth of their first child, Annabelle.

———

In 1982, the Fitzgerald family added a son to the fold. They named him Bobby, after the famous founder of Augusta National, Bobby

Jones. When asked why he and Donna had not made the boy a "Junior," Wish merely stared at the questioner as if to say, "Are you crazy? Another *Aloysius*?"

———

Donna was no longer just a "budding star" in marketing at IBM; she was now the real deal, on the verge of being promoted to vice president years ahead of schedule. The only thing that prevented her from rising even higher into the ranks of corporate superstardom was her refusal to move out of Georgia. For others who had made the same decision, careers foundered. Donna's value to "Big Blue" seemed to grant her immunity.

For some of her colleagues who made the move, the decision was made easy by an eagerness to move out of the South for greener pastures. Others were much more reluctant, feeling the pull of family and the fear of what the non-South could mean for them. Donna's resolve to stay was prompted less by her attraction to her southern heritage than by her pride at what was happening in the lives of her husband and father.

Jameson's Golf Center had grown into a large, modern, full-service golf range and store. The parking lot was paved and well-lit, the dust of the barren range had been replaced by green grass, the stalls and equipment were up-to-date, and the store was well stocked with the latest equipment and fashions. Of course, the golf clothing was replete with garish colors, plaids, and lots and lots of polyester. There was even miniature golf for the children and young couples out on dates. Money was still tight for the two partners, but the future was looking brighter.

Donna's knowledge, drive, and savvy were keys to the growth of the company, but the dynamic duo of Albert and Wish made things work on a daily business. Everything seemed to work seamlessly, and despite the age difference of the two partners, they also became the best of friends. The jokes and insults that flew between them in the office, store, and on the range sometimes had the rest of the staff doubled over in laughter.

Wish had become the face of the franchise. His prowess on the range was recognized around the region. Even high-powered executives from Atlanta who belonged to the best country clubs would make the trek to Waynesboro to seek him out for golf lessons.

Earlier in their relationship, when their business had been sleepier, Wish and Albert could almost always get an afternoon or even two per week to sneak off to the local public golf courses for a game. There, they delighted in suckering some overconfident hotshot into a sizeable wager. It was easy pickings. After all, who would suspect these two black guys could possibly win a golf bet?

But lately, their golf outings were getting fewer and further between. Business and family had pushed the opportunities for five hours of golf on the local public course to the wayside. And with Wish's growing local reputation, it was next to impossible to find some unsuspecting egotist to bite at an offer to place a bet on the game.

Even with all of the recent successes at home and at work, the most memorable development for Wish could easily have been perceived as a giant step backward. He had returned to his roots; the executive vice president of Jameson's Golf had again become a caddie.

Wish had pestered Albert for years to find a way to get him onto the grounds of Augusta National. And for years, Albert's answer remained the same: "I'm just a caddie, pal. Get a ticket to the tournament like everybody else."

Of course, Albert knew that a ticket to the Masters was one of the hardest (and most expensive, at least from scalpers) tickets to get in all of sports. In fact, even the waiting list for tickets was closed in 1978. Additionally, because Albert was usually caddying during the tournament, Wish was forced to mind the store.

Wish was not alone; every golfer in America dreams of visiting the site of the Masters. It is perhaps the only golf course in the world, with the possible exception of the Old Course at St. Andrews, where seeing the course is as important as watching the players in the tournament. Augusta National is the holy grail of golf.

Financially, Albert had no more need to be caddying, and by the early 1980s, he only did it a few times a year. But he, too, had great reverence for Augusta National, so he continued to respond when the caddie master called. And one day, the caddie master said he was short a guy—would Albert's son-in-law, the former caddie, be interested in helping out?

Although he tried not to show it, the excitement Wish felt that first day came close to paralyzing him. Realizing the danger that his son-in-law might screw up the job due to sheer giddiness, Albert suggested that they arrive hours early so they could walk the course and Albert could teach his protégé.

Wish understood his obsession about Augusta National and the Masters bordered on the unhealthy. It certainly bothered him that he was so enamored of a whites-only golf club. Heck, he had a hard time reconciling the fact that his life was all about a sport that was 99 percent white.

But he truly loved just about everything when it came to golf, and this course and this tournament comprised the pinnacle of his sport. Logic told him that his lifelong dream of playing here was unattainable, but Wish had never been a big fan of logic. Merely walking the grounds of this magical place was a step toward his goal. And magic it was.

He couldn't believe how hilly the course was (television didn't do that or anything else at Augusta National justice). He had heard and imagined that the grounds and course would be "manicured," but to Wish, it appeared that every blade of grass must have been individually cut by what, ten thousand greenskeepers? The television coverage began on the back nine, so Wish had only heard about the first nine holes from talking to Albert. Visiting the eleventh, twelfth, and thirteenth holes, known as "Amen Corner" to all golfers, was akin to seeing the Sistine Chapel. Walking up the steep slope of the 18th fairway was taxing, even without the weight of the bag he would soon be carrying.

The welling of emotion, the knowledge that he had finally realized a small part of his dream, actually took a little of his breath away.

Later that day, the two partners caddied for a couple of financial heavyweights from Atlanta and New York. Throughout the afternoon, Albert had to remind Wish to wipe the silly grin off his face. Considering that this was his first time, Wish did a pretty good job. The golfers were good, so there wasn't much searching for errant balls (and there was no truly challenging rough on the course). Wish was able to give his golfer a couple of decent reads of the greens, primarily on the back nine, the descriptions of which he had managed to memorize during his furtive viewings over the years.

On the short ride back to Waynesboro, Wish wanted to recount every moment and every step of the day. Augusta National had been even more magnificent than he had

dreamed it would be; it was vital that he preserve all of the memory.

Wish soon became an experienced caddie
at Augusta National, even if his day job kept
him from being anything but a relief caddie.
But deep inside, he clung to the silent fire:
"I'll play there, someday. Don't know how, but
somehow, some way, I *will* play in the Masters."

Chapter 7

1985

At almost the opposite end of the scale was the local public course that Wish normally played. No one would ever call the Waynesboro Municipal Golf Course a great test of golf or even rank it among the better golf courses, either public or private. It was, in a word, serviceable.

The length was only 6,932 yards from the blue (back) tees, and there was little water and just a smattering of bunkers on the course. There were, however, fairly wide and forgiving fairways and an abundance of pine trees. The town budget did not allow for the best of green-keepers and equipment, so the tee boxes were a bit mangy-looking and the smallish greens rather shaggy. God forbid that the region should experience a drought, because there was no irrigation on the course.

But greens fees were cheap, and the course was popular. The locals came out in force every weekend, resulting in long waits to hit most shots and backups of two or three foursomes on the par-three tees. People were used to this, however, so they usually kept their good humor and did their best to just enjoy the round.

Wish and Albert generally played the course early on Mondays, when their business was at its quietest and they could avoid the crowds. Wish owned the course record of sixty-three, which he had shot twice, along with a couple of sixty-fours and several sixty-sixes. He could play the course in his sleep and often did, in his dreams.

On this particular June weekday morning, Wish arrived early from his home in Greensboro for their usual 8:00 a.m. tee time. Also waiting to play was a thirty-something white insurance broker named Edgar, the inordinately proud owner of a ten handicap. Fortunately for Wish, Edgar had never met or heard of this guy Aloysius, with whom he struck up a conversation as they began to hit balls on the practice range.

"You need a fourth? I'm a single," Edgar ventured.

"Well, it's just me and my dad, but you're welcome to join us."

"You play much?"

"Here and there. I enjoy the game, but I'm still learning."

Wish decided it was better not to hit balls right now. He wanted to see where this conversation was headed.

"Me too," Edgar responded. "You know what I find adds to the game?"

"What's that?"

"A little wager on the outcome."

"You mean, like a bet?" *Keep it low key... don't overact. Let the man do the talking here.*

"Oh yeah. Makes it much more interesting."

"Well, that might be interesting. But what if you're much better than I am?"

"Oh, I doubt that. You already told me you're a player..."

"I don't know..."

"C'mon, live dangerously. How about twenty bucks?"

Still playing things close to the vest, Wish hesitantly took his wallet out of his back pocket and opened it.

"Oh, geez. All I've got is a hundred."

"I could do that," Edgar responded, barely suppressing a grin.

"OK, I guess so. You only live once, right?"

Wish stuck his hand out, and the two shook on the bet.

"This'll be fun," Edgar said. "We'll—"

Edgar hesitated in midsentence, looking past Wish, his eyes getting real large. Wish turned to see what was so surprising.

Approaching the pair was Albert with a middle-aged black man who looked remarkably like Lee Elder. Once Wish's eyes shifted from the Lee Elder lookalike to his father-in-law and saw his patented grin, he realized that somehow, this visitor was actually the real deal. *Lee Elder* was in Waynesboro, Georgia. *Lee Elder* was at the Waynesboro Municipal Golf Course, approaching Wish Fitzgerald with his right hand outstretched. Wish even thought he could hear Albert introducing *him* to Lee Elder.

"And he was in Augusta for some kind of TV thing later today, so I asked him if he wanted to play a round, and I thought you'd like to meet him and—"

"You're…actually…Lee Elder," Wish stammered, shaking Elder's hand for at least twenty seconds too long.

"Yep," Elder replied, an understanding smile on his face. "And you're *actually* Wish Fitzgerald. Been hearing a lot about you for a long time from Albert here. Figured I gotta see the phenom for myself."

"Phenom?" Edgar repeated. He turned to Wish. "You're a phenom?" Albert and Wish laughed.

"Yeah, as in *phenom*enal," Albert said. "Why? You weren't stupid enough to make a bet with him, were you?"

"Mind if I get some of that action?" Elder asked.

"Oh, crap," Edgar whined.

"You're damn right, crap." Albert laughed.

Wish just continued to stare at the golfing legend in front of him.

Wish let Edgar wiggle out of the bet, and Albert allowed him to tag along to make a four-some, a kindness to which Wish would normally have objected.

Clearly nervous, Wish bogeyed two of the first three holes.

"Albert told me you were good, kid," Elder deadpanned. Left unsaid was "When do I see it?"

His pride challenged now, Wish shook off his nerves and began to play his kind of golf. Monstrous drives were followed by accurate, back-spinning wedge shots, sometimes followed by a tap-in birdie putt. In the rare case that a shot went off line into the woods, Wish was still able to save par off of the pine straw. He finished the round with an eagle, five birdies, and the two bogeys for a round of sixty-seven.

Albert and Elder were both three over, with the pro leaving multiple birdie and par putts short. A shell-shocked Edgar shot an eighty-nine. He shook hands with the other three on the 18th green, muttered something about having to get to work, and swiftly departed. Albert invited Elder to stick around for a hot dog and Coke in the ubiquitously named "19th Hole" snack bar.

"Not sure how you did that, kid," Elder exclaimed. "Those damn greens were rougher than an old man's face. How the hell can you putt so well?"

"Local knowledge," Wish said, modestly.

"Seen lots of hotshot 'range pros,' kid, but you look like you might actually have it. You've got the length, that's the easiest part. But you can actually shape your shots, and you've got a great touch around the greens.

"You're right, Albert. He just might have what it takes."

Wish had no idea what his hero was talking about. He looked at his father-in-law quizzically. Albert chuckled.

"Like Lee said before, Wish, I've been telling him about your game for years."

"What are you guys talking about?" Wish asked. "I 'might have it'? What does that mean?"

Elder touched Albert's arm, indicating that he'd answer the question.

"Look, kid, our people look at Charlie Sifford and me, and they call us 'trailblazers' and 'pioneers.' That's all well and good. But I'm forty-nine now. Gonna start playin' the senior tour soon. Jim Thorpe and Calvin Peete are 'bout the only things we still got on the Tour. Calvin's got that bum arm, can't hit the ball too long, but he may be the straightest hitter out there, white or black. Thorpe's got a good game. But that's about it now, and Calvin, he's around forty, I think. I'm not seein' anybody coming up after those guys, you know?"

"I'm not sure I understand your point, Mr. Elder," Wish said.

Albert jumped in. "Lee thinks you've got what it takes to take a shot at the Tour. At least try."

"Whoa."

The two older men waited, self-consciously munching on their food, as Wish contemplated. The only sound was that of an afternoon soap opera emanating from a nearby television set. Finally, Wish returned from his reverie.

"With all due respect, sir," he said. "That's nuts."

"Nuts, huh?" Elder said, looking at Albert for an explanation. Albert was about to speak when Wish cut him off.

"I'm thirty-three. I've got a wife and kids and a business to think about. I'm a pro at a driving range. In Georgia—*rural* Georgia. Not exactly the big time, right? Don't get me wrong, now. To play the Tour, well, to be honest, that's always been my dream—"

"Don't give us that 'wife and kids' bullshit, son," Albert interjected. "And as for the company, I made it without you before, didn't I? You think you're the be-all and end-all of our business? Don't forget whose name is on the—"

Lee Elder interrupted. "Why don't you say what you're really thinking, Wish?"

This suggestion was met with silence.

"OK, I'll tell him," Albert said, staring a hole through Wish. "He's thinking about the things you and Charlie have gone through. And he's thinking it's still a white man's world, golf is."

Albert turned his attention to Elder. "You see, Wish here, he's not a big fan of the white man."

"Well, Al, let's agree on one thing," Elder said. "Wish is right about one thing. The PGA, the tournaments—hell, golf itself—it's white, all right? *All* white. It's as white as white can be. It's better than it used to be, but it's not perfect. Way short of perfect.

"But all I can tell you, Wish, is that it's doable. Tough as hell, even for the best golfers in the country, and they're white. You're not.

"And here's what I say to that: So what?

"What you have to do is work harder than the next guy, and all of the next guys. Work your ass off. And take the racist crap that you'll still run into, without doing what you want to do, and…Well, you know what we *all* wanna do sometimes. You can't do any of that, Wish. You gotta keep that inside.

"But, from what I saw today, and from what your dad has told me, you just might have what it takes. But…and here's the biggest 'but'…You have to want it, Wish. I mean really, *really* want it.

"So, I suggest you think about it. You're building a good life for yourself here, so there's nothing wrong with continuing down that path. Nothing wrong with that at all.

"But you have great potential. I mean *great* potential. But potential is nothing without incredibly hard work, desire, and persistence. Not to mention luck. You'll need all of that if you want to pursue this.

"Like I said, think about it. Think hard. You could make it, man."

———

Late that night, Wish and Donna lay next to each other in bed. Wish stared at the ceiling, oblivious to the fact that Donna was staring at him.

"Quiet down, I'm trying to sleep," Donna said.

Wish glanced at her. "I haven't said a thing, and you're not sleeping." He returned his gaze back toward the ceiling.

"I can hear you thinking, and it's pretty loud, honey."

"Sure you can."

"This is a decision for both of us, Wish."

"And what decision is that?"

"As I was about to say, it's a decision for both of us, because we're a family and we have always handled things that way and this would mean some real sacrifice all around—"

"That's exactly the way I feel. I told Pop today, this entire idea is a nonstarter."

"—and, as I was about to say, Mr. Interruption, I'm not going to be a participant in using any of that as an excuse to not go for it."

Wish turned his body so he could prop his head on a bended arm, mirroring her posture.

"Don't you dare try to use me and the kids as a crutch, Wish. We want what's best for you. I'm sure we can figure out a way to make this work. I've got a bonus and a raise coming soon. I'll bet we could even persuade your mother to move down here and help me out. It's about time she quit working for that family, anyway. This would give her the excuse.

"In any case, we believe in you. All of us, but especially Pop. Apparently even Lee Elder believes in you, and he should know. The real question is, do you believe in yourself?"

Wish resumed his lack of focus on the ceiling. After a couple of minutes of silence, Donna shook her head with a sad little smile of resignation, put her head back down on the pillow, and closed her eyes.

A minute later she smiled as her husband said, "I love you, Donna."

Chapter 8

1986

The route to the PGA Tour ran through a series of "developmental tour" golf tournaments at courses in midsized markets, culminating at the annual qualifying (better known as "Q") school in November. "Q School" was a misnomer of the first order. It was not a school, but instead an arduous six-day golf tournament that rewarded the top thirty finishers with a card that gave them entrée to most of the next year's PGA Tournaments.

And to qualify—to even play in the Q School tournament—one had to do well during the preceding seven months on the developmental tour. Lee Elder had warned Wish that it would be a long and tough road to the Tour.

A hundred such warnings would not have been sufficient to prepare Wish for the real deal.

Initially, optimism reigned throughout the Fitzgerald and Jameson families. Wish was dispatched to his first developmental tour tournament in the spring of 1986 with a ten-year-old beat-up Chrysler station wagon, $2,000 in cash, best wishes, encouragement, and lots of hugs and kisses. His plan was to stay at the cheapest motels and hire a professional caddie at each tournament along the way to help him decipher the local course.

The cash was almost gone in less than a month. He quickly resorted to living out of his car at campgrounds (with showers that occasionally bordered on hot) and eating fast food or hot dogs cooked with a gizmo that plugged into his car's cigarette lighter at one end and through the meat on the other end. He soon developed the first gut of his life.

The caddie idea was also a failure. First of all, if a caddie was good or even available, the more experienced guys had hired him well before Wish arrived on the scene. The most experienced and well-funded players each had their own caddie who toured with them from city to city. Wish couldn't fathom how much that must cost.

So, for the first three tournaments, Wish's caddies were—in order—a drunk, an exceptionally nearsighted man, and a little guy who seemed to be closing in on eighty and who seemed like he might not last until the end of the weekend. Actually, there was no need to worry about making it through the weekend, because Wish missed the cut each time. He was done by Friday afternoon, out of the money, and already on his way to the next stop on his journey.

Checking in at the venue (almost always a country club in the suburbs of smaller markets like Columbus, Ohio, or Knoxville, Tennessee) was invariably awkward, stressful, and time-consuming. Like most of the pros, Wish would arrive early in the week in order to get in some practice rounds. A table staffed by some cheery local club members' wives was the first hurdle. Wish would stand in line behind several of his fellow competitors as the ladies fawned all over them. As soon as Wish stepped forward, the smile froze over. It was still a smile, mind you, just a smile devoid of sincerity and warmth.

"Caddies report around back," blond, pony-tailed, and perfectly made-up and dressed Melissa (or Tandy, Muffy, or Barbara) would command, politely yet firmly.

"Ma'am, I'm not a caddie."

"I don't understand."

"Ma'am, I'm one of the golfers."

"I see. Well, the bags go around the corner. Over there."

"I understand. If you don't mind, I'd like to register. Get squared away here first, then I can take care of my bag."

"Where's your golfer?"

"Ma'am, as I said, I'm the player."

At this juncture, a still confused Mandy would also begin to display just a smidgeon of irritation.

"Young man—"

It was all Wish could do to not display his own impatience. However, he plastered a smile on his face and kept it there.

"Ma'am, I'm one of the players. I don't have a caddie. Right now, I'd like to register, just like the gentleman before me and this guy right behind me here. After you and I take care of this registration task, I'll be sure to take my bag to wherever you wish."

Sometimes that was enough to do the trick. Other times, one of the golf officials who traveled with the tour recognized Wish and hustled over to bail him out. In any case, it was almost never easy.

Likewise, the first time Wish tried to enter the locker room, there was another polite but firm confrontation. Here, the source of conflict was another volunteer, this time a male member of the club. This was his territory, and a black fellow, no matter how much he was dressed like a pro golfer, certainly didn't belong there.

This usually resulted in a quiet but strident conversation between one or more of the local members and one or more officials from the tour. At times, the members had the audacity to recommend "alternative arrangements" for Wish. Each time, the tour officials replied quite firmly that Wish was to be treated no differently than any other player in the tournament. As push quickly escalated to shove, a simple indication that the entire event could be summarily shut down by the tour would put an end to the discussion. Disaster was averted, but just barely.

For the rest of the week, Wish did his best to ignore the stares (subtle and not so subtle) and whispers of far too many of the member volunteers. It wasn't easy.

His competition consisted of flat-bellied, impossibly handsome, country-club born and bred former college golf stars and sometimes cynical, end-of-the-run pros, many of whom had experienced at least one short and unsuccessful stay on the Tour. The former were all twenty-three years old; the latter were all forty-five. Or so it seemed.

And yes, Wish was the only black player.

After a while, Wish's impressively long distance off the tee, as well as his magical command of irons, made him one of the developmental tour leaders when it came to "tee to green" statistics. But that was not enough to bring even a modicum of success.

Suddenly, Wish could not putt worth a damn.

The greens on the tour were vastly faster, trickier, more subtle, and more difficult to read than anything Wish had ever played before. Sure, Wish was familiar with the infamous challenges posed by some of the most famous greens in the world—those at Augusta National. However, he had never *putted* on those greens.

His competitors, of course, had grown up playing on such greens at their country clubs and the many other similar courses they had encountered during countless junior high, high school, college, and other amateur tournaments. They *could* read the greens and, more importantly, most had "the touch."

It's impossible to become a talented putter by merely practicing at a driving range. Prior to embarking on his quest to make the PGA Tour, Wish had played the vast majority of his golf on only two courses—Wee Burn Country Club as a teenager and Waynesboro Municipal Golf Course as an adult. The former had been a suitable training ground for his present task, but it was only one set of greens, and he had played those greens many years earlier. The putting habits ingrained in Wish from his play at the latter course were a distinct part of his problem now.

So, Wish was great at getting to the greens or, to be more specific, close to the greens. The quality of a golfer's "short game"—the nuanced shots from the areas right around the greens, including the sand traps—also depended on an ability to "read" the greens. Once Wish got close to, or on, the greens, his "luck" was abysmal. During one tournament his putts were usually too long. At the next, he over adjusted and continually came up short. Subtle variations in the slope of the green would send his putt rolling well to the left or right of the hole.

Golf is not a team sport. The other golfers Wish encountered were either obsequiously polite or civil but standoffish; there seemed to be no natural, relaxed, middle ground to be had. In any case, they were (understandably) most concerned with their own need to win and hopefully, reach the holy grail of "the show." Being nice to a competitor was not a priority. The fact that Wish was an oddity was noticed and then quickly forgotten.

The caddies, however, were welcoming. It was as if they could smell "brother caddie" as soon as they met him. Some were former pro golfers themselves. Most came from working-class backgrounds, and a few were black.

Wish was civil in his interactions with the few white caddies who attempted to befriend him. However, they quickly got the message that civility was as far as he was going to go. No one seemed to care too much.

Friendships did ensue with some of the black caddies, whom, it turned out, very much wanted to see Wish succeed. After the first few tournaments, they worked out an informal system among themselves to help with that goal. Occasionally, when a black caddie's player took a week off, he volunteered to caddie for Wish—at a substantially lower wage. So, every few weeks Wish actually received accurate, professional advice as to reading his putts, calculating his distance to the green, club selection, and much more.

The rest of the tournaments Wish carried his own bag.

———

Wish put thousands of miles on the old station wagon as he drove from Georgia to Ohio to Michigan to Kentucky to Mississippi to Pennsylvania and on and on. Over a period of eight months, he was home in Georgia a total of twelve days. The budget was so tight that even the long-distance telephone calls to the family had to be short and always late at night, when the rates were at their lowest.

He worried that his absence was placing too much pressure on Albert, Annie, and Donna. How could Albert hold up under the strain of running a newly grown business without his help? How were the kids doing with their grandma during the day and a surely stressed mom on nights and weekends? Did they miss him? *Surely they must, right?* Was this having any irreversibly negative impacts on their happiness and growth?

The toughest part was not his lack of success, although day after day that was certainly

eating away at his confidence. It wasn't the sub-
sistence lifestyle—the lousy diet, uncomfortable
sleeping arrangements, and cold showers. It
wasn't even the enveloping loneliness, assuaged
only a little by his new friendships with a few of
the black caddies.

No, the worst was how much he missed his
family. The easy-going, back-and-forth taunts
and humor with Albert. Kissing the kids and
whispering "I love you" as they slept so angeli-
cally. Being challenged and supported and
loved and comforted by Donna. Brief phone
calls could not replace any of that.

After the first few tournaments, there was
pressure on two principal fronts edging Wish
closer and closer toward giving up and heading home. First was that little voice in his head
that was constantly saying "Maybe I'm just not
good enough to make it on this level. If I'm not
good enough for this level, well, then I'm sure
not good enough to make the Tour!" Second,
and more important, was the lack of money.
The entire family sacrificed for the effort, but
at some point, there had to be a limit.

As he drove to a tournament in Kentucky
in early June, Wish was ready to toss in the
towel. The money had just about run out
(again), and he had not played on the weekend

for a while. "You'll play this weekend," Donna urged. "I've got a good feeling about it." Sure enough, he did make the cut and even finished well enough to make a few hundred dollars. That small amount was enough to get him through another couple of weeks.

Finally, his persistence began to reap just the slightest taste of success. He began to make more cuts and place "in the money"—enough money to keep him on the road.

However, all three adults in the Wish Fitzgerald Fan Club realized that he was subject to a different standard than his colleagues on the developmental tour. For the majority— the young guys—this was a process. Much like minor league baseball players, they had the youth and the resources to give this a few years. The older guys, most of whom also had the resources, were generally just plain stubborn. Just like many aging football, basketball, or baseball stars, they were unwilling to acknowledge that Father Time had graduated from knocking to pounding on their respective doors.

Wish was in a somewhat unique position: at his age, he had only this one year to shoot for glory. If he didn't win his tour card by winning one of the coveted top spots at Q School, the jig was up. It was either on to the PGA Tour next year or back to life as a business owner and driving range pro in rural Georgia. There was no middle ground.

But, he still could not putt worth a damn. And without that, there was virtually no hope for a future on the PGA Tour.

———

Early in November, Wish arrived in Tallahassee, Florida, for the final developmental tour event of the year. His trusty car was on its last legs, as was the driver. In two weeks, those who had qualified would play the Q School tournament in Arizona. At this point, Wish was not one of them. But, if he could somehow manage to finish in the top five in Tallahassee, he would garner one of the coveted spots.

Thanks to his caddie friends, his ability to read the breaks in the greens had some-what improved over the past few months. Competing at this level had taught him that there were a surprising number of factors that had to be taken into account before stroking any putt. The slope of the green (whether the putt would roll from right to left, left to right, straight, or even a combination of these), the speed of the putt (uphill? downhill? both?), the length of the grass, the direction of the grain, moisture (dew, rain), the time of day (have the greens gotten faster or slower as the day has gone on?), even the wind. So much to consider.

Walking each course during the days before a tournament enabled him to chart the greens. In turn, this helped him to better plan his approach shots—whether to hit it short and roll the ball closer to the pin or shoot it past the flag, "yo-yoing" the ball into reverse with a show of backspin.

Unfortunately, his dreadful putting had now reached the point where it had infected his brain. He explored solutions on a daily basis, on the practice greens with his friends and on the phone with Albert. However, nothing could keep him from either leaving his putts short of the hole or powering it too far past. Far too often he managed to do both on the same green.

Wish had switched putters five times, tried four different grips, and even tried putting "cross handed," where he switched the positions of his hands. Nothing had worked.

The first day of the Tallahassee tournament had not produced the results for which he was hoping. As usual, his putting had put him in the unenviable position of having to shoot a phenomenal round on Friday just to make the cut for weekend play. Barring a miracle, it didn't look promising.

Given the fact that this final tournament was do or die for him, Wish decided to splurge with his last few dollars to get some much-needed rest by staying in the cheapest motel he could find. He lay on the lumpy "Magic Fingers" bed that evening, barely watching an episode of *Hill Street Blues* while he stressed about his putting. There was a knock on the door, and Wish, puzzled about who could possibly know where he was staying, hopped off the bed to take the two steps to open the door.

The black man in front of him filled the entire doorframe. Bald, dark-skinned, at least six-foot-nine-inches tall and half again as wide, the man was casually dressed in golfing attire that somehow seemed to fit his gargantuan frame. He offered a huge hand to Wish.

"Name's Tiny," he said. "For obvious reasons."

"Wish Fitzgerald." He shook the giant's hand, wondering what this could be about. He was amazed at how his hand, which certainly wasn't small, was swallowed by the handshake.

"Yeah, been lookin' for you."

Wish waited for an explanation.

"Mind if I come in?"

As if I could stop you? Wish stepped aside to let the man pass. Tiny sat in one of the two chairs at the small round table provided by the motel. He looked like an adult visiting a kindergarten class. Wish sat on the bed.

"Ben Crenshaw sent me," Tiny began. "Ya know him?"

"Ben Crenshaw? *The* Ben Crenshaw?" Wish said, flabbergasted.

"Same one."

"No, never met the man. Big fan, though."

The conversation, such as it was, had already hit a roadblock. Wish realized that he was going to have to ask the obvious question.

"Why in the world would a guy like Ben Crenshaw send you to see a guy like me?"

Tiny slowly sat forward in his chair, which complained loudly under the load.

"Well, ya see, Ben knows some guys who know a guy named Albert Jameson. Lives up near Augusta, from what I hear. We seen him there, at the Masters, ya know? And Albert was tellin' the guys about you, and about how y'all been havin' problems on the greens, and Ben's a pretty good putter, ya know, so Ben offered to help, but I guess Albert says y'all got a problem with white people, and me bein' black and all…"

Holy cow, Wish thought. *This is nuts.*

"And besides that, a coupla my buddies, they been caddyin' on your tour, here, and they got to know you, and they been tellin' me about that same thing, ya know, this puttin' problem y'all been havin'…"

Holy cow.

"So Ben and me, we got ta talkin' 'bout it…"

He stopped again.

"So…" Wish prompted.

"So, I'm here ta fix ya."

"You are."

Tiny nodded. "Yeah, if I can. And if y'all will listen."

It took Wish a moment or so to digest this and few moments to contemplate his answer. The protracted silence was broken by the sound of a couple's argument in the parking lot just outside the door. Neither man noticed. Finally, Wish responded.

"Well, Tiny, everything you've heard is absolutely correct. I suck at putting. The problem is, I'm in a position where I need to fix it immediately. As in, literally, tonight. I've run out of time. If I don't pull off a miracle tomorrow—if

I don't make the cut—it's over." He paused to take a breath. "What I'm trying to tell you is that I appreciate you coming all the way here, but I'm afraid you've wasted your time. There's no chance in hell that this could work, at least not that quickly."

Tiny did some contemplating of his own before speaking. When he did, it was obvious that he had either not heard what Wish had said or that he had chosen to ignore it.

"Did ya suck at puttin' before the tour?"

The question surprised Wish.

"Those were different courses…"

"Every course is different. Every green is different. Ya didn't answer my question. How was your puttin' back then?"

Wish thought about it.

"Not bad, I guess. Matter of fact, pretty good. Really good."

"Why's that?"

Again, Wish was at a loss for an answer for a short while. He smiled as he remembered his successes back in Waynesboro.

"I guess I knew the greens. I sure played them often enough, so I knew what to do."

"You was confident."

"Yes, I suppose I was. No, forget that. I absolutely was. Absolutely."

"I hear tell that y'all been eating these courses up, tee ta green. Crushin' it off the tee, shapin' your shots real nice. Heard that lately, ya even been dialin' in the approach shots."

"Yeah, I guess that's right."

"Why is that, ya think?"

"Sorry, Tiny, I'm not following you."

"Why you so good, tee ta green?"

"Just am, I guess."

"That's a bullshit answer. Not an answer 'tall, ya ask me."

"OK, OK, that's fair. So then, I guess I don't know the answer."

"I'll bet I do, and I ain't never even seen you play a lick."

It was Wish's turn to sit forward on the edge of the bed.

"How many different grips you tried?"

Wish thought about this. "At least four, I guess."

"How many different putters?"

"Oh, yeah, three…no, four," Wish responded, shaking his head. "Maybe five. Geez."

"Still got your putter from before?"

"You mean from before this? From home? Yeah, sure. It's in the car."

"Go get it."

Curious as to where this was headed, Wish ran out to the car and rifled through the mess in the back until he located his trusty old putter. He returned to the room and tried to hand it to Tiny.

"I don't need it," Tiny said, pushing the putter away. He rose from his chair, once again towering over Wish. He took a step to the end of the bed and, without the slightest bit of exertion, lifted it up until the entire bed was standing on one end, against the wall. This created more space in the room.

"Show me your old grip, your old stance," Tiny commanded, pulling a ball from his pocket and placing it on the floor near the door to the room. He went to the opposite end of the room, next to the bathroom door, took a spotted water glass off the counter, and placed it on the floor so that the mouth faced Wish.

"Go ahead, putt."

"C'mon, man. What's this going to prove? Carpet isn't the same as a green."

"Sure is, at least this floor. Just about as fast as some greens, I 'spect. Probably faster, as bare as it is. Go ahead, try it and see."

Wish took a closer look at the dingy, worn surface that barely passed for a carpet. He assumed his old putting stance, took a look toward the glass, and putted the ball. The ball rolled much too quickly, missing the glass, until it bounced off the wall under the sink and ricocheted almost all the way back to Wish. He grimaced.

"I see what you mean."

"Yeah, kinda like that linoleum stuff. Try again. Remember, just like the old days back home. Nothin' different."

Wish's second attempt was still wide right and still bounced back, but just a few inches. Tiny nodded at him to try again and again, until on the ninth try, the ball rolled slowly into the water glass with a pleasing "plink." Wish's smile was short-lived.

"I'm not getting it, Tiny. This isn't a golf course."

"Listen up, my man. Here's what Ben wants you to know. When it comes to putting, *any* stance can work. *Any* grip can work. *Any* putter can work. No magic, no magic 'tall, to none of 'em.

"Ya'll been lookin' in the wrong places, my man. Sure, when y'all got to this level, everything was new. The speed, the reads, the pressure—everything. But you used to all those things now. Can read those greens, right?"

"Yeah, I suppose so."

"See, that right there. *That's* your problem, man."

"Excuse me?"

"Y'all said, 'I suppose so.'" Tiny mimicked Wish's more refined manner of speaking.

"So?"

"So, y'all missin' one thing, man. The main thing. The *only* thing. Confidence."

Wish thought about this and at first nodded his agreement. He then questioned the premise.

"But isn't that obvious?"

"Maybe so." Tiny nodded. "Maybe so. But seems to me, ya'll not gettin' the message, my man."

"OK."

"Ben want you to remember how it was when ya'll were the king of golf. Crushed every drive, made every putt, beat everybody."

"OK."

"Y'all get that attitude back, y'all stop thinkin'. Y'all stop thinkin', y'all will make the putts. Just like the old days."

Wish contemplated this.

"Tell me 'bout y'all on the tee. Whatcha thinkin'? Whatcha thinkin' when y'all swingin' the driver?"

Once again, Wish considered the question.

"I don't know."

"Yeah, ya do."

Wish searched his memory.

"Honestly, I can't think of a thing that's in my head when I actually swing. Nothing, sorry."

"Right."

Finally, the light went on for Wish.

"I'm not thinking about anything."

Tiny nodded, smiling for the first time since Wish had first seen him in the doorway.

"And when I putt, I'm thinking about everything."

Tiny nodded again and shrugged his shoulders as if to say "See how obvious it is?"

"And when I used to putt, back home, I wasn't thinking about a damn thing. I *knew* I was going to make it. I just knew it."

"Y'all was confident."

"I was."

Both men were grinning.

"Tomorrow, y'all gonna kill those putts, my man. Y'all read the putt, y'all decide the line, y'all decide the pace. Then, ya'll stop thinkin'.

"Now, let's practice. Old putter, old grip, old Wish."

For the next three hours, in that decrepit motel room, with its stained, threadbare carpet and its Magic Fingers bed against the wall, witnessed by the giant Tiny, Wish stroked putt after putt after putt directly and softly into the water glass.

The next morning, Tiny greeted Wish upon his arrival at the course. The big man took Wish's golf bag from his shoulder.

A tired but eerily composed and suddenly self-assured Wish spent most of his practice time on the putting green, where stroke after stroke confirmed what he had learned the night before. He even found himself standing taller and straighter, with a newfound smile and an eagerness to hit the course.

As was common, his first drive was magnificently long and accurate. His approach shot left him about thirty feet from the hole. Once he was on the green and could read the putt, he rapidly reached the conclusion that it would break about four inches from right to left. His analysis confirmed by Tiny, Wish took one practice stroke, stepped three inches closer to the ball, and with no delay, stroked the putt. The putt barely lipped out of the cup on the "high," or right side of the hole. It was as close to perfect as a putt could be.

Wish loved having his old putter in his hand, and, oddly enough, it felt surprisingly light. His propensities to freeze over each putt for many seconds, to have multiple thoughts fighting each other ("don't leave it short, but better not slam it past the hole"), and to squeeze the putter tightly were all gone. As Tiny had predicted, as he struck each putt, Wish's thoughts were close to nonexistent.

Wish started the day eight strokes back from the potential cut line for those golfers who would be playing over the weekend—normally, an insurmountable deficit. With the help of ten one-putt greens, Wish shot a sixty-six and made the cut with room to spare.

Over the weekend, Wish finished with two rounds of sixty-nine, good enough for third place, thereby qualifying for a coveted spot in the upcoming Q School tournament. He was one final, yet excruciatingly challenging, step away from qualifying to play on the PGA Tour.

In his slightly euphoric state, Wish failed to notice that for all three days he spent at the course with Tiny, not a single person approached the big man with any sign of friendship, let alone recognition. In addition, the caddie had not helped him to read a single putt. Wish chalked that up to Tiny's strategy to build Wish's confidence. As far as Wish was concerned, that strategy had worked.

Wish made it home for a few days of family time prior to heading to Arizona. Of course, there was much celebrating, including a potluck dinner attended by both family and a few close friends (numbering about fifty). Being of the mind that there was nothing worth celebrating yet, Wish was miffed by what he felt was premature and unwarranted attention. But given Donna's unmitigated joy, he resisted the urge to throw cold water on the festivities.

Late that evening, Wish and Albert, each bundled up against the late-autumn chill, enjoyed a last, quiet cup of decaf as they sat in rocking chairs on Albert's porch.

"I've never spoken to Ben Crenshaw, son," Albert said. "Never met the man. Seen him play, of course. Hell of a putter."

"C'mon, Pop, quit kidding me. Tiny told me you had called Crenshaw—"

"That's another thing. This Tiny fellow— you say he's this huge black guy?"

"Absolutely. Biggest human being I've ever met. Looks like a heavyset Wilt Chamberlain to me."

"Gotta ask, son. By any chance are you blowin' smoke up my ass with this whole fucked-up story?"

"Wish I was."

"This guy said he was Crenshaw's caddie?"

"I thought so. Come to think of it, I'm not sure he actually said he was. I just assumed."

"Well, I can tell you that Crenshaw's caddie is a black fella, but I don't remember him being *huge*. Matter of fact, I've never seen a caddie that looks anything like that in all my days."

"You're serious, right? You're telling the truth this time?"

"Yep."

"Well, that's just weird."

———

The PGA Tour qualifying tournament was known as one of the sternest, most pressure-packed tests in sports. Played over six days, as opposed to the four rounds for the usual PGA tournament, the goal for the contestants was simple: be among the top thirty at the end.

Certainly, not even avid golfers would claim that the game of golf is a tough test of one's physical prowess. Skill and coordination, yes. But strength, speed, and other such indices of physical ability? Definitely not.

However, PGA tournaments, and especially the four "majors" (the Masters, US Open, British Open, and PGA tournaments) are some of the toughest tests in sports of one's *mental* acuity and stamina. To do well, the player has to stay focused for five plus hours, sixty-five to eighty strokes a day, for four days. Because of the stakes involved (one's chances at qualifying for the road toward realizing his dream) and the extraordinary length of the tournament, most pros who have experienced Q School would say that it was indeed the most daunting challenge of their golf life.

Albert's decision to caddie for Wish at Q School was made easier by the onset of the colder temperatures of November, which resulted in somewhat somnambulant business at the driving range. Wish swung by his father-in-law's house to pick him up for the long drive to Arizona. Albert put his suitcase in the back of the station wagon and settled into the passenger seat.

"Need to make a quick stop at the range," Albert said.

"C'mon, Pop. I want to get going. You sure we need to do this?"

"Figured I could check the safe to see if we can scrounge a little more cash for the trip. You said you were tight, son."

This news assuaged the uptight, impatient Wish. Instead of heading directly toward the interstate, he took the right turn for the short trip to Jameson's.

"Every little bit helps," Albert said. "Maybe we can even upgrade to a Red Roof."

"That would be nice."

"Yeah, well, at least this'll most likely be the end of the money worries, right?"

"How do you figure that? It only gets ten times as expensive if I make the Tour."

"Oh, yeah. I meant if things don't work out. No need for money then."

"Gee, thanks for the vote of confidence."

"Hey, c'mon, look at the bright side. I'll have you back at the office, and you can get back to teaching your lessons."

Not catching on to the fact that Albert was pulling his leg, Wish felt his face heat up. As he approached the turn into the parking lot, he was ready to give Albert a piece of his mind.

"Ya know, Pop, you can always stay…"

Wish stopped speaking and stopped the car, so surprised was he to be confronted by the scene in front of him. The parking lot was jam-packed with cars and people. In fact, Wish had failed to observe that cars had been parked alongside the road for about two hundred yards back.

"What the…?"

"Get out of the car, son," a smirking Albert commanded. "People want to say hi to you."

The car was suddenly surrounded by well-wishers of all ages, shouting "You're the man, Wish!" "Right on!" "You're a winner, Wish!" and "You're *our* winner, Wish!"

Someone opened Wish's door for him, and Albert pushed his dumbfounded son-in-law out of the car. A flood of people grabbed Wish's hand and pounded him on the back as the unstoppable flow carried him to the other end of the parking lot, where a flatbed truck with chairs on it was parked in front of the pro shop. Eventually, he was deposited in front of some makeshift steps leading up to the back of the truck, where he was greeted by a beaming Donna and an older black gentleman. Wish recognized the man as the mayor of Waynesboro. Annie and Albert sat nearby on folding chairs.

As Wish took a seat between Donna and Annie, he shot his father-in-law a halfhearted look of disapproval. Albert raised his eyes and shrugged his shoulders.

The mayor stepped up to the front of the "stage" to address the crowd, which numbered around three hundred. He had to raise his hands several times in an effort to quiet the throng. It seemed that each individual wanted to shout his or her own encouragement to Wish, and he smilingly recognized many friends and customers in the crowd.

"Wish, I've been told that you hate this sort of thing," the mayor began. "That's too darn bad." This elicited some laughter.

"The fact of the matter is that we're proud of you!" Loud applause.

"Win or lose this coming week—"

This produced a cacophony of shouts such as "Won't happen!" "He ain't gonna lose!" "Wish is a winner!" and "No chance that boy is gonna lose!"

The mayor chuckled. "OK, OK. Win or win, we are behind you, Wish. We are all here to tell you that we are behind you, all the way. We may not be there in person, but we sure as shootin' will be there in spirit!"

Wish heard the words and appreciated the sentiments being expressed by the mayor and the audience, but, in truth, he was embarrassed by the attention and not a little bit in shock. Donna nudged him and indicated that he should look down at his hand, which was gripping hers so tightly that his knuckles were white and her fingers were red. He sheepishly released her hand for a moment and then grasped it again. With another look, Donna directed his attention back to the mayor, who continued with his remarks.

"Wish, c'mon up here and join me."

The crowd applauded as Wish stood up and stepped forward. The mayor shook his hand heartily as a pair of press photographers snapped flash photos. Wish saw that the mayor held an envelope in his left hand.

"Wish, we've heard tell of your adventures on the road. Sounds like it may have often been a challenge to get a good night's sleep."

The mayor now looked to the back of the parking lot. "And by the looks of it, you've put a mile or two on that limousine of yours."

The crowd laughed.

"Well, we need you to be in fine shape for this tournament—I think you fellas call it Q School?"

Wish nodded, curious as to where this was headed.

"So, your friends here—and I do mean *all* of your *many* friends here—"

The crowd roared its agreement.

"—have chipped in to give you a little gift."

As the applause swelled, the mayor handed Wish an envelope.

"We're not letting you drive all that way to Arizona, Wish. Too tiring—gotta keep our boy fresh! These are roundtrip airline tickets from Atlanta to Phoenix, Arizona, for you *and* that crotchety father-in-law of yours!"

Wish was stunned by this news. His hands shook as he opened the envelope to discover the tickets. The mayor let the crowd express its further approval for a while before once again holding his hands up in a request for silence.

"And that's not all. You boys will also be staying at the *Marriott* hotel, compliments of everyone who loves you back here in Waynesboro!"

When it was Wish's turn to respond, he was unusually succinct.

"This is all so overwhelming," he said, a little too quietly.

"Louder, Wish," shouted someone from the back of the crowd. "Since when you been so shy?"

This produced a lot of knowing laughter and nods from the audience.

"OK, then," Wish began again, his voice stronger now. "If I can just keep from making a fool of myself by crying in front of you…"

This was met by chuckles.

"Let me tell you, this year has been tough. On me, yeah, but more importantly, on my family." The crowd applauded as Wish turned to look at Albert, Annie, and Donna.

"This…you…what you've done for us… This means so much. Your support, your friendship. You have no idea." He bowed his head, trying to collect himself. Other than a few murmurs, the crowd waited patiently.

"I guess this means I'll have to do well out there. Otherwise, I'll never be able to show my face in this town."

His remarks elicited laughter and polite applause.

"So, thank you. I'll do my best, despite the fact that my father-in-law is caddying for me."

The audience erupted one final time as Wish turned into a group hug from his family members. As well-wishers pressed to the edge of the truck's bed, they had to wait for a while for the embrace to end.

The line to wish their hero well was a long one. After twenty minutes of handshakes, kisses, hugs, and backslaps, the very last person Wish came upon was a wizened old black woman, frail and tiny, in a wheelchair. She was dressed in her Sunday best, complete with a large and flowery hat. The lady's grandson, one of Wish's golf students, introduced her as "Miss Maybelle" and told Wish that she was "approximately" ninety-five.

Wish crouched down to shake her hand, which felt like nothing but tiny bones. She applied all of her energy to pull him closer, until he was on one knee next to the wheelchair. It was evident that she wanted to impart something personal to him, so he leaned closer in order to hear her. Her voice was barely louder than a whisper.

"Don't you forget that you are representing us," she said, slowly and distinctly.

"Yes, ma'am, I know," Wish responded, perhaps a tad glibly.

"I'm not sure you do," came her answer. She looked him directly in the eye. "You are representing *us*. *All* of us, not just the folk here in Waynesboro. You'd best keep that in mind, young man. You are representing us."

Chapter 9

Registering at Q School, Wish had to smile. First, with Albert standing nearby, he felt as if he finally had the security blanket he had missed over the previous months. Second, he was well-rested and confident in his game. And third, the personnel behind the registration tables this time were all experienced PGA staffers. They not only knew *of* him, but in many cases they had come to know him somewhat personally. Sure, they were white, but he appreciated the fact they had always treated him with respect.

No excuses, he thought, moments before Albert caught up with him on the first tee on opening day, carrying Wish's golf bag.

"No excuses," Albert said.

"Yeah," Wish responded, his game face firmly in place.

"Let's have some damn fun," Albert ordered, whacking Wish on the butt.

And strangely enough, given the importance of the job at hand, that's exactly what they did. Wish started out with three pars and a welcome birdie. While his playing partners displayed nothing but scowls and furrowed brows as a result of the pressure, Wish had a confident smile as he addressed each shot. His drives were long, and his putts were dropping; he was on his game during the most important contest of his life.

After finishing the fourth of six rounds, Wish was tied for twentieth place in the field of 163. His confidence was sky high, but Albert ensured that his head was not so large that it negatively affected his game.

Even someone from the media, a white reporter from *Golf Digest*, was paying attention to this black man in his thirties who had "suddenly burst on to the professional golf scene." Albert saw this as a great opportunity for Wish.

"What does it feel like, being the only black golfer in the field?" the reporter asked Wish,

"Really? I'm the only one? I hadn't noticed."

"Seriously, Wish. Do you feel like some kind of trailblazer?"

"Other men before me were the trailblazers. I feel like a golfer."

Albert, stationed behind the interviewer so he could be in Wish's field of vision, rolled his eyes.

"So, no sense of being unique?"

"Just qualifying would be plenty unique enough for me."

Giving up, the reporter thanked Wish and walked away.

"Your first chance at national publicity, and you're a first-class jerk with the guy," Albert admonished.

"His questions were asinine, Pop," Wish said. "I'm not a 'trailblazer,' I'm just a golfer. Charlie Sifford, Lee Elder, absolutely, they were trailblazers. But Wish Fitzgerald? Please. The guy needs to do his homework before he asks such a stupid question."

"And you don't feel unique out here?"

"Sure I do. *I* know that, and y*ou* know that, but I don't want *them* to know that."

"Well, son, you sure proved how 'unique' you are with that crap. Remember, you just might qualify for the Tour by the time this puppy is over in a couple of days. And if you do, trust me, you're gonna want guys like that on your side."

Wish's pride kept him from verbally agreeing with this advice.

"Truth is," Albert continued, "the guy was white. So, as usual, you copped an attitude with the man. No, excuse me, *The Man*.

"And what terrible thing was *The Man* doing? His job, Wish. Just his job. And you know what his job is, numb nuts? To make golf interesting to those who care enough to read about it. And guess what? As fucked up as you are with this damn attitude of yours, *you* are an interesting story.

"You think the last year has been tough? You haven't seen tough yet, buddy. Let's say you get your card this weekend—you make the Tour. What do you think happens after that? Ya think the money magically appears for you to travel all over the country to actually play on the Tour? You can't live out of your car anymore, Wish. The Tour stops aren't in the Podunk towns. They're in the big markets, where it costs big money just to stay there. And another thing—you're gonna need a real good, full-time caddie to play with the big boys. And you don't need me to tell you, buddy, that also costs money—lots of it."

"And your point is?"

Albert gave his son-in-law a withering look.

"The point, wiseass, is that if you make it this weekend—*if* you make it—you are going to need all the help you can get. Somehow, some way, we're gonna have to find sponsors for you. Sponsors with deep pockets who're willing to take a chance on a nobody black guy from Georgia who can hit the ball a mile. There's no guarantee that sponsors like that exist, so I suggest you start saying your prayers. I sure as hell have been."

Wish tried to interject, but Albert wasn't done yet.

"You know what could help you find that miracle sponsor? Good publicity. Good press. And a favorable article from 'The Man' you just kissed off could be the first step down that road."

Albert stared at Wish, looking for the slightest sign of enlightenment from the younger man. In fact, Wish's respect for Albert had allowed him to listen, rather than do what he wanted to do, which was to argue. As a result, cold reality was just beginning to trump hot hatred.

"Might be a good idea to go apologize to that guy and see if you can start over."

Wish took a moment to contemplate this suggestion.

"You're right."

"Damn right, I'm right. Now fix it. He's right over there, talking to Paul Azinger. Go kiss some ass."

———

Albert was awakened at 2:15 in the morning on Saturday by the sound of Wish vomiting in the bathroom. Since Wish continued to lead a relatively healthy lifestyle while pursuing his goal, Albert knew immediately that this had to be a bug of some sort. Wish was not a drinker. Even if he had decided to suddenly change, the two men had spent the entire evening together.

This meant nothing but trouble for Wish's chances in the tournament. As he suffered in the bathroom, Wish could hear Albert praying that he be allowed to overcome this obstacle.

After a night filled with trips to the bathroom and no sleep, the two stood on the first tee, ready for the penultimate round of Q School. Wish was exhausted, dehydrated, and completely drained of energy.

"I can do this," Wish said, unconvincingly.

"You'll have to," Albert responded. "You don't have a choice."

It's difficult to hit a three-hundred-yard drive when you have no strength. It's hard to hit an accurate iron shot when you are exhausted. It's hard to baby a delicate chip shot or stroke a great putt when you are so drained that you simply can't focus. Even when you are at your very best, it's extremely challenging to compete against some of the world's best golfers in the most pressure-packed tournament of your life.

Miracles were not to be had on this day. Wish shot an eighty-three and fell from twentieth place to sixty-fifth, well shy of the "cut line" of the top thirty. With one round to go, his position had deteriorated from secure to improbably precarious.

Dinner at Denny's was a quiet affair. Both men were depressed; Wish could barely keep his eyes open. They both realized that the mountain on Sunday was now virtually insurmountable.

"You gave it your best shot, son," Albert muttered, reaching across the table to grasp Wish's forearm.

Wish looked up from his food, disappointment blanketing his face.

"Thanks, Pop. Thanks for supporting me. Thanks for being here."

———

The first five rounds in the Arizona desert had been played under ideal conditions—clear skies, pleasant temperatures, relatively still air. Sunday morning, however, arrived with decidedly un-Arizona-like rain and chilly, howling winds.

As a rejuvenated Wish tied his golf shoes in the locker room, the tension among the golfers was palpable. This was it: their final opportunity to qualify for the 1985 PGA Tour.

Wish thought about how good his life was back in Georgia, about his family's love and the satisfaction of building a solid business with his father-in-law, who also happened to be his best friend. At the moment, his chances of graduating from that lifestyle to an opportunity to realize a lifelong dream were looking dismal. Perhaps that wasn't so terrible. He missed Donna and the kids terribly...

"The hell with that," he whispered to himself, causing a pro at the next locker to glance over at him.

He had worked way too hard over the past year to waste it because of an untimely illness. Sure, it was bad luck. Yes, it sucked. But there was nothing that could be done about it. No sense whatsoever in using it as an excuse. Today, he felt fine.

He was going to make it happen.

He left the locker room and greeted Albert on the practice range with the slightest hint of a smile on his face. Detecting this aura of quiet confidence, Albert decided to dispense with a pep talk. He knew that his charge was fully cognizant of what needed to be done.

With each ball that he struck on the range, Wish uttered a quiet "yes." The drives were once again monstrously long, the iron shots once again landed softly and close to the pins. Each practice putt elicited a quiet "yeah, baby." Virtually every putt was dead accurate.

Wish used every skill in his arsenal to defeat the very conditions that destroyed the game of most of the other golfers. Sometimes he would hit high shots way to the right or left and ride the wind to the spot where he was aiming. On other shots he would hit a screaming drive that stayed a few feet off the ground, keeping the ball under the wind. He calibrated each approach shot and each putt to allow for the soggy, slow greens.

Wish's final round of sixty-three went down as one of the best in Q School history. He had accomplished the nearly impossible: moving from sixty-fifth place to twenty-fifth, from disaster to victory, from journeyman driving range instructor to a spot on the 1985 PGA Tour.

He had done it.

———

A short blurb from the December 1986 issue of *Golf Digest*, written by Jeremy Tuthill:

> *Most golfers trying to make the Tour are PR machines, the very embodiment of self-promotion. Having spent much of their young careers as pros at the nation's best country clubs, they are highly skilled at the art of schmoozing.*
>
> *An exception to that rule is one of the qualifiers at this year's Q School. Aloysius "Wish" Fitzgerald, 35, is a black driving range pro from Greensboro, Georgia, who could not care less what you think of him. One could chalk it up to being an angry black man with a chip on his shoulder, but deep down, for Wish, it's simply all about the golf. The man exudes a drive and determination to not only qualify for the Tour, but to make a statement once he gets there.*

Keep an eye on this guy. He's one of the longest hitters out there who, until recently, was experiencing major problems on the greens. However, he may now have discovered the secret sauce that will help him to consistently drain more putts. If that's the case, he just might be making a very loud and clear statement during the upcoming Tour—with his golf clubs, not his mouth.

———

"Now, it's my turn to make things happen."

Kids in bed upstairs, Donna sat at the head of the kitchen table in the Fitzgerald house, leading a family meeting that she had convened to discuss the way forward for Wish. Now, Wish, Annie, and Albert waited patiently for her to explain the meaning of this opening declaration.

"Wish got his card, with a lot of help from the home front. It hasn't been easy for any of us, but it was worth it."

The heads around the table nodded in agreement.

"The only problem is, we're now back to square one. Wish has qualified to play the Tour, but he can't *afford* to play the Tour. This family cannot possibly afford it, and, as wonderful as the folks have been in supporting Wish, they're tapped out too."

"You know what they say," Annie chimed in. "'The Lord will provide.'"

"I think the Lord has got better things to do, Mom. I'm pretty sure he'd appreciate us taking care of this ourselves."

"How?" All three spoke at the same time, provoking chuckles despite the seriousness of the discussion.

"We've got a little over two months before the PGA season opens at Pebble Beach. We need sponsors, and I'm going to get us some."

"How?" Again, in a chorus.

"IBM has spent a fortune teaching me how to sell. It's paid off for Big Blue, so why can't it pay off for us? I've got six weeks of vacation banked. So, I'm off in search of sponsors."

"Won't be easy," Albert commented.

"Try impossible," Wish lamented. "Who in his right mind is gonna sponsor a black man on the PGA Tour? Maybe we were too naïve about this from the get-go."

Annie gave her son one of her patented disapproving looks.

"I'm not going to pretend that I'm wildly optimistic about our chances either, son. But we gain nothing by being so pessimistic. If I'm the one who taught you this pervasive cynicism, then I apologize for that right here and now."

Wish looked like a crestfallen child.

"Two more things," Annie continued. "First, you owe your beautiful wife a tremendous amount of appreciation, not only for the support and determination she's demonstrating today, but for holding down the fort during the last few months."

"You're right, Mom," a sheepish Wish responded, standing up from the table. He leaned over to Donna and pecked her on the cheek.

"Love you, babe."

"I love you too, Wish. But I wouldn't object if you'd find a way to lighten up a little more often."

Before Wish could respond, his mother interjected.

"As I was saying, there's another complaint I have about my wonderful PGA pro son."

Wish winced as the attention returned to Annie.

"Gonna," she said.

"Gonna?" Wish replied quizzically.

"Gonna. A minute ago you said 'gonna.' You know better, son. I certainly taught you better than that! 'Gonna' is not a word, is it?"

Reverting to his sheepish-son state, head down, Wish responded.

"No, ma'am."

Annie broke into a wide grin, revealing that she had been toying with her son. The family enjoyed a spontaneous and heartfelt laugh.

———

With just a short time until Christmas, Donna hit the phone and the roads with a passion. Her game plan was to call on consumer product and sporting goods manufacturers and retailers until she struck sponsorship gold. Initially, there was reason to take heart. A few companies actually gave her appointments! A hopeful and excited Donna hit the road, photos and promotional materials in hand.

As it turned out, however, Wish's pessimism was warranted. Visiting offices in Atlanta, Miami, Raleigh, and Charlotte, Donna could scare up nary a nibble, let alone a bite.

Undeterred, Donna resorted to cold-calling the many businesses that had not responded to her earlier phone and mail approaches. The initial challenge here was getting past the receptionist or security guard on the ground floor of corporate headquarters. For Donna, however, this was usually a piece of cake. Or, to be more specific, a brownie.

One of the many reasons that Donna had rocketed up the marketing ranks of IBM's Atlanta office was her ability to charm her way into such difficult-to-get appointments. And early on in her career, one of her secrets had been to bring along her world-famous (or, to be more exact, Greensboro, Georgia-famous) brownies for such gatekeepers. The smell of the brownies alone was often enough to obliterate the usual resistance to passing Donna along to the executive suite.

Brownies were also helpful on the top floor, but the receptionist was often a tougher nut to crack. Wizened as she was (and it was always a "she"), the tendency was to accept the brownies but still present a major obstacle to the ultimate goal—contact with the company's VP of marketing.

However, Donna possessed the very wild card that a decade or two earlier would have absolutely prohibited her access—the color of her skin. She was savvy enough to be aware of what she labeled the prevailing "PC sensitivity" and subtly used it to her advantage. The white executive suite gatekeeper (and she *was* almost always white) would be hyper-vigilant to avoid even the slightest possibility that she could be accused of racism.

So for a variety of reasons, Donna was often successful in attaining the nirvana of all cold-callers—a face-to-face meeting with the target company's decision maker. And that's where her successful run consistently hit the proverbial brick wall.

Oh, they listened. Oh, they were polite (usually overly polite, in Donna's estimation). And oh, yes, they often did a fabulous job of pretending to be receptive. But that's where things remained. Not a one was willing to actually consider sponsoring Wish.

A continuing frustration for Donna was the fact that she seldom actually heard the word "no" from anyone. She had no trepidation about hearing the word—God knows, she had heard it plenty in her days as a salesperson. In fact, she respected the few executives who were straightforward enough to say it.

Donna was realistic about her quest. She knew how difficult the task would have been even if she was selling a blond-haired, blue-eyed, well-spoken, college-graduate, All-Star winner of the US Amateur. Some companies already had a stable of golfers they sponsored. Some had never sponsored a golfer. And, of course, Donna was realistic enough to understand that yes, some just might have considered Wish if he was that blond, blue-eyed preppie who was exactly what they needed to advertise their clubs, ball, insurance company, or sportswear.

Donna returned to Georgia for the Christmas holiday week discouraged and empty-handed. She and the rest of the family knew that she had the first couple of weeks in January to keep trying. Otherwise, she would run out of leave time and more importantly, Wish would be unable to play at Pebble Beach or any other tournament during the first weeks of the season that were known as the "West Coast Swing."

There was little joy in Greensboro and Waynesboro, Georgia, that particular Christmas week.

Chapter 10

Early January 1987 brought especially frigid arctic air to New York City. As Donna traipsed from skyscraper to skyscraper, from corporate office to corporate office, she couldn't help but compare the reception she was receiving to the weather outside. But she was determined to keep her spirits up and a smile on her face. *Someone* was going to get it—someone *had* to get it.

The fifteenth company on her list was Emerald Sporting Goods, a manufacturer of high-end sports equipment and sportswear for the wealthiest markets. Donna realized the potentially fruitless task of attempting to sell such a posh company on the idea of using a black golfer to represent their products, but she had a theory. *Perhaps they want to go more mainstream*, she thought. *What better way to do that than to back Wish?* She allowed herself a little smile at how far she was willing to stretch reason in the effort to buoy her spirits.

Allen Tompkins, Emerald's VP of marketing, had granted her a meeting as a favor to a friend at another company. Upon greeting Donna in the reception area, the thin, balding forty-year-old in the pinstriped Brooks Brothers suit—"Is this some sort of uniform in this city?" Donna thought—betrayed his surprise at Donna's skin color for just the briefest of moments.

"Please, come down to my office," he fake-warmly oozed. "I've only got a few moments, but let's see what you have to say."

From fake warm to cold in what, two seconds? Donna followed the man into his office, where framed Emerald ads from *Sports Illustrated*, *Fortune*, and *The New Yorker* abounded. Some of the top names in the world of baseball, soccer, tennis, and even sailing were featured.

As expected, the meeting lasted all of five minutes. As enthusiastic and well-reasoned as Donna's presentation was, it was met with nothing but a wall of artificial nods and pretended interest from Tompkins. It was all Donna could do to not let out a loud sigh of disappointment and disgust. This guy wasn't hearing a word she was saying.

The meeting ended with a second round of handshakes and smiles and the perfunctory promise by Tompkins that he would certainly give a sponsorship his serious consideration. As had been true for weeks, it was in reality the classic "don't call us; we won't be calling you" finish. Donna headed into the elevator for the long ride down to Park Avenue.

Moments after the elevator door closed, another Brooks Brothers suit, this time framing a Hermes tie, appeared in the doorway of Tompkins's office.

"You about ready for the budget meeting?" the Hermes tie asked.

Tompkins leaned back in his large chair, dwarfed by its size.

"Sure, boss," he responded, chuckling, his fingers interlaced on top of his head.

"What's so funny?"

"Oh, this woman who just left. Get this—she was actually pitching me on the idea of sponsoring a colored guy on the PGA Tour. Can you believe that? Emerald, sponsoring a ni...I mean, colored golfer? What a riot!"

The Hermes tie was intrigued by this.

"A *black* golfer? What was this woman's name?"

"To tell you the truth, I don't even remember. But this is hilarious, boss. The golfer's name is Wish. She can 'wish' we'd sponsor her husband as much as she wants, but c'mon, get real. A colored golfer? Ridiculous!"

"How long ago was she here?" The urgency with which the question was asked caused Tompkins to lose his smile.

"She just left. Why?"

"Because I need to see that woman," the suit shouted, abruptly leaving.

A moment later, he reappeared in the doorway.

"And Tompkins, clear out your office. Now. You're fired, you bigoted moron."

———

In the short time Donna had been upstairs at Emerald Sporting Goods, Manhattan's weather had turned from merely cloudy and cold to windy and snowy. And not the pretty snow of movies and greeting cards. Whipped by the fierce wind, this precipitation got into your eyes and almost pelted your face. It seemed to turn from white to gray the moment it hit the pavement.

Perfect, Donna thought. *Matches the mood perfectly.*

She hugged her hopelessly unfashionable plaid wool coat over her chin and began what she suspected might be a trying effort to hail a cab during the afternoon rush hour.

Suddenly, she heard her name being shouted from the sidewalk behind her. She turned to see a florid, out-of-breath, coatless little man running up to her. *Nice tie*, she noted. *Looks expensive.*

"You're Donna Fitzgerald, right?" the gentleman asked, panting.

"Yes, but how do you…" This guy looked familiar. IBM?

"We've met, Mrs. Fitzgerald. Several years ago, at your father's driving range. I'm Jackson Spears. I'd appreciate it if you'd be kind enough to give me a few minutes of your time."

———

After several successful years with IBM, Donna was no stranger to executive suites. Nevertheless, she was unprepared for the sheer size and luxury of Jackson's office.

"Just exactly what do you do here?"

"CEO. I kinda founded the place."

Jackson showed her to a tan leather sofa, in front of which was a spectacular marble coffee table. He took a seat in a matching chair across from Donna. They were uncomfortably silent as a thin assistant introduced as "Tommy" brought in a silver coffee service and poured a cup for Donna and then Jackson. Donna surveyed the office, which afforded a panoramic view of Manhattan (even the snow looked better from this vantage point) and what she guessed was original art on the inside. Jackson's desk was a modern, highly polished masterpiece of good taste.

After taking a sip of the coffee, Donna decided to break the silence.

"Well, this is awkward."

"Oh, I doubt it's nearly as awkward for you as it is for me," Jackson responded.

Both smiled uneasily.

"I have to tell you," Jackson said. "I've been following Wish's progress from afar. He's got a great future on the Tour."

"Not if he can't afford to play on it."

"And that's why I asked you to come back. Perhaps we can be of assistance with that."

"Not according to your marketing guy."

Jackson bristled at this observation.

"Yeah, well, you have my apologies for that. Besides, he's not my marketing guy anymore."

Despite her curiosity about both this comment and where the conversation was headed, Donna decided to bite her tongue for the time being. Anticipation, however, was causing her heart to practically beat right out of her chest.

"You came here looking for a sponsor," Jackson continued. "Emerald would like to be that sponsor."

Elation suddenly flooded every fiber of Donna's being. *We've done it. He can play!*

Almost as suddenly, cold water doused her joy.

"You'd make a terrible poker player," Jackson commented.

Donna realized that she had not disguised her thoughts in the least.

"Yes, well," she stammered, not knowing how to proceed.

"I thought this would be good news."

"And it is. For me, at least."

Confused, it was Jackson's turn to display his thoughts on his face.

"It kills me to say this, Mr. Spears, but with the way Wish feels about you, I'm certain he could not accept such a relationship."

"Yes, of course." Jackson was crestfallen.

"I'm sorry, in more ways than one."

"Hold on, let's think about this for a minute," he said. Jackson rose from his chair and walked over to the window. The two returned to an uncomfortable silence, which lasted for over a minute. Donna had decided it was time to leave and was just about to speak when Jackson, who was staring down and off to the side, raised a finger to ask her to give him a moment. Finally, he spoke.

"When you arrived here, you were clearly unaware of my position with Emerald," he said. "Would I be correct in assuming that Wish is similarly…"

"Ignorant?"

"Not my choice of word." Jackson smiled. "But, yes."

"Oh, believe me, as fine a businessman as my husband has turned out to be, *Business Week* and *Fortune* would be the last publications you'd ever find in his hands," Donna responded, returning the smile. "*Golf Digest*, yes. The *Wall Street Journal*, no."

"So, you came to Emerald seeking our sponsorship. And let's say Emerald, and not Jackson Spears, is interested in exploring such a relationship."

Donna considered this and had just begun to shake her head when Jackson raised his finger again to stop her. He sat down.

"And no, it's not charity, Mrs. Fitzgerald. This would be a business deal—good for you and good for us."

"So, what are you, Mr. Spears?" Donna chuckled. "A businessman or a mind reader?"

"Oh, I am a businessman, Mrs. Fitzgerald. A very good businessman," he responded, casting his gaze around his office.

"Point taken," Donna said, now grinning.

"So, what do you say we talk some business?"

Chapter 11

1969

To say that Jackson had gone on the trip to Europe kicking and screaming would not have been entirely accurate. Rather, he sulked his way through London, Paris, Rome, and the Swiss Alps. Even his father's offer to take a side trip with him to play the Old Course at St. Andrews in Scotland fell on deaf ears. All Jackson wanted to do was finish out the summer playing golf with Wish.

And why the heck had he been swept off on this trip with no warning whatsoever?

When his parents made several attempts to shower him with praise for his club championship, Jackson withdrew even further into his funk. The whole anti-Wish thing had crystallized into a larger issue for the young man. It was obvious that no amount of persuasion or arguments with his parents would have any effect on their approach to the matter.

It wasn't about Wish. His parents didn't even know the guy! They were just prejudiced, through and through. As were their friends. As was, he immaturely extrapolated, most of his hometown.

The trip was timed just right to ensure that as soon as the family returned to the States, it was time for Jackson to return to Choate for his senior year. Conveniently, his footlocker was already packed and ready to go. Hours after the Pan Am flight had landed at JFK Jackson was back with his "friends" in his dorm in Wallingford, Connecticut.

He would have liked to call Wish to explain his sudden and unannounced absence over the last two weeks, but he remembered that Wish and his mom had no phone in their apartment. Jackson didn't know their address, so a letter was out of the question. This was ridiculous!

Call the club. That was it. Sure, with the summer over, Wish was also back in school, but he'd be caddying every weekend. Just call Pete. He'd pass along the message to Wish. Problem solved!

———

"Hello, Pete? I'm so glad I got you. I'm hoping you can help me. This is—"

"Recognize that voice anywhere, young man," Pete said. "Club champ, if memory serves. Never had much of a chance to congratulate ya. How can I help?"

"I need to get a message to Wish Fitzgerald."

"Not sure I can help ya with that, Master Spears."

"I don't understand."

"Wish don't work here no more."

"What? Did he quit or something?"

A pause ensued before Pete spoke again. "No, son, Wish didn't quit."

Shocked and puzzled, it was Jackson's turn to collect his thoughts.

"Did you fire him, Pete?"

This pause was longer.

"We had to let him go, Master Spears."

"Why?"

"Can't say, Master Spears."

"You can't say? Why not?"

"Just can't, Master Spears."

Confused and frustrated, Jackson tried desperately to process this news along with

Pete's reticence to explain. He decided to ask one last question.

"OK, OK. Well, can you at least tell me when this happened?"

The silence lasted at least twenty seconds.

"Pete? Are you still there?"

"Still here, son."

"Please tell me; I need to know. Just when was Wish 'let go'?"

"The day after you two won the club championship."

———

Well, it all adds up, doesn't it, Jackson thought. *I win the club championship with guidance not from my father, but from Wish. Dad is more angry and maybe even embarrassed than he is proud of me. Wish is fired the next day, and we suddenly go to Europe. Holy cow. Somehow I have to talk to Wish, to explain. He needs to know that I had nothing to do with this, that I'm as mad about it as he must be!*

After struggling for days for an answer as to how he could communicate with his friend, Jackson finally realized that there was a way.

Annie, he thought. *Mrs. Fitzgerald. I can call the Johnsons and ask to speak to her. She might even answer the phone! Yeah! Finally, a way to get a hold of Wish. What a relief.*

He grabbed a handful of the change that he kept in his desk and headed for the pay phone in the dorm hallway. *Yeah, at last…*

Receiver in one hand and the first dime hovering just outside the coin slot, Jackson hesitated.

My father got Wish fired, Jackson thought. *Does Wish know that? Would he understand—even believe—that I didn't know? Would that matter to him? He needed the money. He loved the work. He loved golf.*

Damn. I let him down. How can I explain what happened so that he'll still be my friend? Will he understand if I say I'm sorry? Is that good enough?

Gotta think about this. Need to say the right thing…explain it so he'll understand that it wasn't my fault. Gotta think about it.

Slowly, the phone was replaced in its cradle.

———

Shortly after returning to school, Jackson began to notice that the guys at school were treating him differently. They were actually talking to him.

Right off the bat, his roommate, a couple of other guys in the dorm, and even two or three teachers commented on how much he had grown during the summer. He even began to believe it himself, until he asked his roommate to measure him. Jackson held a book on top of his head, and his roommate measured him with a yardstick. No difference whatsoever. Still short.

But sure enough, he really did feel different. Couldn't put his finger on what or why, but yep, there was kind of a different outlook on life these days.

And then there was that incident at football practice.

Now in his third (and senior) year as a team manager, Jackson had risen to the dubious distinction of head manager. Still, each afternoon after practice, he stood by as many of the players dropped their post-shower towels on the floor. This, despite the signs posted around the locker room telling the players to put the used towels in the hampers that were always present. This, despite numerous low-key requests from Jackson and his three other managers that the players please help make the managers' job just a little easier.

One October afternoon as Jackson walked through the locker room, Colton Rogers, a six-three, 240-pound lineman, once again dropped his towel in the much shorter manager's path. This time, Jackson gave the gesture and the towel the slightest of glances and walked on.

"Pick it up, Spears," Rogers bellowed, loudly enough to bring the usual locker room din to a halt of attentive silence.

Jackson stopped, took a breath, squared his shoulders, and turned around to face the beast.

"You're supposed to put it in the hamper, Rogers. You know that."

Rogers stepped forward until he towered over Jackson, a mere foot away.

"Pick it up. It's your job."

Kevin DeLange, a sophomore manager who was even smaller in stature than Jackson, hustled over to pick up the towel. Jackson calmly took it out of his hand and deposited it back on the floor.

He then walked over to one of the wooden benches located in front of the lockers, pushed a wet towel aside, and stepped up onto the bench. Everyone in the room, players and managers alike, waited to see what the hell was coming next. Rogers was not the only boy in the room whose jaw had dropped.

"Listen up, guys," Jackson said, raising his voice a bit. "Starting right now, my managers and I are done picking up after you. We're not your servants. Put your towels in the hampers. Put your tape and other crap in the trash. You wanna keep throwing everything on the floor, that's your business. You can wallow in it, for all we care. We work hard enough as it is, and you know what? We deserve your respect. It's that simple."

Jackson got down off the bench and nodded at his fellow managers, indicating that they were to follow him. Together, they left the room, leaving Colton Rogers and his teammates speechless in their wake.

The four managers gathered in the laundry room.

"Holy shit, Jack," Gary Littleton, a pimply faced junior, exclaimed in the quietest possible voice. "Are you nuts? They're gonna kill us!"

"Yeah, Jack, you gotta go back out there and apologize!" Kevin said.

"Relax, guys," Jackson began just as he was interrupted by Assistant Coach Barrett's appearance in the doorway.

"Coach wants to see you, Spears."

Jackson stood, practically at attention, in front of Head Coach Thompson's desk. The surprisingly diminutive and prematurely balding coach, who had to look up at several of his players, was seated behind the desk.

"What's this I hear that you managers aren't willing to do your job?"

"Coach, we do our job. We wash the uniforms, line the field, bring out the water, give you the stats, everything you tell us to do. But we need more respect from these guys. A lot more. That's what this is about."

There, I said it. It's gonna hit the fan now. This will be worse than whatever the players will do to us.

Ever so slowly, Coach Thompson began to smile.

"Good. It's about time."

"Good?" Jackson was astonished by the coach's response.

"No. Better than good. Actually, it's great, Mr. Spears. I've been waiting for three years for you to grow a pair, and today you did. You stood up for yourself and your staff.

"What you don't know is that I was also a manager when I was your age. And I also put up with all the crap from the players, the disrespect. Only difference was, I never had the cojones to stand up to them like you just did. Congratulations, young man. You deserve their respect. You sure as hell have mine."

———

Howard Spears actually allowed himself to beam with pride when Jackson opened the envelope to find that he had been accepted to Yale. A day later, quite the opposite reaction occurred when a similar letter came from Harvard. And when Jackson had the nerve to defy his father's unceasing lobbying for Yale and against Yale's mortal enemy by enrolling at Harvard? There was verbal hell to pay, including a threat to not pay for tuition. That ended once Jackson's mother put her foot down.

Gradually, a thaw developed in the usually frosty father-son relationship. In fact, during more than one cocktail party, Howard had actually been known to brag to friends whose children were stuck with acceptances from schools like Amherst, Lafayette, and in one notable disappointment, Rutgers. On one memorable occasion during that summer of '70, Howard had even joked with his son that they'd have to sit on opposite sides of the stadium at the Yale-Harvard game.

Finally, on a warm and rainy September day, father and son arrived in Cambridge for Jackson's matriculation. By this time Howard had come to terms with the treason just enough to be looking forward to the freshmen parents' dinner. The two hauled Jackson's footlocker and other gear up two flights of stairs to his tiny new dorm room.

"A bit smaller than my first room at Yale," Howard said. He sat down on one of the two twin beds and picked up a small booklet.

"Look, son, this thing must have pictures of you and your classmates. What did you say was the name of your roommate?"

"I read about that. I think they call that a 'pig book.' His name is Eric Moody. He's from Norfolk, Virginia. We've exchanged a couple of letters. Looking forward to finally meeting him."

"Moody...Moody," Howard mumbled as he thumbed the pages of the directory. "Be interesting to see what the fellow looks..."

Jackson, preoccupied with putting some clothing away, failed to notice the sudden and drastic change in his father's countenance. Howard stood up.

"Son, I'm afraid that I'm going to have to miss the dinner."

"Why?"

"It's a long drive back to Darien, and with this rain, well…"

Surprised by the sudden change of plans, Jackson couldn't think of a response.

"It's just best that I get on the road."

Howard quickly shook his son's hand and practically rushed to leave the room.

"Good luck, son," Jackson heard from the hallway.

Puzzled by his father's abrupt departure and excited about putting his half of the room in order, Jackson forgot all about the pig book. Half an hour later, Eric Moody and his parents arrived.

They were Negroes.

———

Establishing his bona fides as an independent young man, Jackson didn't call home for several weeks. Running low on cash in late October, one evening he stepped into the dormitory hall and dialed home on the pay phone.

"It's so wonderful to hear your voice," his mother gushed. "I've been worried about you. Why haven't you called?"

Before he could respond, Jackson heard his father's muffled voice in the background. His mother came back on the line.

"Your father's going to pick up the other line. How are things? Are you eating well? I'll bet you're turning into a scarecrow…"

Jackson looked down at his pudgy midsection. *No danger of that*, he thought.

The next few minutes of the conversation went as such conversations usually go.

"How's the food?"

"Not so hot."

"Are you getting enough sleep?"

"I guess so."

"Your grades—are you doing OK?"

"I think so."

"So it's not too difficult?"

"For some boys—I mean guys—it's a challenge. I seem to be doing fine."

"Have you met any girls?"

"Not really."

Surprisingly, his father was completely amenable to sending more money. It almost sounded like he had been expecting the request.

Jackson waited and waited for the other shoe to drop. Finally…

"You haven't mentioned anything about your roommate," his mother said. "Do you boys get along?"

Puzzled, Jackson took a beat before answering.

"Yeah, Mom. He's a nice guy."

"Is he from a nice family?"

Jackson cocked his head, trying to read between the inscrutable words he was hearing.

"I guess so. I'm gonna invite him home for a weekend soon." There, he said it.

"Well, I should hope so. We'd love to have him!"

Thoroughly confused now, Jackson paused. *Holy cow. There's definitely something out of whack here.*

"Dad?"

"Yes, son?"

"You haven't told her, have you?"

A long pause.

"No, son, I haven't had a chance."

"Told me what? What is he talking about, Howard?"

Not good. Not surprising, Jackson supposed, *but definitely not good.*

"I've gotta run, Mom. Lots of homework, you know. Bye now."

———

The arguments between Jackson and his parents that ensued over the Thanksgiving and Christmas breaks seemed to fit the very definition of a new phrase Jackson had recently learned: *déjà vu.*

His parents were never going to allow this Eric fellow in their home. And Jackson wasn't going to accept that ruling lying down. The discussions were vociferous, but there was never any question as to the outcome.

In reality, Jackson's campaign was a half-hearted one. There was no question in his mind that he was right on principle. But the fact of the matter was that it didn't terribly matter whether or not he could invite Eric home.

It turned out that the two roommates weren't particularly close.

Jackson looked upon his entrance to Harvard as an entrance to a completely new life. Given the opportunity to run for student government, he did so and actually won a seat. Eric, who had been "Mr. Popularity" back home (he had actually been named so in his yearbook), apparently regretted not having entered the contest. For the rest of the year, he often took the opportunity to kid Jackson about his political aspirations. The strategy worked. Jackson didn't run for office his sophomore year. Eric did, beginning a career that eventually led to his election as the president of the student government in his senior year.

The boys enjoyed a completely civil relationship their freshman year but quickly discovered that they had little in common. They traveled in different circles and joined different clubs and social organizations. At the end of the school year, there was no mention of the idea of continuing to room with each other.

———

Jackson's goal at Harvard was to begin to position himself to get out from under his father's influence as soon as humanly possible. As things turned out, this happened a lot faster than expected.

During his sophomore year, in two different business classes, Jackson found himself sitting next to a Nepali student named Ram Uprety. The two struck up a friendship and eventually decided to room together in a small house near the campus. Both were short (although Ram was substantially thinner), gregarious, and seriously determined to make money—even during their undergraduate days. Ram grilled Jackson on the American market, advertising, and investment banking. Jackson was fascinated by Ram's tales of the incredibly cheap cost of labor and fabrics in Nepal. The fact that neither knew what he was talking about was of little concern to the two young men.

However, both were such excellent students that they needed far less time than their peers to earn decent grades. Making good use of this extra time, they peppered the Harvard Business School faculty (both undergraduate and graduate) with questions and voraciously consumed business magazines and Harvard's myriad case studies. As importantly, they saved what little extra money they had.

In short order, they launched their first business together.

The printed T-shirts and polo shirts the boys imported from Nepal and sold around the Harvard campus were designed by Jackson's girlfriend of several months, a green-eyed, red-haired townie named Margaret O'Sullivan (thus, the original name of the company—Emerald Imports).

The relationship with Margaret didn't last, but Emerald Imports (later changed to Emerald Sporting Goods) did. Within a few short years after graduation, Jackson and Ram had turned their little venture into a Park Avenue-based apparel empire, with manufacturing plants in multiple Asian nations. Their sports celebrity-endorsed clothing and footwear was carried in virtually every boutique, department, and big-box store in America, and they had aggressive plans to expand overseas. The Emerald plan grew from sport to sport. Eventually, its cloverleaf logo was everywhere.

———

Most people never forget the moment they first met the love of their life. Not so for Jackson.

He had contributed to a charity to help underprivileged kids from the poorest areas of New York City. As such, he had been invited to a black-tie event thrown by the charity at some museum in Brooklyn. He planned to put in his obligatory appearance, have one drink, and head back to his home in Manhattan.

Due to his wealth, connections with sports celebrities, and a well-deserved reputation as a philanthropist for such charities, Jackson was so used to attending such events that they had long ago begun to run together in his mind. In any case, wherever he was and whatever he was doing, his mind was usually still back at work.

Rachel Ernst was the equally wealthy founder of the charity, Love Our Kids. Although blessed with a supermodel's height, figure, and blond-haired/blue-eyed good looks, she had eschewed many offers to follow such a career path in order to concentrate on helping others.

They met in the receiving line, where Rachel made it a point to linger over her hand-shake with Jackson to express her gratitude for his largesse. He looked up at her to say something about it being his pleasure—which it was—and thanked her for the invitation. He failed to notice that it took just a little longer than normal for him to extract his hand from hers.

After what he considered to be the requisite hour-long stay to be polite, Jackson began to navigate his way through the cocktail crowd toward the exit. After being stymied a few times by acquaintances and wannabe business contacts grabbing him "for just a moment," his escape was finally in sight.

Just as he was about to make it, a voice from behind stopped him.

"Apparently I didn't rate a moment of your time."

Jackson turned to find that the source of the odd comment was the hostess, Rachel Ernst. He cocked his head to one side, momentarily puzzled as to how to respond. Although he opened his mouth, words still failed him.

"You're one popular guy, Mr. Spears. I've been dying to talk to you, but every time I looked your way, you were taken. And now we seem to be losing you."

"It's a great cause, a wonderful event," Jackson finally said. What was this about? A larger contribution? For him to join her board?

Rachel smiled, bemused by Jackson's reaction.

"Please relax, Mr. Spears. I'm not interested in your wallet or your influence. For the moment, at least."

Try as he might, Jackson failed to disguise his increasing confusion.

A delighted Rachel allowed herself a chuckle before proceeding.

"Actually, I wanted to talk to Jacky."

Now this was really getting out of hand. No one had called him "Jacky" since, when? Elementary school?

Rachel proffered her hand, and a flummoxed Jackson took it.

"Rachel Carter. Carter was my maiden name. I sat behind you in Miss Gleason's class. Third grade. Had a massive crush on you for what must have been two or three years."

Holy cow.

"And you clearly don't remember me from Adam…or Eve, in this case. That's OK. I look a bit different today. Grew up. But then again, we both have, right?"

Social conversation with women, especially such a strikingly beautiful (and tall) woman as Rachel, had never come easily to Jackson. As smooth as he would have been if this was a business discussion, he was positively tongue-tied at this moment.

"Third grade?" he finally managed to reply. "At Hollow Tree? Small world." *Geez, elementary school, small…unintentional pun*, he noted. *Smooth.*

"And a little while later, you were off to private school, like half the kids in Darien."

"Sorry about that." *Was that witty or dumb?*

Rachel laughed. A genuine laugh. *Good, maybe you're not a complete doofus.*

"Growing up in Darien was different, wouldn't you say?"

"You mean like living in a cashmere-lined cocoon?" Jackson answered.

Rachel smiled. "My thoughts exactly. A wonderful childhood, but not exactly the real world."

"Nor is this," he commented, indicating their present surroundings by sweeping one hand and his gaze in a broad semicircle. "I find it's a good idea to not lose sight of that."

"I—" Just then, Rachel was interrupted by a much shorter, older woman, who whispered in her ear.

"Gosh, I apologize," Rachel said, turning back to Jackson. "Apparently I'm needed to make a command appearance elsewhere." *Did she look just the slightest bit annoyed by the interruption?*

"Absolutely. Please, go."

"I'd really like to continue our conversation. Please give me a call sometime."

With a nod, Jackson finally made his escape.

One morning three months later, Tommy appeared in the doorway to his office.

"Rachel Ernst is on the line for you."

"Who's Rachel Ernst?"

"The gorgeous blonde who runs that kids' charity," Tommy answered. "Remember? You donated to one of their events a while back."

"You're gay, Tommy. What's with the 'gorgeous blonde' reference?"

"Hey, gorgeous is gorgeous. Just take the call."

Looking for more money, Jackson thought, picking up the receiver.

"I've been thinking about you" was the first thing Rachel said. "Since you're apparently never going to call me, here I am. Let's have dinner."

———

Throughout the couple's first date at Windows on the World at the top of the World Trade Center, Jackson remained oblivious to the fact that Rachel could possibly be interested in him and not his checkbook. He was fascinated and impressed by Rachel's description of her programs to help disadvantaged kids in Harlem and the Bronx. So much so, in fact, that he volunteered much of his free time to do some actual grunt work at her clinic in Harlem.

Ostensibly, Jackson did this because he thoroughly enjoyed giving back in a way that seemed more tangible than the checks he so often wrote to charities. The fact that this enabled him to get to know Rachel better? Gravy!

And all this did for Rachel was further validate her initial attraction. She cared not a whit that many of her friends could not understand why she was so enthralled with a man who literally had to look up at her.

Within weeks of that first dinner, Jackson finally clued into the possibility that he could have something with this remarkable woman.

Years into their marriage, hardly a day went by when he still didn't spend a few moments thinking how amazing it was that she loved him.

Chapter 12

1987

In February, Wish was packing to leave
for Monterey, California, to play in the
first PGA tournament of the year, the Bing
Crosby Pro-Am. The tournament, nicknamed
the "Clambake," was held each February on
three of the world's best golf courses—Pebble
Beach, Spyglass Hill, and Cypress Point. It was
nationally televised and featured a number of
famous celebrities and wealthy corporate executives who together constituted the "Am" part
of the tournament's official title.

Jackson had been correct about Wish's
obliviousness as to his former friend's connec-
tion to the company sponsoring him. Wish's
gratitude to his wife was boundless, but his

focus was on preparing himself, both mentally and physically, for the Tour.

During dinner the night before his flight to California, Donna commented that Wish apparently had no need for an airplane—his mind had been in Monterey for days already. The kids had a great laugh at this, but Wish barely acknowledged the humor—Donna was correct, as usual.

After dinner, as Wish checked on his clubs for the tenth time in five days, he remembered that Albert was reshafting his three wood and that his father-in-law was still at the range completing some work. Wish called the private number in the office, expecting Albert to pick up despite the fact that the range was closed for the evening.

"Must be in the shop," he said to Donna. "Probably has the television on while he's working—can't hear the phone. That man has got to get a hearing aid!"

They both smiled as Wish grabbed his jacket and car keys to drive over to retrieve his club and say good-bye to Albert.

As Wish pulled into the parking lot, he could see that the lights in the pro shop were indeed still burning and that there was a beat-up Pontiac Firebird parked a few spots away from Albert's Cadillac. *That's interesting*, Wish thought.

Relatively unconcerned, Wish nevertheless approached the glass doors to the shop a little cautiously. In the next moment, he caught the fleeting image of something very negative as it was reflected in a mirror that was situated just inside the shop. A pale, small-boned white teenager with a mullet haircut and half-ass moustache was inside, apparently looking toward the cash register. He was holding a gun.

Adrenaline flooded Wish's system. Albert was in there, and something had to be done to help him—quickly. The outside pay phone was out of order, and there was clearly no time to drive somewhere else for help. *I'm going to have to handle this myself, but how do I stop a guy with a gun when I don't have one myself?*

Wish ran back to his car, where he quietly opened the trunk and pulled out a one iron from his golf bag. He again approached the front doors, this time concentrating on avoiding a sight line from within the shop while also trying desperately to keep off of the noisy gravel. He flattened himself against the wall next to the doors and extended his hand to gently push on the door to see if it was unlocked.

Good, it is. Now what? Have to decide quickly. Where is this guy now? Where is Albert? Is he tied up? Could he jump on the guy if I divert his attention? Could I get to the guy quickly enough before he saw me and took a shot? Take a chance to get a view through a window or door or just go?

No time. Just gotta go for it!

Wish whirled and burst through the door. The bad guy was five feet to his left, his back to Wish. Wish immediately seized upon this opportunity to raise the one iron high over his head and smash it down on the intruder—missing his head, but doing some serious damage to his right shoulder and causing the gun to fly over and behind a display counter.

"Jerry!" a voice shouted. Wish saw his father-in-law, tied up and gagged, his eyes wild with the need to warn Wish about...

Wish felt the pain before he heard the gun shot. *Crap*, was his first thought. *Pop*, his second. He thought he heard another bang, but then...

———

He was outside in the cold air, on his back. Oddly, he was moving. He saw the stars and elsewhere, crazy colored lights, flashing, changing—revolving? What was that about?

———

He was warm, constricted. He kind of wanted to talk, but maybe not. Couldn't, anyway. Tired.

———

Donna was there. Loving, concerned. Maybe even Pop. Good! Not sure about that.

———

Later he understood that it was three days before he awakened from his coma, but that was OK, because the surgeon wanted him in that state so he wouldn't fight the respirator and feeding tube. His system needed time to recover.

———

Five days after he had been shot, Wish was finally off the respirator and coherent enough to communicate. First came the story, from

Donna and Pop (yes, Pop!), of what had happened that night.

Albert and Donna sat by his side in the hospital room, which, for the first time, was not located on the ICU floor of the hospital in Atlanta. His mother was at home in Greensboro, watching the kids, but she had also been a constant presence at the hospital until he was out of the woods.

The two criminals (two, not one, as Wish had originally thought) had knocked on the door of the shop late that evening, and at first Albert had waved them off, pointing to the "Closed" sign on the door. But they were insistent, and finally Albert let them in. They immediately produced guns and tied Albert up. They proceeded to search the store for money and valuable merchandise, ignoring Albert's explanation that he had already deposited the day's cash at the bank located a mile down the road. Irritated by Albert's voice and angry that they were coming up empty, they stuffed a golf shirt in the older man's mouth and kept up their search for cash. That's when Wish had burst through the door.

Wish's assault with the golf club had surprised all three men in the store and succeeded in putting one of the robbers out of commission. The second, however, had recovered quickly enough to begin firing wildly in Wish's direction. Two shots hit Wish, and another had caught the man's accomplice as he was falling to the floor, dazed by Wish's blow. The other three shots shattered a mirror and display case and lodged in some wood paneling.

Panicked by the unexpected turn of events and worried about his friend, the wielder of the gun kept pulling the trigger as the empty revolver clicked harmlessly. After it finally dawned on the young man that his weapon was now worthless, he tossed it to the floor, ran over to help his dazed friend up, and together they hobbled toward the Firebird. Albert, who had not been harmed, heard the car tear out of the gravel parking lot.

While nothing could have ever prepared Albert for what had just taken place, what followed may have been even more torturous. As hard as he tried, he could not free himself from the belts that bound him. He wanted desperately to help his bleeding and unconscious son-in-law but was powerless to do so. No feeling that he had ever experienced—not even the combination of rage and fear that he had just felt—was as horrible as what he felt while he watched his son-in-law dying before his very eyes.

As the minutes and then hours passed, the phone rang several times. Sometime after midnight, Donna pulled into the parking lot, emerged from her car, and cautiously approached the shattered door that had been shot out. As soon as she surveyed the scene inside, she rushed in, uncertain as to which person she should help first.

After pulling the gag from Albert's mouth, she immediately followed her father's instructions and used the office phone to call 911. Weeping and practically hyperventilating, she cradled her unconscious husband's head as they waited for the police and EMTs to arrive.

When the emergency team arrived, Albert was weak and perilously close to having a stroke or heart attack. Having lost a copious amount of blood, Wish was near death. The shock trauma helicopter landed on the golf range, and twenty minutes later Wish was in the emergency room in Atlanta. A team of more than a dozen doctors and nurses worked for over seven hours to save his life.

———

Happy to find that Albert was already back to normal, Wish took stock of his own condition.

The IV drugs enabled him to tolerate the pain, which seemed to emanate from everywhere between his belly and his neck. His left arm seemed to be useless. What did this mean for his career? He was desperate to speak to the doctor.

"You're a lucky man, Mr. Fitzgerald," Dr. Glickfield began. "By all rights, you should be dead right now."

He went on to describe the damage done by the two bullets. "We believe the first bullet was the one that hit you in the left biceps. It spun you around, causing the second bullet to enter from the back, just under the left scapula—your shoulder blade. The first bullet shattered your humerus and did major damage to the biceps."

Wish's mind raced. *What does this mean for my golf game?*

"The second bullet was more serious," the surgeon continued. "It just missed your heart, then ricocheted and punctured your lung, causing it to collapse. The resultant bleeding nearly killed you."

"Doc," Wish interrupted. "What about my golf game?"

Dr. Glickfield looked down at the black man in the hospital gown, IV and full arm cast bent at the elbow. He smiled, thinking, *Good, this guy's got a sense of humor. Bodes well for his recovery.*

"I've heard this one before, Mr. Fitzgerald. You say, 'Will I be able to play golf?' and I'd say, 'Sure.' And you say, 'That's great! I never could before.' Very funny, but I'm not going to bite."

The looks that the doctor received from Donna and Wish told him that his humor had missed the mark.

"So, you *do* play golf."

"I'm a professional golfer. On the Tour."

Glickfield almost made the mistake of uttering the words, "You're kidding me." Instead, his dark countenance said everything.

"Tell me how long it'll be until I can play, doc. I have to be able to play."

Now, the surgeon searched for the proper words. The delay put the exclamation point on the bad news for the Fitzgeralds.

"We spent hours repairing the damage, Mr. Fitzgerald. But there was only so much we could do. With rehab, you should regain most of the function in your arm. Your hand is fine."

This was met with silence. *The bottom line, you're going to have to give it to them. Sometimes this job sucks.*

"I'm a golfer myself, Mr. Fitzgerald. I'm told that the left arm is paramount..." He stopped again.

"To answer your question, I strongly doubt you'll be able to properly swing a club. If you're talking professional golf, I'm afraid the answer is definite.

"No."

———

The answer was not "no" for Wish. He was sure that rehab would bring his arm back.

The work began as soon as Wish left the hospital. Two hours a day of excruciating work at a local orthopedic rehab facility were followed by several hours of additional pain that Wish voluntarily pushed through at home. Within days, his physical therapist was advising him to slow down. Wish backed off for a few days and then resumed his regimen.

After six months of agony, the therapist suggested that they celebrate his progress with lunch instead of therapy. She suggested that Donna join them.

After the waitress took their order, the therapist, a large, middle-aged black woman named Alverta, smiled at her patient.

"You've accomplished a miracle, Wish," she said.

"Yeah, I feel like we've made a lot of progress. Lately, though, it seems to have leveled off. Maybe I just need to push harder."

Smiling on the outside, Alverta was suffering internally. She knew what Wish wanted, what Wish *needed* from this, from her.

"Bottom-line time, Wish." She paused. "You're going to have to start accepting the fact that it's impossible. I've never seen anyone work has hard as you to come back from a trauma like this. You've succeeded in recovering sixty percent of your function—"

"But the arm's still got this bend," Wish said, nodding toward his left arm. "Gotta get rid of that. I know I've got a long way to go, and I'm willing to do it."

"I wish work was the answer," Alverta said, slowly shaking her head.

"Work is the answer for everything," Wish responded.

"There's only so much you can do, Wish. The tissue just isn't there anymore."

"But…"

She reached out and touched his hands, glancing toward Donna for support and then returning her eyes to Wish. It had to be repeated.

"There is no 'but.' This is it, Wish. This is the best that it's going to be."

"But…"

There was nothing more to be said, and Wish knew it. He searched and searched for a way out, but she was right. It was over.

Tears welled in the eyes of both women. Alverta attempted to speak.

"I wish…"

It was Wish's turn to clasp her hands in his.

"You did everything you could. Everyone did. And I appreciate it, believe me I do. I owe you the world for getting me this far."

The tears now flowed freely, just as Wish managed a weak smile.

"I thought I could do it; I really did. But…I keep saying that, don't I? Gotta knock that off. There is no 'but.' It is what it is, and it's time to move on. I get it. Playing golf isn't everything. I have Donna, and the kids, and Mom and Pop, and a great career ahead of me in a business that I love. I've got so much for which I can be grateful, so much to look forward…"

He couldn't continue. The words were hollow, and they all knew it. He smiled sardonically.

"It was a nice try, wasn't it?"

After a few weeks, the façade of optimism came crumbling down. After all, it had largely been a show for the customers and staff at work. Wish tried, he really did, but his heart (the one that the bullet had "just missed") and his head (the one that had never bought into the deal) were just not in it. He made more and more excuses for showing up at work less and less, and the sulking commenced.

He withdrew from his family. Initially, it was the kids who took this the hardest. As their memory of the "bad day" faded, their questions of "Why is Daddy mad?" and "Why is Daddy sad?" increased in frequency. Donna and Annie did their best to explain, to basically make excuses for Wish's dark mood, but this did little to assuage the omnipresent anxiety that spread from child to adult, blanketing his ever-shrinking world.

Wish's self-medication was withdrawal. He retreated into his growing depression, spending most of his time brooding. Under the misapprehension that he was "dealing with it" and protecting everyone else by keeping things to himself, he was, of course, harming everyone who loved him.

The business suffered, at first because Wish was no longer Wish and then because

Wish just wasn't there. Albert and the staff had valiantly made up for his absence during the previous year. That had been a team, even a community effort, gladly undertaken as a matter of great pride.

This was a horse of a different color. Employee morale bottomed out. Since Jameson's Golf was as much a service business as a retail business, the malaise spread to the customer base. It just wasn't as much fun to visit the range to hit balls or play miniature golf when everyone who worked there was in a bad mood. Cash dwindled.

Hardest hit, of course, was Donna. She had dedicated herself to helping Wish attain his dream. She had sacrificed tremendously, trying to maintain her high standards at IBM while acting as two parents to her children at home and even covering some shifts in the office at Jameson's Golf. It had been exhausting, but even more than everyone else, she had believed completely in the cause.

Much like her husband, the death of Wish's dream crushed Donna. The previous year had sapped her energy, but the events at the store that night in late January and the finality of the aftermath had momentarily brought her to her knees. However, she could not afford to swim in a morass of pity like Wish. Pride, coupled with necessity, would not allow any more damage to her career with IBM. Her instincts forced her to protect and nurture her beautiful children. She recognized and reacted to the fact that she was needed. Her wallowing was short-lived because it was simply not an option.

She missed Wish. She tried mightily to shore up her husband's spirits, but her patient efforts went unrewarded. He had retreated so far into himself that he could not be reached. Her requests that he seek professional counseling fell on deaf ears.

One of the more frustrating and unattractive aspects about Wish's decline was what Donna privately called his "bigotry fire." Out of respect for his wife, in recent years Wish had tried to keep most of his toxic attitude toward whites to himself. She knew what he was thinking, of course, as she had witnessed such actions as his not-too-subtle campaign to get rid of the Norwegian-born physical therapist he had originally been assigned.

But up through the lunch meeting with Alverta, the vitriol of overt bigotry had been largely sublimated. Of late, it was incessant. As irrational as his reasoning was, Wish blamed the recent U-turn in his fortunes on

"The Man." Even Annie, as cynical as she could be about whites in general, had long ago ceased to support Wish's brand of intolerance. Unfortunately, motherly talks with him had just produced more of the same.

The Thanksgiving holiday brought things to a head. The family tradition for the blessing was for each individual, children included, to say what they were grateful for. Albert always started it off, and this year he thanked God for the fact that he and Wish were alive. Annie followed with similar sentiments. All eyes then turned to Wish.

At first he sat mute, avoiding eye contact with any of his family.

"Wish, it's your turn," Donna said.

Still, there was no response from the frowning Wish.

"Please, honey, for the kids," Donna whispered into his ear.

After a few more moments of deliberation, he cleared his throat.

"Sorry, I'll pass."

Mortified, the adults did their best to move on. Unfortunately, the day had been ruined for everyone concerned. The children weren't stupid; they sensed the enveloping tension, and it affected them. The repast was consumed in silence.

———

Later that evening, the kids fast asleep in their rooms, Albert found Wish at the kitchen table, nursing a cup of coffee and staring off into space. The older man poured himself a cup and sat down across from Wish. A few moments passed before either man spoke.

"If you'd manage to extricate that fat head of yours from your posterior," a decidedly unsmiling Albert said, "maybe you could stop being such an ass."

Returning to this world, Wish met Albert's eyes across the table.

"I'm not kidding, Wish. This crap has got to stop. This family has done just about nothing but take care of your sorry ass and worry about you and put up with you for two years now. Enough is enough, man."

For just a moment, it appeared that Wish might actually be considering someone else's perspective.

"And another thing. It's way past time to cut all this 'The Man's out to get me' crap. We're all tired of it, Wish. All of us."

"Tell me something, Pop," Wish said, fighting back. "What more evidence do you need than this?" He lifted his withered left arm.

"Oh, 'The Man' shot you, did he?"

"That's right."

"No, son. I guess you didn't hear us back when you were coming out of it in the hospital. Either that, or you've got a selective memory. Truth is, you clocked the white kid with your iron. Things happened so fast, you never did see the other guy, did you?"

"No, but—"

"The other guy was black, Wish. Remember? We explained that to you, months ago. The other kid was one of us. *Not* 'The Man.'"

Reality filtered through Wish's defenses, but he wasn't nearly willing to give up his argument. After all, he had depended on this for years.

"Still," he retorted, only to be immediately interrupted.

"Still, but, whatever, Wish. It's all bullshit."

Albert hesitated, debating with himself before he made the decision to plunge ahead.

"I promised my darling daughter that I'd keep her secret, but what the hell. You're always railing against the white man, Wish, and sure, there's plenty of screwed up folks out there. But for the umpteenth time, son, they're not out to get you. And I can prove it to you."

"Not possible, Pop."

"Who sponsored you for the Tour, son?"

"Dad, please don't." The two men were startled to find that Donna had been standing in the doorway between the kitchen and the dining room.

"Nope, it's high time the truth came out, honey," Albert said. Donna held her tongue as her father turned his attention back to Wish.

"C'mon, son. Give me an answer. Who sponsored you?"

"You know as well as I do."

"Humor me."

"Emerald Sporting Goods. Why? What's your point?"

"Who owns Emerald Sporting Goods?"

"Well, it's one of those big corporations," Wish responded, simultaneously defensive and curious. "I guess a lot of people own it."

"A *white* man owns Emerald, Wish. A *white* man, who wanted to help you. A white man named Jackson Spears."

It took a moment for this news to take hold of Wish. The rage showed first in his flared nostrils and then in his widening eyes. Neither Albert nor Donna could ever remember hearing Wish raise his voice to either one of them, but they now prepared themselves for the worst. Instead, Wish slowly stood up and walked over to within inches of his wife, seeming to tower over her. He spoke in a whisper, with a tone of disgust and disappointment that cut far deeper than any scream.

"You *spoke* to that man? You made a *deal* with that man?"

"Wish, I…" Donna was defenseless in the face of Wish's fury.

"You *sold* me to that man."

Donna was crying, her father unable to help.

"You don't even know me, do you?"

He left the room, taking great care not to touch his wife as he brushed past her.

Chapter 13

Home for Jackson and Rachel Spears was a four-story townhouse on Fifth Avenue overlooking Central Park. In short, one of the more expensive homes in Manhattan.

Early in the evening that post-Thanksgiving Friday, Jackson was sitting in his favorite leather wing chair in front of a warm fire in his mahogany-paneled study. He heard the chimes of the front doorbell.

As the door opened, the two men who faced each other were immediately confused by a sense of "Where have I seen this guy before?" Their initial surprise was quickly replaced by recognition.

"Tiny?" Wish exclaimed to the man in the black suit, white shirt, and black tie who towered in front of him. "What the hell are you doing here?"

"Mr. Fitzgerald. Good to see you again. Please, come in. I imagine you're here to see Mr. Spears, so let me announce you." He escorted Wish through the marble-floored, high-ceilinged foyer into an ornately decorated parlor and indicated that he should make himself comfortable on a red velvet settee. Thoroughly confused by the unexpected meeting with his old caddie mentor and Tiny's suddenly refined speech and manner, Wish chose to remain standing. *Focus. This won't take long.*

Wish, who had arrived with a scowl, was prepared to make a brief, angry statement in the doorway and then leave. Now, a little disoriented, he was already off his game plan.

Jackson appeared in the doorway, dressed in a burgundy V-neck sweater, khakis, and sockless loafers. A disconcerting thought popped into Wish's head. *He looks sharp.*

"This is a nice surprise, Wish," Jackson said. Remembering that years earlier Wish had rejected his offer of a handshake, he just smiled.

"Actually, I'm not here to surprise you, Jackson," Wish said. "Just have a couple of things to say, and I'll be on my way."

"OK, fine. We might as well at least make ourselves comfortable."

"No, I..." Wish started to say, but Jackson had already left the room and was heading up the obscenely grand staircase. Unless he wanted to yell, Wish had no choice but to follow. When he caught up, the two had entered another obscenely furnished room. *What's this? A study? Library? What do you call this? Looks like something out of a damn movie.*

"Please, have a seat." Two chairs were positioned in front of a crackling fire.

Again, Wish had little choice. *This is killing my plan! What happened to my fire, my anger? Stop accepting this asshole's hospitality! Stop being impressed by this place!*

"You wanted to tell me something?" Jackson asked.

Ahh, here we go. Let him have it.

"You were—"

They were interrupted by Tiny, who wheeled in a cart with a tray of various cold drinks, a bucket of ice, and a beautiful plate of fruit, cheese, and crackers. He took a few moments to arrange everything on a table between the two men and quietly departed. Wish waited until he was out of earshot.

"You've been interfering in my life."

"I'm not sure I'd use the word 'interfering,' but if that's how you perceive it, then OK. I'm guilty."

"You had no right to do that."

"OK, I accept that."

"And you need to stop."

"OK, I will. I have."

"Fine."

Now, Wish was at a loss. This hadn't gone at all like he expected. *He's manipulating me. I haven't had my say! Just say it and get out of here! Maybe if I stood up...*He rose from his seat and looked down on Jackson.

"You screwed up my life, Jackson. At least for a while, you did. I trusted you, man. I trusted you. You were my best friend! The best friend I ever had!"

Wish suddenly realized that he was shouting. Now Jackson had stood up to face him.

"And that's the way I felt about you," Jackson shot back, his voice also rising. "I tried to tell you that, that time in Georgia, but you wouldn't give me chance!"

"Why would I want to do that?" Wish shouted.

"Daddy?" A little voice startled both of them. The two men, red-faced, turned to see a little boy, a little *black* boy, perhaps three years old, who had entered the room.

"Why are you mad, Daddy?"

"Come here, little guy," Jackson said, his face having morphed from anger to a warm smile. The boy ran to his father, who lifted him into his arms.

"Who are you?" the boy asked Wish. "Are you mad at my daddy?"

To say that Wish was confused would be the grossest of understatements. He was embarrassed that he had been shouting in front of this tyke and had absolutely no idea where to go from here.

"I'm Wish."

"You're not *my* wish. Who wished you?"

As angry as both men had been, they couldn't help but smile.

"No, buddy, this is Mr. Fitzgerald," Jackson said to the little boy in his arms. "His first name is Aloysius, like your first name is Tyrell. But people call him 'Wish' for short, just like I call you—"

"Buddy?"

Both men smiled again. Tyrell smiled back.

"Something like that."

"Is he your friend? He doesn't look like your friend. He seems mad."

Rachel entered the room.

Is this Jackson's wife? Wish wondered. *Can't be! She must have six inches on him!*

"Oh there you are, little guy," Rachel said to Tyrell. "Mommy's been looking all over for you."

"Mommy! This man is a wish!"

"Yes, honey, Mommy guessed that," she said, taking Tyrell from his father's arms. "Gentlemen, dinner is ready. Mr. Fitzgerald, you'll join us. And both of you will keep your voices and your emotions in check while we dine."

"No…" Wish began before Rachel abruptly turned and departed with Tyrell, obviously expecting the two men to follow. Again, Wish was stymied.

During dinner, Wish and Jackson took an extended break from what they had previously thought was important. Wish learned about how Jackson and Rachel had met and all about Tyrell's adoption. He was astounded to be told that, having had an addict for a mother, Tyrell was himself born addicted to crack cocaine in a rough neighborhood in the Bronx. The mother graduated to even more serious drugs and eventually died, found with a needle still in her arm. Tyrell, who had fortunately been rescued from that environment shortly after he was born, still had to deal with a torturous infancy.

Adopting Tyrell seemed like a no-brainer to the Spears. In reality, they had to deal with the perception that they were white, dilettante do-gooders, the worst thing for a black child. They *were* do-gooders, but because of Rachel's charity, they were also realistic about the challenges of an interracial adoption. In the end, their sincerity and love for Tyrell won the day.

By the time Wish and Jackson resumed their discussion in the study (or was it a library? Wish never did learn the proper name for the darn room), much of the poison that had polluted Wish's mind before he arrived had dissipated. The two were now at least willing to listen to each other.

Jackson began by telling what had happened after he had won the junior championship back in 1969. He apologized profusely for his father's actions, and Wish began to understand things from the perspective of a powerless kid with a powerful, controlling father.

"So, you were hauled off to Europe, against your wishes."

"Very much so."

"And you had no idea that your father had gotten me fired."

"I found out much later. I hated him for that."

"But you never contacted me, Jackson. You never explained all that to me."

"And that's where I failed, Wish. I was embarrassed. Actually, I was completely ashamed. I owed you that much, as a bare minimum. I'm so sorry. Since those days I've lived my life regretting that and wanting to make it up to you, somehow, some way. I wanted so badly to apologize in person."

"Why did it bother you? It would have been easy to blow it off."

"That's exactly the point."

"So?"

Jackson collected himself by pouring another serving of aged port into his glass. He gestured to Wish to see if he wanted more, but Wish declined. Jackson took a sip.

"My friendship with you was the most important relationship in my life; that is, at least until I met Rachel. Looking back, I realized that before I met you, I had just about zero confidence in myself. Was that my father's fault? I suppose, to some extent. My weight? My height? The fact that I sucked at sports?

Probably a combination of everything. Who cares what the reasons were? I had the self-assurance of a pet rock.

"You were the first person who truly believed in me, Wish," Jackson continued. "My father wanted me to be what I could never be; I was a disappointment to him. My mother? Well, my mother was wrapped up in…Darien. I don't know how else to explain it. In hindsight, winning that championship was a watershed moment in my life. We both know that it would never have happened without your help, without your friendship."

"I had no idea, but thanks for saying that," Wish responded. "Those were happy days. While they lasted, at least."

"They sure were."

"So that's why you hired that guy to find me." Something clicked in Wish's mind. "And *you* were the one who sent Tiny!"

"Jerome. His name's Jerome."

"A hell of a golfer."

"Actually, he doesn't play the game. He played football for Alabama."

"No way," Wish said.

"Hear me out. I had been following your progress from a distance. I knew you wouldn't give me the time of day if *I* showed up. We were in the process of breaking into the golf market, so I had some friends on your mini-tour, and they told me that you were a potential superstar. They said the only thing you were missing was the ability to putt."

"Pretty important."

"Sure, but you had been practically flaw-less in your putting before."

"But a crappy public course in Waynesboro, Georgia isn't—"

"Right! But you had all the tools, all the knowledge. You could read the greens, Wish. You lacked one thing—confidence. Coincidentally, the very thing you taught me."

"And you figured all of this out from here in New York?"

"No, no way. You, better than anyone, know I'm not a great golfer, Wish. A good businessman, yeah. But sports…Anyway, I had developed some relationships in golf, and one of them was Ben Crenshaw."

"Holy cow. So, that was real?"

"That's right; Ben found out about you through me. He asked around as a favor to me, kinda took an interest in you, actually looked at some video footage of your game."

"There was video of me?"

"Well, it was hard to arrange when there's little to no audience, like on your tour, but I managed to get some. Anyway, Ben's the one who figured out the answer. We used Jerome—Tiny—to deliver the message."

"And it worked."

"Yes, it did."

"OK, but that's an awful lot to assuage your guilt over what your father did, Jackson. You went through a lot to find me, and I shot you down. Despite that, you went through so much to keep track of me and then to help me with Tiny. And then, the sponsorship? That's quite a bit to make up for a childhood mistake."

"Look at it this way." Jackson sighed. "Let's say I indirectly helped you regain confidence in your putting, and that led to…what?"

"The PGA Tour. At least, it should have."

"And you helped give me confidence in myself, and that led to…what?"

Wish shrugged his shoulders.

"Emerald Sporting Goods. And…this!" Jackson spread his arms and looked around, indicating the very building in which they were sitting.

"You would have had the money anyway, from your parents."

"Maybe so, but this is *my* money, *my* success. *I* earned it, not my father."

It was a lot for Wish to take in.

"I owed you, Wish. It's as simple as that."

Wish considered this for a few moments.

"If so, consider the debt paid."

———

They had been talking for a while; it was time for Wish to leave. Tyrell had long ago been put to bed, so Rachel joined them at the front door. The good-byes were awkward. Rachel looked as if she might be about to offer a hug, but Wish evaded the gesture with a nod and thanks for her hospitality. He did shake hands with Jackson.

"If you two don't kiss and make up, you're both idiots," Rachel admonished. "Stop wasting time. I mean it."

Wish sidestepped the issue. "Please tell Tiny I said thanks," he said, with a sheepish smile.

Wish was halfway down the front steps when the door reopened behind him. It was Jackson.

"Hey, Wish. Was that another one of your patented non sequiturs?"

Wish reached the sidewalk and turned around, again allowing himself a begrudging smile.

"I suppose so." He smiled. "I suppose so."

———

After grabbing a few hours of sleep in a flea-bag motel in New Jersey, Wish hit the road for what should have been a sixteen-hour drive home to Greensboro. Unfortunately, most of the day and evening were spent driving through torrential downpours, adding three more hours to the trip. He arrived home around four in the morning, dead on his feet, hungry, and in desperate need of a hot bath.

It was still raining like crazy. Much more importantly, he needed to go to the bathroom in the worst way.

The front door was locked. The front door was never locked, so Wish didn't even carry a key. He went around back to the kitchen door and discovered the same thing. Puzzled and soaked to the skin, he returned to the front door and knocked quietly so as to avoid waking the children. Nothing. He scratched his drenched head and knocked again, a little louder this time. Still no response. Concerned, he now pounded on the door.

Hearing a window on the second floor right above him open, Wish stepped back to see Donna. As soon as he looked up, raindrops started hitting him in the eyes.

"Go away, Wish."

"What?"

"I said, 'go away.'"

It was hard to look up at the bedroom window through the driving rain. He had to shout to be heard above the sound of the weather.

"Stop kidding around, Donna. C'mon, open the door. I'm tired and I'm hungry, and I need to use the bathroom. Badly."

"No."

"Have you lost your mind, woman?"

"No. Now just go away. Perhaps we can talk about this tomorrow."

"But I live here!"

"Not tonight, you don't. And the way things are going, I'm thinking maybe not for good."

"I don't get this!"

"I'm sure you don't, Wish. Please, just go."

"Open the door so we can talk! We're going to wake the children, Donna!"

"They're at your mother's house."

"Please." He was getting desperate.

"No, *you* please. I've had it with you, Wish. I've tried to understand your situation, believe me, I have. You have no idea how much I— we—all of us have…how patient we've tried to be. But when you basically accuse me of auctioning you off like a slave, well…"

She could no longer hold the tears back.

"I…I'm your wife, Wish! I love you, at least I did…You say things like that and then you just up and leave, without telling anyone anything! Do you have another…?" She gulped. "We can't live like this, Wish. I am just not going to accept this any longer. Neither is Dad, or even your mother. You need to go away for a while, or live somewhere else, but somehow, some way, you need to get your head on straight. I don't know how you're going to do it, but I won't be treated like this, and I won't allow my children to watch you treat me like this!

"So…just go away."

"I went to New York, to see Jackson."

She gasped. "Oh, God. What happened? You didn't say anything…You didn't do anything…"

"It took me sixteen hours to get there. Sixteen hours of anger, just building and building. And it started out exactly as how you would probably picture it. But it ended up differently. And now is not the time to talk about it. At least, not like this.

"I had another twenty hours today to finally think the right thoughts. I've had a lot of time to think about things, Donna, and I have been wrong, in so many ways. Like Pop said, I've been a perfect ass—a self-centered idiot. I don't deserve you, and maybe I don't deserve the kids. And I am so, so sorry for what I said about you selling me.

"But right now, I really need to use the bathroom."

He waited for a response, practically hopping to take his mind of his bladder.

"I understand how you're feeling. I promise, I get it! I'll go to the Holiday Inn, and then I'm going to do my best to win you back, but first, for God's sake, I really need to use the bathroom. Please?"

He looked up, and Donna was no longer in the window. Taking that for a no, Wish trudged over to his car and opened the driver's side door.

"Wish."

Donna was standing in the front doorway wearing a fluffy pink robe and matching

slippers. He liked it when she looked like that—
domestic and slightly disheveled, like the wife
and mother that she was.

"Yes?"

"Do you mean that? About understanding
what you've done, how you've been? You're
really sorry?"

"Yes, very much so."

"You *really* mean it?"

"I do, Donna."

"And you'll change?"

"All I can promise is that I'll try. But believe
me, I've already started."

Arms folded, Donna considered this. Wish
looked like he was in pain.

"You still need to go?"

"Well, yeah. That hasn't changed."

"Go ahead."

Breathing an audible sigh of relief, Wish
hurried toward her, attempting a kiss that she
deftly sidestepped. He rushed into the powder
room and closed the door behind him.

"And you can stay tonight," Donna said to
the bathroom door. "But don't you even think
about coming upstairs, Wish Fitzgerald. This
isn't over because of a few nice words. Get to
know that sofa, because you'll be sleeping there
for a while."

With that, she padded her way upstairs to the master bedroom and closed the door.

———

A man's pride is a funny thing. The ability to admit that one has been wrongheaded, let alone wrongheaded for years, is tough to come by. The admission to one's self is challenging enough, but actually "coming out" to everyone else? Problematic, to say the least.

The first steps for Wish started with letting go of the depression that had suffocated him since the shooting. The easiest way to do that was to return to work. Albert and the staff happily welcomed him back, and, within weeks, life began to return to normal at Jameson's. Although Wish couldn't swing a golf club, he was still prized for his golf lessons. He also began contributing more on the administrative side of what was becoming a thriving business.

One of the healthiest signs that the "old Wish" was back was the increase in the insults, needling, and pranks between Wish and Albert. One morning Wish greeted Albert's arrival at the store with the theme song from *Sanford and Son* blaring from a boom box. Albert good-naturedly grabbed his chest and mimicked Red

Foxx's "I'm coming, Elizabeth" pretend heart attack.

The two loved the acidic byplay between fictional father and son, Fred and Lamont Sanford. They often recreated the popular television show's routines for the employees.

Wish: "You're a dirty old man, ya know that?"

Albert: "And I'm gonna be one till I'm a dead old man."

Or:

Wish: "This idea is going to put us on easy street."

Albert: "Is that the one with the poorhouse?"

Or:

Albert: "You just dumb, son. You just dumb."

What Albert failed to appreciate was the fact that he always seemed to leave his audience in stitches not necessarily because of the quality of the humor or his ability to mimic Red Foxx, but just the opposite. While he believed that he was recreating Foxx's voice perfectly, the high pitch of his voice made for a hilarious mockery of each performance.

The business, moribund during Wish's absence, took off again within months of his return. Little by little, joy and pride returned to Wish's demeanor and visage. The old Wish was coming back at last.

Chapter 14

Echoing Rachel, Donna was now urging her husband to reconnect with his childhood friend on a regular basis. Having established a relationship with Jackson herself, she was sorely tempted to jump-start the process by concocting a reason for the two couples to get together. Instead, she concluded that she had already done enough meddling in the relationship between the two. She decided to lay low while she waited for Wish to overcome his stubbornness on the subject.

Otherwise, Donna was happy to have the old Wish back. Productive at work and involved at home, Wish was his old self again—even better. The kids vied for the closest position to him during bedtime stories. Despite the age difference, eight-year-old Annabelle loved hearing her "old" stories retold again and again to five-year-old Bobby.

Wish often encouraged Annabelle to read the stories herself. Big sister beamed with pride as little brother listened, squirmed, and eventually dozed off. In that moment, Wish actually felt that his life wasn't half bad.

Little by little, his view of what was important evolved. His quest to become a touring pro had become all-encompassing, to the point where his life was truly all about him. It had become too easy to accept the adulation of the people of Waynesboro and Greensboro and, more importantly, the sacrifices made by his family and even his colleagues at work. After all, wasn't everyone working for a common goal?

He had awakened to the realization that making everything about him just didn't work. Now, he dealt with an odd dichotomy. At the very time that he felt guilty about his past behavior, he was also happier than he had ever been.

———

But the reality was that he couldn't play golf.

Every day, golf was in his face. He ran a growing company that was all about the game.

The company first added a state-of-the-art miniature golf course, then a matching facility in Greensboro and gradually expanded the size of both stores and ranges. Soon snack bars were also added, and with some recipes from Annie, those facilities gradually morphed into locally popular restaurants. In addition to overseeing the growth, Wish purchased golf equipment and apparel for the stores and oversaw the company's other teaching pros.

Although he refused to discuss it, Wish missed his old friend terribly. Much too often a random memory would filter through the defenses he had consciously constructed. A shot, a winding putt, the shape of a green, the beauty of a memorable hole, the challenge of a match, the creativity and skill he had employed to meet that challenge. The feel of a swing. The satisfying sound of a ball well struck. The camaraderie of the game, especially—especially—the back-and-forth, the trash-talking, a game with Albert. Winning.

It hurt.

No matter how hard he tried, he could not suppress the ache, the longing. It was a war between wishes and reality, desire and the cold truth. Reality always won. The truth was final. No way around it. No appeal.

Those who were closest to Wish realized what was happening and wanted desperately to help. But what was there to do? This was his battle; surely he would find a way to adjust, to deal, to accept.

There was a measure of relief when he was playing with the kids and thankfully, he could always lose himself for a while in Donna's arms. Home was a refuge.

And some solace came from the strangest of sources, probably the last place one would expect Wish to look—caddying at Augusta National.

A few months after the shooting, he decided to return. At first, the thought was to caddie one more round in order to drink in the beauty and the peace and the tradition. That way he could perhaps bottle the memory and drink it later a sip at a time, savoring it for years to come.

Inexplicably, his tension—the sense of loss—disappeared for the few hours that he walked the course. Rather than mourn his private loss in the one place where one would expect it would hurt the most, Wish breathed. He concentrated on each shot and each putt as if it were his own. He shared his stories with the golfers in the foursome, and he reveled in his golfer's properly crafted shots and the putts that dropped as a result of his wise guidance. For whatever reason, he wasn't even jealous.

He really did savor each moment on the course, appreciating the meticulously manicured grounds with their brilliantly placed bright-white bunkers and the sometimes glassy surface of the pond between the tee and the diabolical green on the sixteenth. Rae's Creek, the Eisenhower Pine on the seventeenth and the Hogan Bridge near the fourteenth. The steep climb up the 18th to the clubhouse, with the "Big Oak" tree nearby. And, of course, Amen Corner.

He knew the names of every hole, from Tea Olive to Chinese Fir to Magnolia to Redbud, and he loved them all.

Donna was shocked when Wish returned that day a happy man. The smile lasted for only a few hours, but it was a smile. She urged him to continue caddying at Augusta National. Two weeks later, Wish was back.

———

With Bobby's sixth birthday on the horizon, the Fitzgerald family sat around the kitchen table to make plans for the big day. Important decisions abounded—where to have it? What kind of cake? How many guests? And most importantly, who to invite?

Big sister Annabelle, a confident and already irrepressible fifth grader, did her best to take charge of the meeting. After all, she was knowledgeable on what and who were cool, even for first graders. She even knew something about several of Bobby's peers, since three were siblings of her friends. Although her parents were happy to see how much Annabelle cared about her little brother, they needed to remind her that it was *his* party and not hers—several times.

Several venues favored by either Annabelle or her parents were discussed and rejected. McDonald's was not cool enough, and the miniature golf course at Dad's place of business was "lame." The lake or a pool party? No and no. Pony rides? C'mon, Dad! Bobby's heart was set on the new Chuck E. Cheese at the local strip shopping center, and Chuck E. Cheese it would be.

Given that, Donna and Wish set the guest limit at ten—not including Annabelle ("...and a friend, Dad! I can't be alone there! And she can help out!").

The final challenge was winnowing the guest list from Bobby's initial two dozen to ten.

The first seven, all of them on Bobby's T-Ball team, were easy. Then Bobby mentioned his eighth choice, a boy named Jimmy. Annabelle immediately reacted with an adamant shaking of her head, her ponytail flying.

Wish and Donna wondered what the problem could be with this kid. Not cool enough?

"No, Bobby, not Jimmy," Annabelle said sternly.

"But he's my friend!" Bobby pleaded.

"No!"

"Why not?" Bobby whined.

Annabelle, who was seated next to her brother, leaned in to whisper her answer. Curious, the parents strained unsuccessfully to catch a word or two.

"I don't care!" Bobby whispered back, loud enough for the parental units to hear.

"You have to!" Annabelle whispered back. Things were at a standstill.

Wish and Donna looked at each other. What could be the problem?

"Annabelle, honey, it's your brother's party," Donna said.

"Yes, Mom, but he can't invite Jimmy. He can't."

"Why not, sweetie?" Wish asked.

"You know…"

Again, the two parents looked to each other for an answer. Finding none, they turned back to their daughter.

"I guess you'll have to tell us, honey," Donna said.

"But you know!" Annabelle was adamant.

"C'mon, honey," Donna said, getting frustrated. "Just tell us. Why shouldn't we invite this boy Jimmy?"

"He's white."

Her parents were still clueless.

"You know. Daddy wouldn't like that."

For Wish and Donna, it was if a bomb had gone off in their kitchen.

A proud Annabelle looked expectantly to her father for approval. Bobby, who didn't get what was happening at all but just wanted to invite Jimmy, was on the verge of tears.

Also on the verge of tears was Donna. Anger and shame battled for control of her system. Anger was winning.

Wish was stunned. Despite his bigotry, he knew this was wrong and that it was his fault. But his daughter was merely parroting him; she had done no wrong. Donna was staring—no, glaring at him.

"Dad?" Annabelle said. "That's right, isn't it?"

"Daddy?" Bobby said plaintively, his voice quivering.

"Fix this, Daddy," Donna said in the most forced sweet tone of voice ever concocted.

Overwhelmed with chagrin and feeling flushed, Wish stood up from the table, forcing a smile. He reached across the table to take his daughter's hand, guiding Annabelle to her feet.

"Sweetheart, your ol' dad has some explaining to do. Come with me. We're going for a drive. Mommy will help Bobby with the birthday plans while we talk."

"Mommy?" Bobby said.

"Am I in trouble?" Annabelle asked.

"Absolutely not, sweetheart," Wish answered. "But I am," he muttered to himself as they left the room.

As epiphanies go, this one was a doozy.

During the short drive to the Friendly's in Greensboro, Wish searched for the words to explain himself to Annabelle. Meanwhile, he was oblivious to the fact that she was on the verge of tears, still certain that she had done or said something terribly wrong.

It was a weeknight, so the restaurant was relatively empty. Wish steered his daughter in the direction of a booth in a far corner. As soon as they were seated, he finally tuned into Annabelle's distraught appearance.

"What's wrong, sweetie?" he asked, through a strained smile.

"I'm sorry!"

"For what, sweetie pie?"

"For...for...for...I don't know!" The dam burst; tears flowed.

Oh, geez, Wish thought. *Can this get any worse?*

"You have nothing to be sorry about, Annabelle." He reached across the table to grasp her hands, wet from brushing away tears. "Daddy is the one who should be sorry, not you."

This revelation stopped up the dam.

"Wh...wh...why, Daddy?"

"Guess what. Daddies make mistakes, just like kids do. And your daddy has made a big mistake, for a long time."

The waitress stopped by, interrupting the conversation just long enough to enable the pair to order their traditional father/daughter banana split to share. Not wanting to embarrass herself in front of others (God forbid a classmate should walk in), Annabelle gained control over her emotions.

"Daddy has been wrong about something for a very long time," Wish said. "And Mommy was right."

Wish made note of the fact that he had the rapt attention of his growing-up-too-quickly daughter. He continued.

"No one should dislike a whole group of people, honey."

"But you do. You hate white people."

A damning indictment, and he was guilty as charged. Why did it hurt so much? Why was he embarrassed? No, check that! This was outright shame!

"I did feel like that, honey—before. And that is wrong. I was wrong."

"Really, Daddy? Does this mean that you've changed your mind?"

He needed to be honest. How *did* he feel? Taking a moment to consider this, he realized that, amazingly enough, the hatred was now gone.

"Yes. Really and truly. I've changed my mind."

"I'm glad, Daddy."

The waitress arrived with the banana split, producing a wonderful smile on his daughter's face. The crisis over, they attacked the dessert.

The introspective lesson that Wish had hurriedly prepared on the way over wasn't needed.

———

Wish and Donna often had their most transparent conversations in bed. Wish was oblivious to this, while Donna wondered if it had something to do with the relative absence of clothing.

"So, problem solved, right?" Donna prompted a brooding Wish.

"Yeah, I suppose so." Wish pretended to return his attention to a barely audible ESPN broadcast of *SportsCenter* on the nearby television screen, hoping for some golf highlights. Donna decided to wait out the silence. She didn't have to wait long.

"No."

"Excuse me?"

"No, the problem is not solved."

"But I thought you said—"

"Annabelle is fine. At least I think she is."

"She's like that."

Once again, silence.

"You're about to give me that 'I can hear you thinking' line again, aren't you?" Wish finally remarked.

"I didn't say a thing."

"It's not pleasant to realize that you've been a first-class idiot," Wish confessed. "For the second time, and for many years."

"Idiot? I don't think so, Wish. Wrong, yes. But an idiot? That's pretty harsh. There were reasons you felt the way you did."

"Geez, what the hell was I was doing to the kids? How could I have been that…that…"

"Blind?"

"Stupid. Stupid and blind. Blindly stupid. It took a nine-year-old girl—my baby!—to make me see that I've become the very people that I hated. I'm Jackson's father!"

As always, it pained Donna to see her husband suffer. At the same time, she was overjoyed to hear that he was finally getting it. After all these years, there was hope for her flawed, wonderful man.

As she searched for the right words, Wish interrupted her thoughts.

"I don't want to be that person, Donna."

"So don't."

Both returned to their silent reverie, each thinking the same thing. *Easier said than done.*

Minutes later, just as Donna was finally dozing off, Wish had one more thought to share.

"Donna?"

"Yes, honey."

"Thanks for not saying 'I told you so.'"

"Never crossed my mind."

"You're an excellent liar, sweetheart."

———

"Hello?"

"Jackson?"

"Wish?"

"Yeah."

"Wow. I mean, hello, how are you?"

"Good question…"

"How's that?"

"Never mind. I'm fine. Listen, something happened yesterday that kind of opened my eyes about…Well, I guess about life, in a way."

"Sounds profound."

"Sounds like you've been working on your vocabulary."

"Yeah, well, I had a good example in that regard."

"Hey, look. What I called to tell you is that you had a pretty…profound effect on my life, like you say I had on yours. If you remember, I was a bit of a loner myself back in those days…matter of fact, I still am.

"But the point is, the kids in South Norwalk thought I was pretty strange. Hell, even their parents thought that. Just about everyone but my mother…Well, in any case, people didn't like the way I talked, and they thought I was really strange, I guess because of the golf thing."

"Yeah, I remember."

"But *you* got me, Jack. We got each other. You were my first real friend. Thinking back on it, you were the best friend I ever had, man."

"And I screwed it up."

"No, your dad screwed that up. For both of us. I get that, now. Took me a long time, I admit, but I do get it. I also get that I was a knucklehead to not let you explain yourself when you came down to Georgia that time."

"Wish—"

"No, Jack. When I was in New York, you ended up doing most of the talking. Now it's my turn. OK?"

"Absolutely."

"I'm just beginning to realize the mistakes I've made, big mistakes that I've been making for a lot of years. First thing I want to…actually, the second thing, after a bunch of apologies to my wife, who shouldn't have had to put up with me all these years, is apologize to you for not giving you a chance."

"No need, but thanks. I—"

"And speaking of thanks, if I didn't say it before, thanks for all that crazy stuff you were doing behind the scenes. Considering what a jerk I had been to you, that was way beyond—"

"You're welcome. I—"

"Still talking here, Jack."

"Yeah, right, I forgot. Your turn this time."

"Yep. I can tell you, man, hatred takes a lot out of you. It's not a good way to live your life. Gets you nowhere, and turns out, it even hurts the ones who love you. I guess I can't promise that I'm all of a sudden gonna be all lovey-dovey with you white folk, but I do realize that something's got to change.

"And I also understand that I need my friend back."

This was met with silence.

"You still there?"

"Yeah."

"Then say something!"

"Oh, so it's my turn now?"

Wish laughed. "C'mon, man!"

"Well, I don't know what brought this about, but whatever it was, I sure am glad to hear it. I'm glad you're back, man."

They talked for another hour. Wish learned that Jackson's father had died years earlier from cirrhosis of the liver and that his mother had remarried. Jackson talked about how the decision to adopt Tyrell had been both joyous and stressful, with the primary source of the stress stemming from his certainty that his mother would vehemently object to the adoption of a black child.

"But she shocked me, Wish, she really did. She loved that little boy from the get-go."

"This was *your* mother, right? Your mother from *Darien*?"

"Yep."

"So, what happened to change her?"

"Best guess? Maternal instinct. At least I haven't been able to come up with a better explanation. She saw that this little boy needed us and just plain needed love, and she just… loved him. The woman can't get enough of her little grandson and he of her. It's a damn love affair!"

"Wow. Who woulda thunk?"

"Well, who woulda thunk that we'd ever be having this conversation?"

"Maybe we can chalk it up to 'better late than never.' Whatever. I'm all for making up for lost time. Hope you are too, my friend."

———

To say that Wish and Jackson picked up exactly where they left off in childhood would be an exaggeration. After all, people in their thirties are far different than they were in their teens.

But over the next ten years, especially given the initial physical distance between the two friends, the relationship did grow steadily back to where each claimed the other as his best friend. Rachel and Donna also hit it off, speaking to each other often on the phone. Even Tyrell and Bobby became best buddies, bonding, just as their fathers had, on the golf course.

Emerald Sporting Goods kept growing, reaching Fortune 500 status by the end of the decade. Although he was on the cover of numerous magazines and was a much sought-after motivational speaker, Jackson remained essentially a private man. He treasured his time with Tyrell and Rachel and his many getaways, most often with the Fitzgerald clan.

Jameson's Golf was successful in its own right, although limited to the two operations in Waynesboro and Greensboro. Albert officially retired in 1998 and handed the reins of the company to Wish.

Under the tutelage of his father and grand-father, Bobby became one of the hottest junior golfers in Georgia. Annabelle was also so good at the sport that she was offered full-ride golf scholarships to a couple of ACC and SEC universities. However, since money was not a problem for her parents, Annabelle decided to head north to Brown University to study business and marketing. It turned out she wanted to grow up to be Donna, not Wish.

In the early nineties the Fitzgeralds moved into a large home overlooking the twelfth and thirteenth holes on one of the golf courses in the new, nationally recognized Reynolds Plantation development in their very own town of Greensboro, Georgia. Wish took great pleasure in noting that he owned one of the finest homes in a development that featured the word "plantation" and that was located in the heart of Dixie. "We've come a long way, baby!" he would crow to Annie, who would laugh at her son's enthusiasm.

The Fitzgeralds' next-door neighbor at Reynolds Plantation? The Spears' vacation home. The two families got together often, with Jackson entertaining everyone from the kids to Albert and Annie with his dead-on impersonations of Wish and Albert. He imitated their seriocomic arguments perfectly, with special attention to Wish's glowering countenance and Albert's excitable, unmanly voice.

Despite the success of the business, Wish found that he was still happiest among the other caddies at Augusta National. Although much more comfortable financially than his colleagues, he could identify with them.

The mere fact that Wish wanted to hang out with the guys was a subject of much discussion and pride. At their request, Wish often regaled them with stories from his year on the developmental tour. Some also wanted to hear about how he had become a success in business.

Another hot topic in the caddie shack (although it was a stretch to describe the pristine building at Augusta National as a "shack") was that Wish always declined to caddie during the Masters Tournament and even chose not to attend as a spectator. The guys couldn't believe that, as much as Wish loved the tournament, he still turned down such opportunities. However, they respected their "wealthy" friend too much to press him on this issue.

Once you had managed to establish yourself as one of the guys, you were awarded a nickname by the others. Wish, however, was given a pass, since one nickname was enough for him.

Just as in a school cafeteria, black caddies generally hung out primarily with blacks and whites with whites. This didn't necessarily mean there was animosity between the two groups; it was just a fact of life in the caddy shack. Oddly, Wish bridged this artificial gap. For instance, Mike "Modesty" Rogers was the caddie with whom Wish enjoyed chatting the most. Modesty hailed from the Smokey Mountains ("not sure what state exactly, ta tell ya the truth"). A deeply tanned sixty-year-old white man with few remaining teeth and lots of lines in his face, Modesty had earned his nickname with his incessant claim to be "the best damn caddie ever at Augusta National, or any other damn course you care to name."

As many stories about Augusta National as Albert (who had been dubbed "Buckets") had shared with Wish, it seemed that Modesty had ten times that number. Stories about Arnold Palmer, Gary Player, Lee Trevino, Tom Watson, and even such legends as Sam Snead, Byron Nelson, and Ben Hogan abounded. Each time Wish was tempted to chalk one of these tales up as BS, he managed to ascertain the accuracy of it from another source.

After a while, Wish himself became a walking fount of information about Augusta

National. He possessed an encyclopedic knowledge of what the best options were in terms of shots from any point on the course, based on the player's demonstrated ability, loft and length of each shot from each club, the wind direction and speed, softness of the green, and other variables. He had memorized the sometimes insane nuances of every square foot of every green, which gave him the ability to accurately predict the speed and path of each putt and its odds of ending in the bottom of the cup. He took into account such variables as the direction of the grain, the time of day, the weather (especially wind strength and direction), when and how short the greens had been mowed, and references to his monumental library of how putts had rolled, both from his personal experience as a caddie and the innumerable putts he had witnessed during decades of Masters television broadcasts.

Of course, all of this put Wish in great demand as a caddie for the extraordinarily wealthy and successful members of Augusta National. For those who cared to scratch the conversational surface with this particular caddie, they were shocked to find the savvy, successful businessman who carried their bag and read their putts. It made for an even more intriguing round at what was arguably the world's most coveted golf course.

Sometimes, even some of the lesser-known PGA players who had earned the privilege of playing the Masters asked Wish to caddie for them. In each and every case, the answer was a polite but firm "no."

Chapter 15

2000

Wish had never heard his friend so stressed. Jackson was apparently on the verge of tears.

"Tyrell's missing. He never came home after school yesterday. We don't know where he is, Wish."

"That's terrible, Jack," Wish said. "Have you spoken to the police?"

"They came over, and I filled out a missing-persons report. We gave them a couple of pictures of him, but they seemed kind of nonchalant about the whole thing. Said with a kid this age, it's almost always a false alarm. He's probably at a friend's house, or embarrassed about something he's done wrong and doesn't want to face up to the consequences…"

"So, I'm sure you've contacted all his friends."

"Yes, but that's just it. He hasn't been hanging out with his old crowd for quite a while now. He's sixteen, and we can't get through to him anymore, Wish," Jackson said. "We've lost him. School, his friends, sports—nothing means anything to him these days. He's sullen, a real wise-ass to both of us. We live in fear that the phone is going to ring, and it'll be the cops calling to say that he's been arrested, or even… and now this."

"He's a teenager," Wish responded, trying to be reassuring. "Hopefully, the cops are right. It might be a phase he's going through; maybe this is easily explicable, and he's just hiding out somewhere safe."

"It's way beyond that. He's gotten mixed up with a gang. These are serious people, Wish."

"Damn, I had no idea. Is there anyone you can talk to, get some advice on how to handle this? Maybe they could figure out what's going on here."

"Believe me, we've tried. Found the best therapist in Manhattan. We got him to one appointment, and he practically spit on the poor woman."

"When this is over—after we find Tyrell safe and sound—you might have to move, Jack. The suburbs, or better yet, come down here permanently. He's out of their reach way down here. I know the business is there, but…"

"We're willing to try *anything*. Tyrell is the most important thing in the world to us, Wish. He doesn't understand what he's gotten himself into. Those bastards have gotten complete control over him! They've convinced him that *they* are his family—not us." Wish heard Jackson take a deep breath. It sounded like he was stifling a sob.

"Can you believe that?" Jackson continued. "We can't lose him. We can't."

"I'm on my way. I'll grab the first plane out of Atlanta and should be there late tonight."

"Thanks."

———

As Wish dialed his travel agent, Donna was upstairs packing a bag for him.

"Dad?"

It was Bobby. Without turning around, Wish waved his son away.

"Not now, son. I'm in a rush. There's a problem with Tyrell."

"Tyrell's here!"

"What the..." Hanging up the phone, Wish whirled around to see the two boys standing side by side.

"He wants to see you, Dad. He says he needs to talk to you."

Wish was shocked by Tyrell's appearance. For years Tyrell had hung out at the Fitzgerald household during his family's frequent trips to Greensboro. Until today, Wish had never seen the boy in anything but a golf shirt and khakis or golf shorts. The young man in front of him was decked out in what Wish could only assume were gang colors along with immensely baggy jeans barely holding on halfway down his rear end, a bandana on his closely shaven head, "bling" hanging around his neck, and huge, unlaced, red Air Jordan basketball shoes on his feet. The sight was jarring to Wish, and, judging from the saucer-like eyes on his son, to Bobby also.

"Bobby, please get your mother," Wish said.

Wish turned his attention to his guest, who had already plopped down on the overstuffed sofa across from Wish. Wish, who was still standing, said, "Thank God you're OK. Do you have any idea what you've done to your parents?"

"Wassup, Uncle Wish?" Tyrell asked, ignoring the question. He slumped sideways on the sofa, swaying his head and gesticulating with his hands the way Wish had seen the rappers preen as he channel surfed. Wish ignored his greeting.

"Tyrell, what are you doing here?"

"Jes chillin'."

Wish's head was spinning. The boy was safe, so the first priority was to let Jack and Rachel know that. The second priority was to keep him here and find out what the hell was going on. In the hundreds of hours that Tyrell had been around Wish, he had never spoken like this and had certainly never displayed such an attitude. As much as he wanted to immediately address all of these issues, Wish decided it was better to first see where this was headed.

"How did you get here?"

"The usual. Delta. Took a cab from the airport."

"That must have cost a pretty penny. Who paid for it?"

"Like always. Plastic, man." He disdainfully tossed his wallet on the coffee table.

"And your parents? Are you under the impression that this is OK with them?"

"Doubt it. They ain't got nothin' ta do wid it."

"Do you have any idea how concerned they've been about you?"

"Don't know, don't care."

Donna had quietly entered the room behind Tyrell. Upon seeing the young man, her eyes showed the same astonishment that Wish was feeling.

"Excuse me for a moment." Wish walked over to Donna.

"Whatever" came Tyrell's answer. He shifted in his seat just enough to see Donna, but if he acknowledged her presence, it was impossible to tell.

"Call Jack and Rachel," Wish whispered to Donna. "We need to let them know that the boy's OK. I'll try to figure out what's going on here."

"Of course. He's…he's…"

"Yes, I agree. Let's just take this one step at a time."

Donna cast a worried look at the back of Tyrell's head before departing the room.

"Let's go for walk, Tyrell."

———

It was dusk on the deserted golf course, a nice breeze cooling off a late-spring day. A multihued sunset was visible over the abundant trees. The air was fragrant with the scent of magnolias. Wish couldn't help but reflect on how many rounds the angry teen walking alongside him had played on this very course, most often with Bobby.

"OK, young man," Wish began. "You've done something exceptionally stupid, but we'll deal with that later. Apparently, you came here to talk. So talk."

"I be—"

"And I know that you know how to speak perfectly good English, so save that crap for your new friends in New York. If you want me to listen to you, speak intelligently."

"This be *my* English," Tyrell retorted.

"Be that as it may, it's not *my* English, young man. And I'm gathering, since you came all this way, you wish to communicate with *me*. Your choice. We can always cut this short right now. I've got plenty of other things that I can be doing with my time."

A glowering Tyrell clammed up for the next fifty yards before finally deciding that his silence was counterproductive.

"I be…I mean, I'm leaving my parents."

"I see."

"And I thought I could live with you, Uncle Wish."

Wish's shock caused his gait to slow for the briefest of moments. Collecting himself, he moved ahead.

"What's going on with you, Tyrell?" Wish asked, struggling to keep his demeanor and tone of voice conversational, despite the fire in his mind.

"I can't live with them no more."

Wish chose to ignore the poor grammar in order to focus on the message.

"And why's that?"

"They don't understand me, Uncle Wish. Especially Da...my so-called father."

"And your new friends? They understand you, right?"

"That's right! See, I knew you'd understand!"

"Because I'm black like you, I suppose. And I'm assuming they're black, right?"

"African American, that's right."

"And how do they show you that they understand you, exactly?"

"They got my back."

"I understand. They *say* they have your back. But I asked, how do they *show* that they are your friends? How have they demonstrated that?"

"Like, if we're in a fight, or say some dude disses me, they got my back. Like that!"

"And let me ask you this, Tyrell. Let's say you had never met these fellows, would there be any reason for you to be fighting? Were people at school, for instance, 'dissing' you?"

Tyrell considered this for just a moment.

"I guess not, but they ain't no African Americans at school, least not many. Anyhow, they all kiss ass."

"So this gang, that's your new family."

"Damn right."

"I'm going to ask you one more time to watch your language."

No response.

"Because I assume they're black, at least minorities, and your parents aren't. *Especially* your dad."

"Yeah."

"But you're here. Right now, I mean. You're here, and this gang—your gang—they're way back in New York, aren't they?"

No answer, but the sullen attitude seemed to have been toned down a bit.

"Because I'm black, is that it, Tyrell? So I'm better able to understand you?"

"Yeah. Somethin' like that."

They walked along in silence for a few moments. The sun had set, and it was rapidly getting dark. However, both of them knew their way around. Finally, Wish renewed the conversation.

"I'm going to take a wild guess here, Tyrell. You tell me if I'm right or wrong."

"OK."

"I'm guessing that one of two things happened with your boys—your 'family' in New York. Either they told you to do something to prove yourself to them, like beat someone up, or they wanted money from you. I'm guessing they see you as pretty valuable to them. Am I right?"

Tyrell mumbled something unintelligible.

"Excuse me?"

"Yes."

"Which was it?"

Embarrassed, Tyrell hesitated. "Both," he whispered. "You're supposed to kick someone's ass, I mean really beat them up, hurt them badly, to prove that, well, I guess, that you'll do anything for your brothers…"

"Yeah…"

"And they wanted me to steal from my parents."

"And you wouldn't do either."

"No. I mean yeah, I guess so."

"Why not?"

"I don't know."

"Yes, you do."

Nothing.

"You wouldn't do either, because you knew better. You knew it would be wrong."

Still nothing.

"Tell me, Tyrell. Tell me where you learned that."

Nothing.

"Let me help you, although I'm sure you know the answer. You learned that from your parents, those people who 'don't understand' you."

Still, silence from Tyrell, whose earlier swagger had now vanished.

The two had returned to Wish's house, where they sat down across from each other on the expansive patio. For the first time in a few minutes, they could look at each other. Wish pulled his chair up close enough to Tyrell so that he could reach out and touch the boy. His hand rested on top of Tyrell's.

"Listen, you don't need me to tell you that you did the right thing. You already know that."

Wish could see that Tyrell was still fighting himself. It was obviously hard to relinquish the recently obtained "bad boy" persona and return to some semblance of normalcy. At the very least, it was tough to back down. Nobody knew that better than Wish himself.

"And let me tell you something else you are right about," Wish continued. Tyrell looked up from staring at the flagstone, interested to find out what, if anything, he could possibly also be right about.

"Your dad *doesn't* understand you, at least in some ways. No matter how hard he tries—and take it from me, he does try hard—he can't."

"What do you mean?"

"Your dad is not black."

"Damn right about that."

This language was met by a stony glare from Wish.

"Sorry, Uncle Wish."

"Now, I don't want you to misunderstand what I'm saying here. Ever since your parents adopted you, you've had all of the benefits of an extraordinarily fortunate lifestyle. Today, Bobby and Annabelle have the same good fortune. You're blessed, and so are they. We all are.

"But you are black, and because of that, there are some things that, try as he might, your father will never be able to understand. You know what I'm talking about. That feeling you get from some white folk when you're the only black person around, and a black *male teenager* to boot. Doesn't matter how you're dressed, even if it's much better than those folks. They're *afraid* of you, even if they are probably trying not to show it.

"And I'm sure there have been times when you can't get a cab, when the white folk can."

"Yeah, stuff like that."

"I hear you. You know that I know. We've all been through crap like that."

"That's right, Uncle Wish."

"But…"

"But what?"

"It's not like it *used* to be, son. Not nearly like what my mother and her parents went through many years ago. Not what folks in much poorer, much tougher neighborhoods live through every day, even these days. Like I said, Tyrell, we've got it good. You need to understand. We are extraordinarily blessed."

He had the boy's attention now.

"But, like I said, your father cannot truly understand what it is like to be a black man. He never will."

"That's my point!"

"But I want you to listen carefully to me, son. Whether he is black, white, or purple, you could not possibly have a better, more loving dad. You couldn't possibly have better parents. And your father is the finest man, the best friend, I've ever known."

Wish's hands were gripping the boy's knees, perhaps a little too tightly, as if to emphasize his point.

"So, enough of this nonsense, Tyrell. You made some mistakes, but you were intelligent enough—*and* you had enough character—to realize that before you did something really wrong. You're a teenager, and teenagers will always have disagreements with their parents. That's part of growing up. Bottom line, that's what this is mostly about. You don't know it now, but someday you will. Trust me on that."

Wish stood up and clapped Tyrell on the back. "So, you go find out where your buddy Bobby is, and then we'll get some food in you."

"OK, Uncle Wish." Tyrell stood up.

"We square?"

"Yeah, Uncle Wish. We all square."

———

After a hastily arranged flight via the corporate jet, Jackson and Donna arrived at the Fitzgerald house just before midnight. Emotionally and physically exhausted, they practically collapsed into the arms of their friends.

After looking in on their son, who was sleeping peacefully in Bobby's bedroom, the Spears joined their hosts for breakfast. As they ate, Wish found himself deflecting the praise that Jackson and Rachel tried to give to him.

"Let's see how things work out, but I'm guessing he pretty much managed to solve things for himself," Wish said. "Hopefully, the worst is over."

The Spears spent the rest of the night next door at their house. Weeks later, they moved to Greensboro permanently. Jackson commuted to Manhattan for about a year, after which his corporate headquarters made the transition to Atlanta.

And Wish was right; the worst *was* over. Nothing more was heard about gangs, and the relationship between father and son gradually returned to the somewhat less turbulent (but nevertheless choppy) waters of a more typical teenager/parent voyage.

The gunshot Wish had suffered thirteen years earlier had seriously damaged his left arm, which is the dominant arm for any right-handed golfer. From outward appearances, however, few people would be able to detect that he had any disability.

Shortly after his recovery, Wish had tried off and on for several weeks to prove his medical team wrong by attempting to hit golf balls. Eventually, he was forced to admit that the doctors and therapists were right. He could not play right-handed any more.

The fact that Wish was a natural lefty was not lost on those closest to him. Eventually Albert, later joined by Jackson, broached the idea of attempting a return to recreational golf, this time from the left side. Their many entreaties were met with deaf ears.

From a slightly selfish standpoint, both Albert and Jackson wanted Wish to give it a try so he could once again join them on the golf course. Their usual argument came from the "What Have You Got to Lose?" school of reasoning, as in:

"Just get out there and swing the club a few times. If it doesn't work, so what? You're no worse off than you are today, right?"

"You live and breathe the game, numbskull! You have got to be frustrated not actually playing it!"

"What about Bobby? Doesn't he deserve the chance to play with his dad?"

"I need you to try these new clubs we just got in. I just want your feedback. Help me out here."

"Even Donna/your mom/Bobby/Annabelle/the dog wants you to try, Wish! You owe it to yourself/them!"

"You miss it. We know you miss it."

"I know what this is really about. If you can't be a PGA pro-caliber golfer, what's the point? But you should take your own advice for once. Remember how you often you've told me that golf should be about having fun? How about that? You don't *have* to be as good as you used to be…"

But for Wish, *that* was the bottom line. If he couldn't be "that good," what was the point in even trying?

But God, did he miss playing the game. They were right about that. They were right about the fact that he was surrounded by the game virtually every single day of his life, whether at his business, at home, when caddying at Augusta National, or even on vacation. Golf was his life, but he couldn't even play the game!

The big news in golf in the summer of 2000 was Tiger Woods's historic win at the

US Open at Pebble Beach. Dominating the field like no golfer had done in the history of professional golf, Tiger almost lapped the field, winning by an unheard-of fifteen strokes. Suddenly, here was a young *black* man setting the golf world on fire.

None of the irony of this was lost on Wish as he watched the tournament unfold from his easy chair in Greensboro, Georgia. He coulda, shoulda, woulda been that black golfer, if only. In fact, his first PGA tournament, the tournament for which he was supposed to leave the day after that fatal night in the pro shop, was to have been at Pebble Beach.

On the one hand, he was so happy and proud to see what Tiger was accomplishing— finally! On the other hand, man, it was just so darned hard. *That was supposed to be me.*

Later that night, as Wish climbed into bed next to his sleeping wife, he did his best to not disturb her.

"How was the tournament?" she asked, sleep making her voice a little raspy.

"Oh, fine, fine. Pretty amazing, actually. He's quite a golfer."

A few minutes passed. Wish was just about to drift off when Donna whispered to him.

"My husband is also an amazing man."

For some crazy, inexplicable reason, that moment changed everything. Wish was now wide awake. After lying there for another two hours, growing further and further from the peace that he needed to fall asleep, Wish got out of bed, got dressed in a polo shirt and jeans, and headed to the garage. Hopping into his cherry-red Porsche, he drove the five minutes to his Greensboro driving range. By now it was two in the morning, but the first thing Wish did was turn on the lights to illuminate the range. Inside the shop, he tried on a few pairs of golf shoes until he found the ones he liked. He then went over to the golf equipment section and tentatively picked a left-handed Callaway six iron off the display wall and swung it a few times. Going down the line, he did the same thing with a Mizuno club, then a Taylor Made, and finally an Emerald Sporting Goods iron. Smiling, he then also grabbed a three wood and a pitching wedge from the same display and headed out to the range, which was now lit as brightly as day.

The first few swings simply didn't work. As expected, it was as if his left arm was dead—no energy and, unfortunately, a quick pain came with each swing. Stubbornly ignoring the discomfort, Wish sprayed weak shots right, left, and along the ground with the six iron. Surprisingly, he was not frustrated by the experience.

I'm a teacher, he thought. *Figure this out.*

Shortly thereafter, the solution occurred to him. For years, he had told his students to relax their grip. "Let the club do the work," he'd say. "Watch the pros. Do they look like they're swinging hard? No. But do you see how far the ball flies?"

Wish realized that because of the pronounced weakness in his left arm, he was overcompensating by the strength that he was applying with his right arm and grip. He relaxed everything and swung again. Lo and behold, it worked.

The shots weren't long, especially by Wish Fitzgerald's old standards. But some were straight, and a few were even, in an odd way after so many years, satisfying. *I might be able to do this.*

As he climbed back into bed a little before five, Wish made sure that he was quiet enough so as not to awaken Donna. She had never known that he had left in the first place.

Likewise, no one in the extended family knew that Wish was now practicing on a regular basis. His cover-up consisted of an extended

campaign to visit other driving ranges in the
region to check out the competition. It was
during those visits that he would hit a couple
of buckets of balls. With each session he was
hitting the ball straighter and more cleanly, thus
building his confidence. On the negative side,
he soon reached the conclusion that he would
never again be able to hit a ball nearly as far as
he had. Yet it was incredibly satisfying to hit the
ball well and accurately. He even reached the
point where he could shape his shots, putting an
accurate fade (for him, a movement of the ball
to the left at the end of its trajectory) or draw (to
the right) on the shot.

The negative to all of this was that each
and every swing was still painful. But taken in
moderation and considering the rewards, he
decided that the pain was bearable.

Incredibly, it was coming back to him. He
was once again enjoying the game that he so
loved.

———

Many of the residents of Reynolds Plantation
drove from place to place within the development via golf carts. This was especially true
if you were headed from home to the golf

course. There was no need to load up the car to travel such a short distance.

One September afternoon in front of Jackson's house, Wish observed as Albert and Jackson loaded their clubs onto the back of Jackson's golf cart. The trash-talking had already begun.

"You know I feel guilty beating an old man," Jackson said.

"Then I guess you'll feel just fine at the end of this day, sonny," Albert fired back. "In any case, haven't you heard? Seventy is the new sixty."

"I admire your spirit."

"You're gonna be admiring my golf game."

"One should always hold onto one's dreams."

"I think you need a lesson, young fellow. Tell you what, I'll take you to school today, free of charge."

And so it went, with the non-golfing Wish an afterthought, until suddenly he joined the conversation.

"You're both talking nonsense."

"Another country heard from," said Albert. "What's up with you?"

"Nothing," Wish replied. "Just thinking, that's all."

"About what?" Jackson asked.

"Oh, just about how you fools are both full of hot air."

The other two men were confused. What dog did Wish have in this fight?

"Matter of fact, I'll bet even an old, one-armed guy such as myself could whup the two of you."

"Ouch!" was Jackson's reply. Albert stared at his son-in-law curiously.

"Yeah, betcha I could," Wish continued.

"I'd take you up on that, but it's a moot point, isn't it," was Jackson's retort.

Albert stuck his hand in front of Jackson in a gesture of restraint. "Hold on, Jackson," he said. "Don't either one of us want to be making any kind of damn bets with this boy. Something's going on here. He's got some shit up his sleeve, sure as shootin'."

Jackson looked from one to another, catching the slightest bit of a wry grin emerging on Wish's countenance.

"Yeah, what's going on, Wish?"

"Don't care to bet, gentlemen?"

"You been holding out on us, Wish?" Albert queried, the truth dawning on him. "You've been holding out on us, haven't you!"

By now, Jackson was thoroughly perplexed. "Will you guys please explain what's going on here?"

"Here's what's going on, Jack," Albert said. "My knucklehead son-in-law here has been practicing, or playing—"

"Golf?!" Jackson exclaimed.

"Golf," Albert shouted. "Right?" he said to Wish.

"Last chance," Wish replied, deadpan. "You can bet the disabled guy, straight up. Not *even* asking for any strokes."

"Holy cow, you're gonna play with us," Jackson exclaimed. "You're really gonna do it!"

The three slammed together in a group hug.

Wish's first drive was a beauty, about 250 accurate yards over a fairway bunker, cutting the corner on a dogleg. Jackson whistled his approval. Albert was more reticent.

"Ya winced. It hurt, didn't it?"

"I did not wince!"

"Ya damn sure did. Crap!"

"Well, keep your opinions to yourself, old man. Maybe I did wince, but it was a nice shot for a cripple, don't you think?"

As he studied a putt on the fifth green, Wish was already up two strokes on Albert and four on Jackson.

"OK, I'm impressed," Albert admitted.

"Me, too," Jackson chimed in.

"But y'all lost your length," Albert said.

"Geez, Pop, what the hell did you expect? I gotta bum arm, I'm playing left-handed for the first time…Come *on*!"

"And don't forget he's no kid anymore," Jackson contributed.

"You, too?" Wish complained.

"The pro expected a free ride, Jack," Albert teased.

The outcome of the match, such as it was, was never in doubt. Wish's lead over the other two grew as the day wore on. Also growing was their concern over the undeniable pain that Wish was experiencing, but they ignored it for Wish's sake. The old Wish was finally back.

———

An additional and immense benefit of Wish's return to golf was the fact that he could now play golf at Augusta National—on only one very special day a year.

Surprisingly, the course was closed for play all summer. On the day after it was closed to the members, the caddies got their opportunity to play the historic track. And play it they did—for as many holes as they could possibly get in between dawn and dark.

Wish always played with the same guys, Albert and Modesty. Early in the day, the repartee was rapid-fire and nonstop. But there was a difference between the kidding in the caddie shack and these conversations on the course. Within the confines of the caddie shack, the back-and-forth was loud and often ribald. On the course, the tone was quiet, almost reverential. "Like the patrons during the tournament," Albert would observe.

By the time the group reached Amen Corner for the first time, the banter had ceased. Although the financial terms of the inevitable wager were as low as a dollar per hole, the bragging rights were invaluable. As a result, the play got deadly serious. Just like the pros in April, each shot was strategically aimed; each putt was assiduously studied. These caddies had seen every shot and every putt from every spot on these grounds. They knew better than the pros how the course should be played, and they played it pretty well.

Each of these matches was treasured by the participants. It seemed like every swing and every putt was remembered and analyzed over and over during the next twelve months.

And no matter how many holes he played on this day, Wish's arm seemed to hurt far less than when playing any other course.

For Wish in particular, this was his definition of heaven.

Chapter 16

2002

In the world of professional golf and even in sports in general, Tiger Woods was now the hottest star on the planet. Friends in Wish's decidedly smaller orbit often couldn't contain their curiosity. How did Wish feel about this?

"Why do you ask?" was Wish's standard response.

"Well, you know" was often the comeback, accompanied by lots of hemming and hawing.

"No, help me out," Wish would say, enjoying the subtle bit of torture he was inflicting.

"Well, you know...I just thought, you know, that that's what *you* wanted, to be the first black superstar in golf. And now Tiger's come along, and he seems to be doing just that. C'mon, how does that make you feel?"

Eventually, Wish let them off the hook.

"First of all, I'm happy for him. If he isn't already, someday soon he's going to be exactly that—a superstar. What a talent.

"As for me, I just wanted to be a professional golfer. A golfer who was good enough to compete on the PGA Tour and maybe, just maybe, play in a major or two."

"Like the Masters."

"Yeah, ya got me there," Wish would say with a chuckle. Then, turning serious again, he would add, "It was a different time for black people, especially when it came to golf. Couldn't join most clubs, so most of us didn't even consider playing. People thought my father-in-law was crazy for even considering opening a driving range for folks in our community. But he made it happen, didn't he?

"Look, some kids wanted to be president, and some wanted to be Mickey Mantle or Frank Robinson or Walter Payton. Doesn't mean it's going to happen, does it? You just dream, sometimes even if you don't have a role model. You just dream."

And so the truth finally emerged.

And the deeper truth was that Wish was at peace with his life. He had passed fifty years of age, and he was successful at business. He had a loving family and a great friend, and yes, finally, he could enjoy his passion again. As challenging as it was, he could play golf.

———

Fortunately, Wish had the financial freedom to enjoy golf as much as he chose, and he wanted to make up for lost time. If he could have played four or five times a week, he would have. Unfortunately, his disability prevented that. When Wish pushed the envelope by playing two days in a row, he paid a dear price. He'd be groaning through each swing of the club on the back nine and recuperating with sharp pain that very gradually diminished to a constant ache for at least another week. While he had multiple golf courses from which to choose at Reynolds Plantation, his golf was limited. So, at most he enjoyed the game once a week, usually with some combination of Jackson, Albert, Bobby, or Tyrell. Here and there he'd treat his caddie friends from Augusta National to a round. Wish played often enough to get back down to scratch golf. He even won the club championship, although that multi-round test took its physical toll.

The greatest joy came from the simple, recreational rounds he played with Albert. The sandbagging before the round and the trash-talking on the course were legendary.

"You're only gonna give a seventy-four-year-old man *twelve strokes*? That's just wrong, son!" Inevitably, Albert's uniquely high-pitched voice ruined Wish's ability to keep a straight face as he listened to his friend and father-in-law rant and rave.

"What's wrong is your nonsense, old man. If you think you're gonna get *twelve* strokes from a cripple like me, you've got another thing coming…"

Or…

"That was a truly feeble shot, Mr. Club Champion! I mean *truly* feeble."

"No wonder you're retired from the golf business, old fella! I promise not to tell anyone at work about how badly your game has deteriorated. They'd be sending you flowers, and I *know* you don't want to be smellin' no flowers unless they're on top of your damn casket and you're inside."

Yes, it got pretty brutal when it was just the two of them on the course. It went so far that they frequently breached one of the cardinal rules of golf etiquette—remaining quiet when a fellow golfer is striking a shot or hitting a putt. Albert would slowly pull the Velcro of his golf glove in the middle of Wish's backswing, and Wish would whisper "Yip! Yip! Yip!" during Albert's putt. Somehow, both golfers usually managed to survive the fusillade of bad manners. In the end, the only truly effective technique to throw the opponent off his game was to make him laugh. Unfortunately (or fortunately) enough, this happened often.

One spring day, Jackson, of all people, came up with the best move ever to throw Wish off his game. He, Wish, and Albert were coming to the end of a match on which some pretty hefty cash had been bet, and Jackson and Wish were tied (Wish had given Jackson a dozen strokes). Wish prepared to hit a tricky approach shot over water. As Wish addressed his ball, Jackson spoke up.

"Oh, hey, Wish, I forgot to mention this to you, but I lined up a sponsor's exemption for you to play the Greater Hartford Open in July. We decided to become one of the sponsors, and lo and behold…"

Wish backed away from his shot.

"What did you say?"

"I'm pretty sure you heard me, Wish."

Jackson and Albert smiled. Albert had known about this for days and wondered when Jackson would choose to reveal it. "Good move to save it until now," Albert said to Jackson. "Messes his game up. No way the boy will recover from this."

"The Greater Hartford Open," Wish said.

"Yeah, the Greater Hartford Open," Jackson parroted. "The first tournament won by a black man. Charlie Sifford, 1967. Pretty cool, huh?"

Wish tried to play it cool. "I'm an amateur. Why the hell would I be playing in a PGA tournament?"

"Because, in my opinion, you're good enough. And given the fact that my company is sponsoring this shindig, that's all you need."

Still playing it cool, Wish stepped back over his shot. Normally a quick player, he wiggled and waggled his club over the ball, clearly distracted by the news. Finally, he stepped away again.

"Hit the damn ball. You're holding up the foursome behind us," Albert admonished. Wish turned to look behind them and couldn't see a single player in sight. Shaking his head, he directed his attention back to Jackson.

"What if *I* don't think I'm good enough?"

"Tough. I do."

"What if I don't want to do it?"

"Just say the word," Jackson answered, calling the bluff. "And I'll pull the plug. Can't guarantee you'll get a shot at something like this another time, though."

Wish shook his head. "Pretty presumptuous of you."

"Yep."

Finally, Wish stepped up to his ball and swung. He shanked the shot badly, and the ball ended up rolling right into the pond.

"Nice shot," his two opponents said in unison.

Half an hour later, the three were shaking hands on the 18th green; Jackson had beaten Wish by two strokes and Albert by five. No one had mentioned the exemption to the upcoming PGA tournament since Wish had shanked the earlier approach shot. The three headed off the green on the way to the clubhouse locker room.

"You know, I should be mad at you," Wish said to Jackson.

"Oh, really? What for this time?"

"How many times have I told you to step interfering in my life?"

"I've stopped counting."

"Then why do you keep doing it?'

"Probably because I love you, you ungrateful asshole," a smiling Jackson shot back.

"Never said I wasn't grateful."

"Never said you were, either."

"Well, I am."

"Good."

"Not going to say I love you, though."

"That's OK," Jackson responded. "It's enough to know that you're thinking it."

———

The fact that Wish was as inconspicuous in the TPC locker room in Cromwell, Connecticut, as a fifty-two-year-old black man could be was of little help to his nerves. The local press had seized upon his status as the oldest golfer in the tournament and an amateur to boot. They made note of Wish's travails in the early eighties, but, to Wish's great happiness, glossed over the fact that he was the only black golfer in the tournament.

Despite the many offers from caddie friends to haul his bag during the tournament, Wish made the improbable choice of putting Albert on his bag. "He's still in great shape"

was all he would say to his friends. The reason
for the selection was that he knew Albert was
the only caddie on earth who would make him
focus, or laugh, or simply breathe, at the appro-
priate times.

The other great debate was whether or
not to have family and friends attend the tournament. Of course, everyone wanted to be
there. In the end, however, Wish determined
that having Donna, the kids, Annie, and even
Jackson's family present would only negatively
affect his focus. Besides, he was convinced
that this wasn't going to go well. Putting on an
embarrassing performance in front of strang-
ers was one thing; doing it in front of loved
ones was a different story entirely.

Wish tried hard, but unsuccessfully, to
keep history off of his mind. "Charlie Sifford.
First win. Charlie Sifford. Oh, man." When he
realized that the tournament was at a different
course than the tourney in 1967, it helped a bit.

Just before he went out to the practice
area, Albert handed Wish a cell phone.

"What's this?" Wish asked.

"Someone wants to talk to you."

"Who?"

"What difference does it make? Just answer
the damn phone, fool!"

Exasperated, Wish put the phone up to his ear. "This is Wish Fitzgerald."

"Charlie Sifford here. I just wanted to wish you good luck today."

Wish stared over at Albert. The old man wasn't laughing.

"C'mon, who is this, really?"

"Hey man, this is Charlie Sifford. For real."

Wish couldn't respond for a moment, then managed a "Wow."

"Listen, I heard about you years ago from Lee. Was expecting big things from you, young man. Shame what happened, but now at least you can get a taste of the action, right?"

Speechless, Wish just continued to stare at Albert.

"You still there, Wish?"

"Yes. Yes, sir. This is an honor."

"The feeling's mutual. Have fun out there. Hit 'em long and hard. Show those suckers what ya got."

———

In his heart, Wish knew he had about as much chance at actually winning this tournament as any other fifty-two-year-old, let alone any fifty-two-year-old *amateur*, which was to say, absolutely no chance at all. In reality, he had only two goals—to make the cut (meaning he would play on the weekend) and to not embarrass himself. Deep down, he believed that neither of those goals was terribly realistic, and, given the level of competition, sticking around for the weekend bordered on a fantasy.

Wish recognized a number of players from his days on the developmental tour (of course, they had been the youngest guys back then). Remembering that he had most likely given them the cold shoulder way back then, Wish decided to go out of his way to approach each to offer a handshake and congratulations on his career. In each case, a potentially awkward moment was diffused. To his surprise, Wish found that he actually enjoyed the conversations.

A little later, Albert overheard a conversation near the putting green between two of the pros with whom Wish had conversed.

"He was actually nice to me!"

"Yeah, weird, isn't it?"

"Maybe we had him wrong back then."

"I doubt it. I think he must have changed, that's all."

"Be interesting to see how long he is off the tee these days. Remember what a monster he was?"

"Way past me, that's all I remember. Waaaay past me. He couldn't still be doing that, could he? I mean, the guy's got a few years on him…"

"Wasn't he right-handed? Coulda sworn he hit from the right side."

Wish began to gain confidence as he drained putt after putt on the practice green. But his time on the driving range told the tale: he was hitting his drive much shorter than the majority of these younger players. Phil Mickelson, for instance, often seemed to have as much as a hundred yards on him. He quickly decided to limit his practice shots. The pain was already creeping into his arm, and he hadn't even played his first hole.

No biggie, it's exactly what you expected, Wish told himself. *You're not a kid anymore, and you've got a bum arm. But you've got game. It's still golf, right? These guys aren't playing against you; they're playing to beat the big boys. They couldn't care less about Wish Fitzgerald; don't even know you're here. So, just play your kind of golf and see what happens. Make the cut. Just make the cut.*

Fortunately enough for Wish, his playing partners for the first two rounds were two youngsters, aged twenty-three and twenty-four, who didn't know him from George Washington

Carver. He didn't know anything about them either. Less pressure that way. *Just play your game.*

For the next two days, Wish played a brand of golf he liked to call "old man's golf." His drives were indeed relatively short but usually smack dab in the middle of the fairway. He didn't always make the green in regulation, especially when it came to the longer holes. But he avoided trouble by staying out of the rough, the woods, the water, and the sand. And most importantly, he played a younger man's game on and around the greens. If he laid up short of the green, his approach shots usually ended below and close to the hole. And he made his putts, one-putting a surprising number of greens.

And he made the cut. Comfortably. However, his left arm felt anything but comfortable. He gritted his teeth and toughed it out through the stabbing pain, one shot at a time.

When he and Albert arrived at the course a few hours before his tee time on Saturday, Wish found that a few members of the golf press wanted to talk. The fact that he had made the cut and was actually tied for thirteenth at two under, six strokes off the lead, was a curious little story for some—what the print press called a sidebar, a human-interest story. Older golfer, black guy, amateur, former PGA Tour qualifier. Five different reporters approached him for "a moment of your time" as he went about his pregame preparations.

"How does it feel to be in contention, Wish?"

"Oh, I wouldn't go so far as to say that. Had some luck, been putting well."

"How do you like your chances?"

"At what?"

"To win the tournament!"

"I'd say it's about as likely as you winning this tournament. And since you're not playing…"

"Where does your name come from?"

"My mother."

"No, c'mon. 'Wish,' that's a nickname, right?"

"Short for Aloysius. Guess you could call it a nickname…"

In each case, the interview, which was less than stimulating for the respective reporter, was abruptly cut short when a famous star such as Fred Couples or Phil Mickelson happened by. Suddenly left alone, Wish shook his head, chuckled, and returned to tying his show, putting, or driving. He understood.

By the end of the day, it was a different story entirely. Literally.

Suddenly, shockingly, Wish was in third place, only two strokes behind Phil Mickelson and Sergio Garcia. Every reporter, whether from print or electronic press, wanted a piece of Wish. He was *the* story of the tournament. There he was, front and center at the press center podium, bright lights and all, for his fifteen minutes of fame. Albert grinned from the sidelines.

"Where does the name come from?"

"I understand you were shot? Tell us about that!"

"What does it feel like to be in contention, Wish?"

"How does your arm limit you?"

"Think you can keep it up?"

"Think you can win?"

And finally, "How old is your caddie?" to which Wish answered, "Too old." That brought the house down and a wave of derision from Albert. As Wish stepped off the stage, he whispered to his father-in-law, "Sorry, I couldn't resist."

Reporters pursued him as he left the press center. Even Albert was corralled for questioning by some reporters. This was now hotter than your run-of-the-mill human interest story.

That evening Wish and Albert enjoyed a meal at the nearby Applebee's, not because they were on a budget, but because Wish just happened to like Applebee's. In contrast to the old days, though, they were staying in a luxury suite at the local Marriott hotel instead of sleeping in the car in an empty parking lot.

"I know you can do this, Wish," Albert said.

"No, you don't, and neither do I."

"Well, yeah, but it sure is fun."

Easy for you to say, Wish thought, once again trying to disguise the pain that never stopped emanating from his left arm.

"Mickelson and Garcia, Pops," he said. "And how about the guys right behind me? Geez."

"You giving up already?"

"Nope. I got myself this far, I might as well see what can happen. The way I've been putting...pretty strange, huh?"

"Pretty fun, is the way I look at it."

"That too, Pop. That too."

By Saturday afternoon Jackson had decided to override Wish's ban on having family members present at the tournament. He arranged a flight on the Emerald corporate jet and ground transportation in Connecticut to bring the balance of the Fitzgerald and Spears family members to the course. Since Emerald was a tournament sponsor, passes were the easiest thing to provide. So Sunday, the families were on the course all day, always careful to stay out of Wish's eyesight.

And it was certainly a good thing they were there, because by the 18th green, the outcome was a foregone conclusion. It wasn't even close. Wish won the tournament by three strokes.

The next few minutes were a blur. The applause for Wish was thunderous, growing even louder when his family surprised him for what was actually a rather painful group hug. Phil Mickelson came over to offer his congratulations. Some famous announcer from CBS or ABC interviewed him, and then there was the presentation of the trophy and a gigantic check, right there in the middle of the 18th green.

Throughout, Wish was aware of two things: Donna was by his side. And his left arm hurt like hell.

Shortly thereafter, he was back in the press room, the television lights seemingly brighter and hotter than the previous afternoon. The questions came fast and furious for ten minutes. Wish felt that he was doing a decent job answering them, until…

"How does it feel to know that you've qualified for next year's Masters?"

The question didn't register.

"Could you repeat that, please?"

"I was just asking how it feels to know that you'll be playing in the Masters next April."

"I will?"

"Well, yeah…"

The assembled press waited patiently for an answer. At the back of the crowded room, Donna, Jackson, Rachel, and Albert also watched. The moment the question had been asked, there had been a collective intake of breath by the four, followed by whispered variations of "Oh my God."

Up front, Wish struggled to contain himself.

"I…"

He bit his lip, which didn't help at all.

"I…"

Wish stood up.

"Please excuse me," he mumbled, the sound of his heavy voice a little too far away for the bank of microphones and recorders to pick it up. He then left the stage and exited through the closest door.

———

Much to Wish's chagrin, the people of Waynesboro welcomed him home that Monday with what could only be labeled a hero's welcome. Held at the original Jameson's Driving Range, the parking lot was packed from one end to another with well-wishers. Politicians made speeches, keys to the cities of Waynesboro and Greensboro were presented, and, unbelievably, some members of the national press were even in attendance.

As Wish looked out over the crowd, he thought back to the day many years earlier, when many of these same folks had been present to send him off to Q School. This crowd was two or three times as large and as loud, but the memories of that day were particularly acute at this moment. Bittersweet memories—joy interspersed with what might have been.

At one point he spied a former student of his, the grandson of Miss Maybelle, the wizened, tiny lady who had lectured him from her wheelchair so many years ago. The grandson was now middle-aged, which made Wish realize that Miss Maybelle must be long gone from this earth. He smiled at her memory and silently hoped that he might finally be doing her proud.

The interest in Wish's success story had stunned the whole family. When Wish finally made it inside the building and proceeded to his office, he discovered what could best be described as ecstatic chaos. Everyone on the staff vied for his attention simultaneously.

"One at a time, guys!" Wish begged.

"*Sports Illustrated* wants an interview! They're thinking about putting you on the cover! And CNN, and ABC, and geez, just about everybody—"

"Who's your agent, boss?"

"What kind of question is that?" Wish responded. "I haven't got an agent! Why would I need an agent?"

"Well, looks like you're gonna need one now, and quickly! I must have gotten calls from every PGA tournament for the rest of the year. They all want you to play. And the Senior Tour…"

"Champions Tour," someone corrected.

"Yeah, yeah, the Champions Tour. They want you, big time, boss!"

"Yeah, you're a celebrity, boss!"

It seemed like everyone was speaking in exclamation points.

"OK, everyone calm down," Wish said. "I'm not going to be playing any more tournaments, and I don't see any reason to do any of these interviews. I'm puffed up with myself enough as it is."

"But—"

"Why not?"

"Could be good for business—"

"Look, everyone," Wish continued, raising his hand to command silence. "I was lucky. I got on a streak, and I won a tournament. And because I'm an old man, and maybe a little because of the color of my skin, I'm a novelty. For what? A few days? Believe me, this is nothing to get excited about."

"But—"

Wish raised his hand again.

"No 'buts.' Thank you all for your well wishes and encouragement throughout the last many days. Thanks for covering for me here at the office. It was a blast, and now it's over. Let's try to settle down and get some work done."

He met with hesitation.

"And I sure as heck don't need an agent!" he said with a smile.

This was met with laughter, and finally, the knot of employees dispersed. Several patted Wish on the back or gave him an affectionate hug or squeeze of the arm as they did so.

Wish turned toward his office door to see Albert, who had quietly observed everything. He followed the old man into his office and shut the door.

"You gonna explain this to any of 'em?" Albert asked as Wish collapsed into the chair behind his desk.

"Explain what?"

"Why you're not jumping at these opportunities. Especially the chance to get out on the Tour, PGA *or* Champions."

"Nothing to explain, Pop. Doesn't make any sense."

"Thought this was your dream, son."

"*Was* my dream. *Was* my dream, a long time ago."

"OK, we'll keep it our secret. You gonna tell Donna, Annie, Jackson?"

"Tell them what?"

"The real reason…"

"C'mon, Pop," Wish said, irritation and impatience in his voice. "What're you getting at here?"

"You were in pain throughout the god-damn tournament. Then you were wincing when those folks were hugging you. It *was* worse outside, just now, wasn't it? And yesterday, all those people congratulating you…"

"Your point?"

"You seem to forget that your ol' father-in-law was with you every step of the way this weekend."

"I sure as hell couldn't forget that."

"You barely made it, Wish. That friggin' arm of yours nearly came off."

Wish sighed. The last bit of energy that had sustained him through the tournament and the craziness of the past twenty-four hours finally drained out of him.

"It hurts, Pop."

"I know, son. Proud of you, prouder than you will ever understand. You showed a ton of guts out there, playin' through it like that."

"Don't think I can do it again."

"Yeah, that's what I thought."

They sat for a while in silence. Finally, Albert raised the matter that weighed on both of their minds.

"Except for the Masters."

"Yeah, exactly. Except for the Masters."

Chapter 17

Wish insisted that the rest of the family be kept in the dark about how much pain he was in, knowing full well that he'd face an ultimatum that he stop playing. With the Masters on the horizon, that was not an option he was willing to entertain.

In the end, only Jackson was added to the conspiracy of silence. Wish and Albert decided that he met the "need to know" criteria, partially because it was hoped that he could help Wish get in to see the top sports orthopedist in the country—Dr. Frank Jobe. Jobe was the man who had performed the most famous sports surgery ever, the legendary "Tommy John Surgery," which saved the career of the major league pitcher of the same name. When top athletes needed a diagnosis or operation, more often than not, Dr. Jobe got the call.

Sure enough, Jackson was able to work his wonders, and within days Wish was in Birmingham, Alabama, meeting with the doctor. After a thorough physical examination and MRI, Dr. Jobe sat down with his new patient. First, he told Wish that it was pretty miraculous that he had been able to play golf at such a high level, given the condition of his arm. Then he gave him the bad news.

"Unfortunately, I have to agree with what your doctors reported after your initial rehabilitation. In fact, I'm not in favor of you playing golf at all."

"I don't understand," Wish answered. "So much has happened in medicine since I got shot."

"I wish I had better news than this," Dr. Jobe replied, shaking his head, "but there haven't been the kind of advances that pertain to the massive trauma that you suffered. It's wonderful that you've had the amount of function that you've been able to enjoy. But you need to understand, you're pressing your luck. There's not much left in there, and every time you swing, you're putting stress on what limited muscle tissue you still have."

"Can't give up golf, Doc."

"I can see that. Since that's the case, the best advice I can give you is to do it in extreme moderation. Even then, you're probably playing a version of Russian roulette with that arm."

"Meaning?"

"At some point, you could lose all of the remaining function."

"I qualified for the Masters."

"I understand, Mr. Fitzgerald, but I'm telling you that playing in any tournament is the *worst*-case scenario for your long-term health. Several rounds of golf in a row, not to mention all the practice swings on the range before each round…I strongly recommend against it."

The doctor had dealt with plenty of stubborn patients in his long and distinguished career, and, without a doubt, professional athletes were the worst. Most of his patients were far younger than Wish, the best athletes in the world, and thought they were invincible—that they could overcome any obstacle. The doctor thought that this patient, being more mature, would be wiser. He had hoped that his advice would fall on receptive ears.

He was wrong.

"I have to do this, Doc."

"Nothing's for certain, Mr. Fitzgerald. But, I'll repeat myself. I don't think you should be playing golf or any other sport, for that matter, that puts stress on that arm. But if you have to do it, do it in moderation. Once a week, for recreation. No time at all on the range. And above all, no tournaments." He paused. "And I can tell that you're not going to take my advice. So, I wish you the best of luck, and I'll be rooting for you next April."

———

Wish returned to Georgia to discover that the jig was up with Donna. Smelling trouble, Donna had spent the day grilling her father to get at the truth about Wish's little trip. Albert did his best to fend her off, but he never stood a chance.

"What did he say?" were the first words out of Donna's mouth when she picked her husband up at the airport.

"Who?" He could tell immediately that his fake innocent look was not getting the job done.

"Knock it off, Wish. Spill it. What did Dr. Jobe say?"

Geez, Wish thought. *I'm gonna kill Pop the moment I see him.*

"Wish? Tell me everything."

"He said that he'll be rooting for me next April."

"But he can't fix you."

"No, he can't."

"And you'll still be in pain."

"I'm not in pain, Donna."

"Don't try that parsing of words nonsense with me, Wish Fitzgerald. I realize that you may not in pain *right now*. What do you take me for, an idiot?"

"OK, yes. I'll still be in pain. And that's OK with me."

"And…"

Wish grimaced. This was worse than the damn pain. He searched his mind for a way to avoid giving his wife the whole truth and finally gave in. He had never lied to her, and he wasn't about to start now. So, he gave it to her, chapter and verse.

"You know I completely agree with Dr. Jobe, Wish."

"I don't doubt it for a moment."

They drove the rest of the way in virtual silence, with Donna debating what to say and do and Wish dreading the rest of the conversation. Sitting in the car in the garage at home, they finally finished the conversation.

"I could argue against this idiocy for the next few months," Donna began. "And we'd both be miserable, because this is the most important thing in the world to you, and that's not going to change."

"Yeah, other than you guys, I guess it is."

"You're willing to risk losing the use of your arm for a game."

"The Masters is not exactly a game, Donna."

"Yes it is, Wish. It's a *game*."

Wish kept his mouth shut. The old saying "Discretion is the better part of valor" crossed his mind.

"I get it, Wish. It's your dream. It's *always* been your dream. In your mind, especially after all you've been through, you want to be able to at least try. That's it, isn't it?"

"Yeah, baby, it is."

"Sometimes loving you can be so damn hard," Donna whispered, a catch in her voice. Her voice grew stronger with her next words.

"This is not a good idea, Wish. It isn't. But you're my husband, and *you* are the most important thing in *my* life…and I'll be rooting for you in April, too."

———

As he prepared for the tournament over the next few months, Wish did his best to follow Dr. Jobe's advice. As difficult as it was, he limited his golf to two rounds per week, always separated by days of rest. Practice on the driving range was out, but hours on the practice greens, always with the greens of Augusta National firmly in mind, helped build his confidence.

Likewise, he envisioned each shot at Augusta during the rounds he allowed himself. Rather than just playing a game, he'd place the ball in different spots on the course he played to replicate as much as possible the yardage and potential predicaments he expected to face during the upcoming tournament.

He sought the advice of his fellow caddies. Players in the Masters had always been required to use only the caddies that worked at Augusta, but that was changing, starting next year. Several of Wish's buddies had caddied for the greats over the years. Wish invited them to join him during his practice rounds and picked their brains while they played. If there was little he could do to prepare himself physically, there was much he could do to prepare himself mentally.

Given the fact that Albert would again be his caddie, he played most of these practice rounds alongside his son-in-law. Wish wanted him to also soak up this information. Having already caddied during a number of Masters tournaments, Albert was of the opinion that this was entirely unnecessary. However, he usually went along with the game plan in an effort to prove that he was a team player.

The two men hit one of the Reynolds Plantation courses early one October morning for another practice round. The air was just crisp enough to require a light sweater, and even the hyper-focused Wish took a few moments to drink in the sharp fall colors and the beauty of the glistening dew on the grass.

Wish and Albert had the course to themselves, which enabled Albert to ratchet up the usual flow of insults he threw in the direction of Wish. Albert was not cooperating with Wish's instructions to help him achieve the Zen-like state that was his goal. There was no way that he was going to allow Wish to take himself too seriously, Masters or no Masters.

Halfway through the round, Wish's tee shot was seriously errant, producing delighted derision from Albert. He wouldn't even help the younger man search for his ball, which had flown deep into the woods. After all, Albert's tee shot had ended up in the middle of the fairway.

"Well, lookee here," Albert shouted to Wish. "The little old man's in great shape. And where is the young hotshot? The *Sports Illustrated* cover boy, the star of golf, stage and screen? Oh my gosh! He's deep in the woods and well on his way to *losing his bet with the little old man*!"

Wish, who had finally located his ball, was enjoying every bit of the diatribe. As he prepared to hit a shot out of the trees, he shouted back at Albert.

"If I were you, I wouldn't be counting those chickens quite yet, little old man!"

Hearing nothing in return, Wish concentrated on the task at hand. He could just chip the ball out sideways and onto the fairway, granting the course a one-stroke win in this case, or he could attempt to hit an incredibly accurate, full draw through a narrow sliver of daylight between several trees and try for the green. Naturally, he chose the latter course of action. His shot ricocheted off of at least three trees and ended up weakly bouncing out onto the fairway to pretty much the same spot he would have reached had he taken the more cautious alternative.

I'm sure as hell going to hear it now, Wish thought as he walked back through the woods. He emerged to discover Albert facedown in the middle of the fairway, motionless.

"Pop!" he shouted, rushing toward the body, sliding the last two feet on his knees.

"Stop kidding around," Wish said aloud, turning Albert over. *My God, he's heavy! What the hell happened?*

He felt for a pulse, but found none.

Where do you check for this? It's there; I'm just not checking in the right place!

"Help!" he cried. "Please help me! Someone please call 911! My father has had a heart attack!"

Given their location on the golf course, there was no one around to hear his pleas.

Albert was turning blue. Wish struggled to remember what he had seen so many times on television—CPR. Open his mouth...pinch the nose? Blow into his mouth, push on his chest three times, blow into the mouth...

Wish did just that, for he didn't know how long, all the while not thinking, but praying and begging and begging and begging...

Finally, physical and mental exhaustion simply overwhelmed the adrenaline that had driven him. Wish collapsed, sobbing, on top of Albert's lifeless form.

I love you, Pop was all he could think. *I love you so much.*

"Thank you," he whispered to Albert. "Thank you."

———

No one was surprised when over two hundred people turned out for the funeral. The procession of cars from the church to the cemetery seemed like it must have been miles long. The family took comfort in the fact that so many people had loved the man.

———

Donna put on a stoic face in the presence of friends and the kids, but she was unable to keep up the façade when finally alone or with Wish. The two would sit on together on the porch each evening, nursing a couple of drinks and rocking each other. Little was said; they were both lost in their memories and pain.

———

Even Annie was somewhat disabled by her grief. Several days after the funeral, she finally had the energy to share with Wish and Donna.

"I know everyone wondered," she began. "And the answer is yes, I loved him, and I believe he felt the same. We talked all the time, but never about that.

"Why? Because he still loved your mother so much," she said to Donna. "And I respected that. To tell the truth, the friendship was enough.

"I will miss him so much. So very much."

———

Two weeks later, as Wish cleaned out Albert's home office, the memories of their relationship flooded his very soul.

He smiled as he recollected some of the names Albert had called him over the years. Knucklehead, Nimrod, Pretender, The Great Black Hope, and, Wish's favorite, Bupkis. He'd had to look that one up just to find out what it meant.

One by one, he took the many award plaques and trophies from community associations and business organizations off the walls, wrapped them in tissue paper, and placed them in boxes. Then he did the same with the family pictures, which produced a few more tears from eyes that had done almost nothing but cry for days. The last thing to come off the walls was a large framed photograph of Albert arm-in-arm with his fellow caddies at Augusta National. Wish was there, at the back of the group. Wish decided to hold onto this one for himself. He couldn't stem his sobbing.

In a side drawer of the desk, Wish was surprised to find two sealed business envelopes, one marked "Wish" and the other "Donna." He secured the latter in his lapel pocket and then opened the one addressed to him.

Dear Wish:

I've known for years about this bum ticker of mine. I hope you, Donna, and the kids will forgive me for not sharing the news about it with you, but truth be told, I figured not a lot could be done about it. It was my choice to just keep on living my life my way. If you're reading this, I'm obviously done doing that by now.

Anyway, if I had told you about my health, you would have taken me off your bag at the Masters. Sorry, I wasn't going to miss that experience for anything. So you need to understand that that was my choice, and my choice alone, son.

I also want you to remember that no father in the world could be as proud of a son as I have been of you. Although it took you a while to figure out how to do it, you eventually made my beautiful daughter as happy as could be. You're a great father to my grandkids. You took my rinky-dink little driving range and built it into a successful business.

And although I never admitted it, you're a GREAT golfer, despite everything you've been through. You're not just physically skilled, you're downright brilliant in how you adapt to conditions and physical limitations and all the nuances that make golf the game that both of us love so much.

Outside of Donna and the kids, the greatest joy of my life has been sharing my love of golf with you.

Now, I know that at this time, you and everyone else might be thinking that because of my death, it wouldn't be proper for you to play the Masters. Well, pardon my French (which you know damn well I can't speak a word of), but bullshit! That's the last thing that I would want.

You play it, Wish, and you do your best to win it. Whether you know it or not, you can do it!

Just keep that focus of yours. Don't be thinking about me, or dedicating the tournament to me, or anything like that. The only time I want you to think about me is when you arrive that first day. You know what I mean—when you drive down Magnolia Lane, instead of coming in the back way, the way we caddies always do. I want you to hear me that morning, son, because I'll be saying, loud and clear, "Way to go. Way to go!"

Love,
Pop

———

Within weeks of Albert's passing, the competition among his caddie friends at Augusta National for the honor of carrying Wish's bag at the upcoming tournament had come to a boil. During the late fall and early winter, Wish played with first one, than another, until he had gone through a total of six candidates.

The subject came up one evening in February after a family dinner at the Spears residence.

"Seems to me it shouldn't be too tough a decision," Jackson said with a chuckle. "If

Modesty's half as good as he thinks he is, it's a no-brainer."

"I'm a better caddie than Modesty," Wish shot back. "In any case, he'd drive me crazy with all that talking."

"Dad wasn't exactly quiet on the golf course," Donna said. "Nor modest, for that matter."

"That's for sure," Jackson and Rachel said simultaneously, drawing a laugh from everyone.

"Actually, to answer your question, I *have* picked a caddie."

"Who is it?" Jackson asked. All three leaned forward expectantly.

"You."

"Me? You're joking, right?" Jackson said. Judging from the looks on their faces, Jackson, Rachel, and Donna all seemed to think that he was.

"Nope. And I'd advise you to start working out, because that bag's heavy, my friend."

"I think he's serious, honey," Rachel said to her husband.

"Oh, believe me, I am," Wish said.

"But…but…I'm not a caddie," Jackson stuttered. "I've never even played Augusta National, and not for a lack of trying, I'll tell you. How would I be able to help you?"

"Well, I *am* a caddie," Wish answered. "And since I know the course better than any caddie I know—including my friend Modesty—I figured I don't need a caddie. Leastwise, I don't need a caddie to caddie, if that makes any sense."

"Not really," Jackson responded.

"Look at it this way, Jack. When it comes to everything *but* carrying the bag and cleaning the clubs and the ball, I'm perfectly fine being my own caddie. I know the distances. I can read the greens. What I need out there is a friend, pure and simple. Someone who understands me and can help me get the most out of me those four days."

"Someone like Dad," Donna said softly, finally understanding her husband's reasoning.

"Exactly. And there's only one person left who fits that bill, Jack, and that person is you."

———

Later, the two men enjoyed cigars outside on the back patio, seated close to the glowing fire pit.

Wish chuckled to himself.

"What?" Jackson asked.

"Nothing."

"Yeah, right. C'mon, spill."

"I was just thinking about something you said a few minutes ago."

"Which was…"

"You're a lousy liar, Jack."

"What's in that cigar? Mine seems to be plain tobacco."

"'Not for lack of trying.' You couldn't play Augusta National, even though you really wish you could, right?"

Jackson was quiet, waiting for the other shoe to drop.

"Jack, I know you were invited to join Augusta."

"Oh."

"And you told them no."

"I did."

"No one in his right mind says no to that invitation."

"Well, I did." Jackson crossed his arms.

"C'mon, Jack."

"OK, OK."

Jackson got up from his seat and paced for a few moments, but he quickly returned to the warmth of the fire.

"It was the late eighties, around '88, I guess. Yes, you're right, I got the call that every golfer dreams about. They offered me a membership.

I couldn't believe it, and what's more, I couldn't believe how cheap it was. I figured it'd be a bloody fortune to join."

"The contract with CBS pays for a lot."

"So I've heard. Well, in any case, I didn't see the point."

"Why not, for God's sake? Any sane person would kill for that!"

"Wish, I wasn't about to join any club that my best friend couldn't join. Don't you remember? They didn't invite the first African American until what, '90?"

"I see," Wish said, smiling. He considered this for a moment until hitting upon another thought. "But, you could have joined after that."

"Don't think it works that way. And to tell you the truth, even if it did, think about it. I'm gonna be a member and what, you're gonna be my caddie there? I don't think so. It would have been a bit too much déjà vu for my taste."

"So, you turned them down, and on top of it, you didn't tell anyone."

"What would telling anyone have accomplished?"

The two sat in silence for a minute, their cigars just about finished. Finally, Wish startled his friend with an outstretched fist.

"Thanks, buddy."

They bumped fists.

"No problem. You would have done the same thing."

No response was forthcoming from Wish.

"Did you hear me? You would have done the same thing, right?"

Still nothing.

"Wish?"

"I'm thinking, I'm thinking."

They both laughed.

———

From an article in the April 2003 issue of *Golf Digest*, written by Jeremy Tuthill:

> One of the more interesting stories of this year's Masters is the tale of its most unlikely contestant, 53-year-old Aloysius "Wish" Fitzgerald. One of the few African Americans ever to play in the tournament, his road to Augusta likely qualifies as the most unusual in the long, storied history of this treasured tournament.
>
> I first met Wish back in 1983. He was in his thirties, a journeyman driving-range professional who, like so many other wannabes, was struggling on the back roads of professional golf's developmental tour. Like his fellow competitors,

his holy grail was a PGA Tour card, and the path to that achievement was through Q School.

Wish was known on the developmental tour as a diamond in the rough, an extraordinary long-ball striker who also possessed tremendous skills around the green but was flat-out pathetic once he actually made it onto the green. In fact, he was a terribly ineffective putter until just before Q School, when he experienced some sort of mysterious epiphany that turned him into the second coming of Ben Crenshaw.

Wish qualified for his card at Q School that November, despite having to play through a serious illness in the middle of the tournament. Sadly, life then threw Wish Fitzgerald a monstrous curveball.

The night before Wish was to leave his home in Georgia for his first PGA tournament at Pebble Beach, he was shot during a botched robbery at his business. The gunshot practically destroyed the young man's left arm. In the blink of an eye, this lifelong golfer's career, his dream of playing on the Tour, his ability to play even recreational golf—everything—was destroyed.

Wish has gone on to have an excellent business career, helping Albert Jameson, his father-in-law, grow his little country driving range into two modern and successful businesses near Augusta,

Georgia. And despite his wealth, he actually caddies at the course he has worshiped since childhood—you guessed it, Augusta National.

But deep down, Wish never lost his love for the simple act of actually playing the game. You see, Wish is a natural lefty who was forced to learn to play the game as a right-hander with mismatched, discarded clubs he found during his teenaged years, when he worked as a caddie at a country club in Connecticut. In his late forties came another epiphany, when he decided to try playing as a lefty. Although often painful as hell, it worked, and last July, as you may have heard, astonishingly—improbably—Wish Fitzgerald won the Greater Hartford Open.

In the months since, no one has heard or seen anything of this enigmatic man. Sadly, the only news to report was the death of his father-in-law, business partner, and caddie, Albert Jameson. Just another roadblock for this man to overcome.

More than likely, this will be the only mention of Wish Fitzgerald at this year's Masters. Despite his win on the Tour last year, and even considering he knows this course better than most, it is highly improbable that he'll make the cut to play the weekend, let alone contend for the title. But I can tell you that this reporter, along with the few others who are familiar with the trials and *tribulations of Wish Fitzgerald, will be rooting for him to do as well as possible and most of all, to enjoy the experience.*

———

Chapter 18

In order to preserve his health for the four days of the actual tournament, Wish had made the unusual and risky decision to skip the days of practice rounds and the traditional par-three tournament on Wednesday. As a result, it was Thursday morning, April 10, 2003, when Wish and Jackson turned off the nondescript Washington Road in Augusta, Georgia, and drove through the main gate at Augusta National Golf Club.

The drive down Magnolia Lane, the driveway to the clubhouse, is reserved for use by a privileged few. Only tournament participants, officials, club members, and the members' guests are allowed to use the hallowed entrance. Only 330 yards in length, it is a drive that is prized and dreamed about by all professional golfers.

Remembering Albert's instructions, Wish did his best to drink in the experience, making note of each of the sixty-one magnolia trees that flanked the roadway and blocked the sunshine that morning. His first thought was random: he noted the fact that the trees had been planted way back in 1850. As Jackson quietly concentrated on driving the car, Wish's private reverie continued.

He thought about Albert, certainly, and how much he would have loved this ride. Next, the long journey that had brought him to this moment in time. Lastly, as the bright yellow flowers that comprised the giant map of the United States that is the famous Augusta National logo came into view, he thought of his mother, who he knew would be tuned into the broadcast from her home in Greensboro. He hoped against hope that he might get some air time so she could see him in action.

At that moment, arriving at the clubhouse itself, his attitude changed. *Oh, she'll see me*, he thought. *She'll see a ton of me, right through to Sunday evening, when that kid Tiger Woods helps me on with the green jacket.*

The car doors opened, Jackson popped the trunk, and the two friends emerged from the car.

"Let's win this thing," Wish said.

"Let's," Jackson responded.

The sixty-year-old black gentleman who helped Jackson remove the golf bag from the trunk smiled. He had never met Wish, but he and everyone else who worked at Augusta knew his story. Given that, his smile was born not of derisive skepticism, but of pride. Wish was one of them; he had a lot of fans, both black and white, in the clubhouse this week.

———

The weather at any golf course can have a big effect on scoring. Wind and rain make the game of golf more challenging; calm, dry conditions are conducive to low scores, but the drier the greens are, the faster and more difficult they are. Rainy conditions preceded the opening round of the 2003 Masters, making the greens much more receptive to approach shots and much easier to putt. With the weather conditions that Thursday—calm and sunny—the television commentators had the temerity to label the course at Augusta National as "defenseless."

Wish had wondered which players he would be joining for the first two rounds. One was a young Danish phenom who played principally on the European Tour; the other was a thirty-year-old journeyman golfer from the PGA Tour who had not yet won on the Tour but had earned sufficient money during the previous year to qualify for the Masters. Wish was relieved to find that he knew neither golfer, leading him to believe that it would be easier to concentrate on his game and less on being social with his fellow competitors.

All three golfers were playing in the Masters for the first time, and, since they were relatively unknown to the American golf audience, Wish was sure that they'd have a tiny gallery following them. Good. That would make it easier to concentrate.

The threesome drew an early afternoon tee time. By that time, a number of golfers had already finished their first round. For those just teeing off, the news was already discouraging. The scores were indeed very low, with some of the most famous golfers in the world already atop the leaderboard.

"Hey, there's no stopping you from following suit," Jackson said, trying to encourage his golfer.

"Not likely," Wish said with a frown. "Look at those names. Mostly the young guns, the long hitters. Need some wind, maybe some rain, to challenge those boys, because we both know that there's no way I can match their length."

Wish had planned to remain calm and under control during this first round. Instead, as he stood on the first tee ready to—finally—hit his first shot at the Masters, he felt as if his heart was beating somewhere close to his mouth.

"Relax," he thought, not realizing that he was also saying it out loud.

Good luck with that, thought Jackson.

The tee shot was decidedly not according to plan. With his adrenaline pumping, Wish swung too hard. Hoping to hit the ball close to 275 yards down the left side of the fairway on the slight dogleg right, he failed to make clean contact and left the ball short of the bunker on the right side of the fairway.

Having been the last of the group to tee off, Wish growled and immediately began walking quickly up the fairway. The much shorter Jackson, burdened by the heavy golf bag, practically had to jog to keep up.

Wish now had no chance to reach the green on this par-four hole in regulation. On in three, he two-putted for a bogey.

"Not good," Wish grumbled to no one in particular.

The next few holes were played in a similar funk. After six holes, Wish was four over. A tremendous score for a really good country club golfer, but not in this tournament, against the best in the world, on a day when the course was "defenseless."

With his tunnel vision in full force, Wish failed to notice that, surprisingly, his threesome did have a small gallery following them. And interestingly enough, the face of that gallery was black.

Just about every aspect of the Masters experience, especially for the fans, is uniquely Augusta National. The ticket holders are not "fans." At Augusta National, they are *always* to be referred to as "patrons." And God help the reporter or CBS announcer who forgets that, because such a mistake can lead to being banned from the coverage.

Food, beverages, and souvenirs are exceptionally reasonably priced. No cell phones or cameras are allowed on the course. Patrons are better dressed and better behaved than at other

PGA tournaments. Rarely will you hear the obnoxious and sadly ubiquitous shouting of "Get in the hole" by the drunks at other tournaments who want to tell their friends "Didya hear me on TV?"

For golf lovers, walking the grounds of Augusta National is the summit of one's involvement with the sport. Tickets to the Masters are among the hardest to come by in the world of major sporting events. By contrast, it's relatively easy to see the world's best golfers at the many annual PGA tournaments taking place from New York to Hawaii and even to get tickets to major tournaments such as the US Open and the PGA. For the Masters, though, families actually will their annual tickets down through generations. If anyone is caught scalping, either outside the grounds or on such sites as Craigslist or eBay, the privilege is yanked away from them by the powers that be at Augusta National.

But it is possible, if you know someone, and for a hefty price, to get tickets. And somehow, some way, three or four dozen folks from Waynesboro and Greensboro, friends of the Fitzgeralds and the Jamesons and employees of Jameson Golf, most of whom had never attended the Masters or any other golf tournament, were on the grounds of Augusta National today.

Even in the days of the rising black phenom known as Tiger, golf audiences were white, and the patrons at Augusta National were even whiter. But the group following Wish Fitzgerald and his fellow competitors, *that* group of at least fifty "patrons" was of a different hue altogether. And while they might have started the round as sedate as the other patrons, after an hour or so on the golf course, it became a whole different story.

This was a vocal bunch, composed of folks who were there to cheer on their friend and hero, no matter how he was playing. Many were public golf course (commonly called "muni," for municipal) players, others played most of their golf at the local driving range, and many had never held a golf club in their hands. But Wish here, now Wish was their boy.

While Wish was so focused that he was oblivious to their presence, the other two golfers, their caddies, and Jackson were well aware of it. The thirty-year-old was annoyed by the atmosphere, Jackson was enjoying every minute of it, and the poor Danish guy didn't quite know what to make of the somewhat raucous scene.

"Nice shot, blondie!" one of the patrons in the gallery yelled at one point. "You kinda cute!"

But mostly, the words were ones of encouragement for Wish, who acknowledged none of them.

"Don't get down on yourself, son!"

"Show 'em summa those trick shots, Wish! You remember them tricks ya used to do!"

"That man taught me how to play golf!"

"You can't play no golf, girl!"

"Well, I can putt! Right, Lucas? Tell the girl I can putt the ball! That's golf, ain't it?"

Exclamation points ruled the day.

As much as the gallery entertained Jackson, he was worried about Wish and searching for a way to help. His friend seemed to be intent on beating himself up mentally, inwardly cursing stroke after mishit stroke. This approach, of course, merely resulted in Wish beating himself on the golf course. He was as tight as could be, trying to prove to himself and others that he belonged here, while at the same time trying to catch up to the multitude of seemingly streaking golfers whose names were above his on the leaderboard.

The thirteenth hole at Augusta National is the third of the three holes that comprise "Amen Corner," the most famous stretch of golf holes in the world. Named "Azalea" for the magnificent beauty of the many azaleas that are usually in bloom at this corner during the Masters, the hole presents one of the most infamous risk/reward decisions in the game. The hole is not overly long, so long hitters can easily reach the green on this par five in two shots. However, that choice can be disastrous. The small green is protected in front by Rae's Creek, which has claimed more than its share of the best golfers' balls. The drama commonly plays out during the often tense battles between the leaders on Sunday. Many a dream of victory has been drowned in Rae's Creek.

In the months leading up to this day, Wish had highlighted the decision that would have to be made on the second shot here many times. "When I was young, it would have been an easy decision," he had said. "I had the length back then, and I would have gone for the green in two to try for the eagle. But not now. If I'm dumb enough to try a stunt like that today, I deserve the consequences."

Wish's first shot on thirteen was good enough, but it left him with a daunting 250-yard shot to reach the middle of the green. At that point in the round, Wish was already +7, thirteen strokes behind the leader, Mark O'Meara. Based on what Jackson had heard Wish say about this very situation, he was confident that the golfer would lay up well in front of the creek. He reached for the five iron to hand it to Wish.

"Gimme the five wood," Wish said, hand out, staring intently toward the green.

"But—"

"The five wood."

Jackson took his hand off the iron, extracted the five wood from the bag, and put it in Wish's hand. When Wish pulled it away, he met resistance for a second before Jackson released the club. The caddie was trying to send a message, but the golfer refused to acknowledge it.

Predictably, the shot didn't come close to making it. Rae's Creek had won again. Wish was disgusted with himself.

After the penalty stroke and drop in the fairway, Wish pitched a decent shot onto the green and two-putted for a bogey. Another shot lost to par. Wish was at +8 through thirteen holes on his first round of the Masters. He had dug himself a hole that was so deep it almost didn't matter how well he played on Friday. Making the cut and playing the weekend was already looking like an impossible goal.

With the threesome ahead of them still waiting to hit their second shots from the fairway ahead, Wish's group was forced to wait a few minutes on the fourteenth tee. Jackson decided to use the opportunity to speak up.

"I've got an idea," Jackson said, addressing the still-seething Wish for about the first time during the round.

"Oh, you do, do you?" Wish responded sarcastically.

"Yes I do, numb nuts."

Wish actually did a double take at this impertinence.

"Numb nuts?"

"Oh, did I say numb nuts? What I meant to say was knucklehead."

A slight smile cracked Wish's irritability, giving Jackson the courage to go for the gusto.

"How about you stop trying to be Tiger Woods and start being Wish Fitzgerald?"

Wish glared at his friend for few moments. Gradually the glare changed to a blank stare.

It was then that Jackson realized that he had succeeded in penetrating his friend's artificially tough rind. Wish was considering what he had said.

"You all of a sudden trying to be a caddie?" Wish asked. "Or are you trying to channel Pop?"

"Little bit of both, I suppose," Jackson replied with a laugh. "How am I doing?"

Wish laughed. They were forced to cut the conversation short as they observed the other two golfers hitting their respective tee shots. Wish then pulled his driver out of the bag and began to set up for his shot.

"And by the way, I *have* been trying to be Tiger Woods," Wish said, looking down the fairway. "Him and Jack Nicklaus, Arnold Palmer, Sam Snead, and a few others."

Before hitting the ball, Wish looked back at his friend.

"But apparently that isn't working so well."

He hit a nice, controlled tee shot that landed in the middle of the fairway about 250 yards out and bounded forward for another thirty yards. Pleased with that result, he walked the few steps to his bag and replaced the driver.

"I think I'll try being Wish Fitzgerald for a while. What have I got to lose, right?"

The pair proceeded on down the fairway, with Jackson clearly struggling to keep up under the weight of the golf bag. Although short of breath, the smaller man nevertheless continued to drive the conversation.

"You're not enjoying this, are you?"

"I'm not here to enjoy myself, Jack."

"No? You've looked forward to this your entire life, and you're not going to enjoy it? Not too bright."

Wish had no answer for that. However, as they arrived at his ball, he noticed the gallery for the first time.

"What's going on?" he asked Jackson. "Who are all these people?"

"From what I can tell, they're here for you, Wish."

"I doubt that."

"Take a good look at the faces, Wish. You think they're here for Lars? They've been cheering for you the whole round."

Wish took a more encompassing look. He smiled when he spied Donna, Rachel, and the kids in the gallery.

"Holy cow. You know what, I think you're right!"

Jackson shook his head and muttered to himself.

"There's focused, and then there's oblivious."

———

Finally, Wish began to relax a bit. He stopped pressing. Once he did that, his "luck" completely changed.

He birdied the fourteenth, fifteenth, sixteenth, and seventeenth holes, all by getting on the green in regulation and one-putting. After parring the uphill 18th, he ended the round at +4, riding a newfound wave of confidence.

"Not gonna win anything, buddy, but at least I might not embarrass myself," Wish said as he settled back into the passenger seat of Jackson's car during the short drive home. "Might—just might—still make the cut tomorrow. It probably depends on the weather."

"Yep," Jackson responded. "C'mon, rain."

"Yeah, c'mon rain, and even more, c'mon wind. Hail, tornado, whatever. Make it *Wizard of Oz* time. Mess with their games, just one time. Just one time."

———

After dropping Wish off, Jackson drove another forty yards to his driveway and pulled into the garage. As soon as he turned the engine off, he wondered how Wish's arm was holding up.

At that same moment, Wish was standing outside the front door to his house, wincing as he felt more pain from his left arm. The day's adrenaline had worn off a couple of hours earlier, and the four ibuprofen tablets he had taken in the clubhouse hadn't yet kicked in full force. He made a mental note to take the pills again in the morning.

"Not so bad," he said to himself. *One more day. Better yet, three more days. Then you can fall off, for all I care.*

Chapter 19

True to his name, Wish awoke the next morning to find that he had gotten his wish for bad weather, in the form of a howling, chilly northeast wind. As a result, he and Jackson were both smiling broadly all the way to Augusta National.

Once again, Wish eschewed the driving range, choosing to spend all of his practice time on the putting green in order to get the most mileage possible out of his bad arm.

He noted that many of his fellow competitors were quieter and grumpier today. Was it the weather or the fact that many of them would not be seeing the weekend at Augusta National? Probably a little of both, he thought.

Several players wished him good luck in passing, and Wish actually returned the favor instead of answering with his usual self-absorbed grunt. This surprised more than one player who remembered Wish from the eighties.

As the two friends headed to the first tee, Wish realized that the previous day's load had been lifted from his shoulders, while Jackson clearly struggled a bit with his bag.

"How's the arm?" Jackson asked.

"It's faring a hell of a lot better than your body," Wish answered. "Sure you're up for more of this?"

"If it's *three* more days, I sure am," Jackson responded.

This time Wish immediately noticed the small, bundled-up crowd of friends and neighbors that flanked the first tee box. He grinned when he caught Donna's eye and tipped his cap to several of his employees.

Today, I'll give you a better show. Wish stepped up to his first tee shot of the day.

And remarkably, he managed to do just that.

While the near-constant wind frustrated and tortured his playing partners, Wish welcomed every thirty-mile-an-hour gust. He made sure that he played like Wish Fitzgerald rather than Tiger Woods. This meant that his shots were shorter but generally more accurate than the younger, stronger players. He played his shots low and under the wind, while the wind often pushed the higher shots of his competitors off-line and into the water or woods.

But most importantly, Wish was a short-game demon on this Friday in early April. If he did not manage to get on the green in regulation, he was virtually assured that his wedge shot would end close to the pin. Whether it was an approach shot or a putt, Wish used his knowledge of the greens to perfection. He even calculated the affect of the wind into his very few longer putts. As a result of all of this talent and strategy, he one-putted all but three greens and actually chipped in for a birdie on one of the remaining three.

Meanwhile, most of the rest of the field was coming back to Wish. No matter their talent or experience, those who had run away with especially low scores on Thursday struggled to keep close to par today. Two of the lesser known golfers who had started the day in the top ten actually matched Wish's near-disastrous +4 of the previous day.

At the close of play, three players had managed to shoot under par for the day. Fred Couples shot one under par and was now one shot behind the tournament leader, crafty veteran Vijay Singh, who had shot par for the day. Left-handed Canadian Mike Weir had played his way to -2 for the day and three shots off the lead.

The little-known fifty-three-year-old from Georgia, Wish Fitzgerald, shot a five-under-par sixty-seven, easily enabling him to make the cut at -1. Since he was now relatively close to Vijay Singh's tournament leading -5, Wish was actually, improbably, in the hunt for the title. Two more days of bad weather, and he just might be fitted for the green jacket of a Masters champion. The only problem was the weather forecast. Calm winds, fair skies…perfect weather for the weekend.

Remembering his performance at his previous press conference, Wish tried mightily to talk the Masters officials out of insisting that he appear before the press late Friday afternoon. Unfortunately, his score left them and him no choice. As he sat down at the table on the platform in the press room, his right foot immediately began a nervous tapping behind the table's skirting.

"Barry Culman, *Golf Magazine.* Were you surprised by how well you played today?"

Wish had decided in advance to take the time to carefully consider each answer before speaking. He figured that that way, even in the worst-case scenario, he might avoid making a fool of himself. So, as innocuous as he thought this first question was, he took a moment to debate just how to answer it.

"No, not really," he replied. His hubris elicited some chuckles from the assembled press, who clearly viewed Wish as a temporary oddity.

"David Melugin, Associated Press. How do you feel about making the cut?"

"Happy."

Another collective chuckle. Now, what had started as a bored "Let's ask him a couple of perfunctory questions and get on with the stars" press conference started to get a little livelier. This Wish guy had an attitude. The reporters began to shout out questions without the formality of giving their name. They actually interrupted each other.

"Wish, Wish! Do you think you actually have a chance this weekend?"

"Actually?"

"Yeah, do you think you have a chance?"

"To do what, win?" Loud laughter now.

"Yeah!" from the irritated reporter.

"Well, that depends."

"On what?"

"On how well I play."

The audience was eating this up.

"C'mon, Wish. Do you think you can win this?"

Wish paused for a few moments. *Oh, what the hell.*

"Yes, I do."

Wish had created a feeding frenzy. Modesty was clearly not one of his virtues. This guy beating Tiger Woods, Phil Mickelson, Ernie Els, Fred Couples, Vijay Singh? He must be kidding!

"You really think you can win? Why so confident?"

"I know the course, and I'm a good player."

"But you're the oldest guy to make the cut."

"So I hear."

"That doesn't bother you?"

"I have no choice in the matter."

"But what about your arm?"

"Again, I have no choice in the matter."

The conference went on for another ten minutes before an official put a stop to it, explaining that Tiger Woods was waiting in the wings. Still, several reporters followed Wish as he left the room. He did his best to be patient and polite with them, but after fifteen minutes, he excused himself. His arm was killing him, and he didn't want the press to see that.

Donna and Jackson were waiting with a special sleeve that had been kept on ice to help with the swelling and pain. Donna had called Dr. Jobe the day before, and Jackson had dispatched a staff member to pick up and deliver the sleeve to Augusta National. Wish began to feel a little relief almost immediately.

"Dr. Jobe's not happy with you," Donna reported.

"Can't say that I'm particularly giddy myself right now," Wish said as he grimaced.

"So…"

"So, I've got to finish this, honey. I appreciate what you guys did to get this for me; it feels great. Well, that's an exaggeration, but it helps. But even if this puppy is about to fall off, I'm gonna see how far it can take me."

"You're sure about this?" Jackson asked, only to receive a dead-serious stare from his friend.

"He's sure," Jackson said to Donna.

The next morning, Wish discovered that he was again an instant celebrity, although this time on a much grander scale than after he had won the Greater Hartford Open. So many reporters approached him as he arrived and later walked from the clubhouse to the putting green that officials from Augusta National had to fend them off. His impromptu remarks at the press conference had caused people to take notice of him, bad arm, aged body, and all. According to some members of the press, he now had fans from all over the world interested in his progress.

Wish's story even merited the attention of the CBS announcers.

Jim Nantz: "Wish Fitzgerald, the local guy. Interesting name, interesting fellow. Fifty-three years old and a caddie here at Augusta National. And to top it off, he's got a Fortune 500 CEO on his bag. Somehow, he managed to make the cut, with room to spare. Now, there's a story we'll be following this weekend."

Lanny Wadkins: "This guy was something else at his press conference yesterday. Best round of the day, despite the terrible conditions. Cocky as all get out. As a caddie here, he has the benefit of knowing this course, Jim."

Jim Nantz: "So, what's your take on this? Do you think we'll find Wish Fitzgerald among the leaders here tomorrow afternoon?"

Lanny Wadkins: "That would make a great story, but to be honest, it's not gonna happen. Sunday at the Masters almost always boils down to the biggest names in the game. Guys like Ernie, Phil, Vijay, and of course the new kid on the block, Tiger. Wish Fitzgerald had an impressive day yesterday, but Saturday is 'moving day,' and I'd be very surprised if he manages to do anything positive with the spotlight on him. Hate to say it, but history says that he's had his one day in the sun. Good story, though. I wish him the best."

While Wish was oblivious to the mounting media attention, he definitely noticed that there was a larger gallery following his twosome. He chalked that up to the fact that he was paired with the left-handed Canadian, Mike Weir. Wish's small posse of neighbors and friends was still there but far less noticeable among the hundred or so other "patrons."

Contrary to Wish's hopes, the day had dawned with sunny and relatively calm conditions. He ignored the lack of help from the weather and decided to stick with his game plan—playing within himself from tee to green and putting lights out.

His plan worked. Wish was able to shoot a stunning sixty-five, and at the end of the day, he found himself in second place, two shots behind the hottest golfer in the world—Tiger Woods. This meant that on Sunday he would be paired with Tiger and his legendarily large and loyal gallery.

Judging from the questions at the press conference (which had double the number of press denizens compared to the previous afternoon), the only person who wasn't in shock over this development was Wish himself.

"Can you catch Tiger?"

"Hey, I'm a golf fan like everyone else," Wish said. "I know all about Tiger Woods. He's a tremendous young golfer, great for the game. But c'mon now, he's two strokes ahead. Pretty sure he's a human being. So, we'll see. And guess what? There'll be a bunch of other great golfers out there tomorrow too."

"How's the arm, Wish?

"It's still there."

"Does it hurt?"

"Like I said, it's still there."

In reality, the pain had reached the point where it was almost debilitating. Each day's adrenaline had helped him get through, but as the tournament wore on, the pain was stronger while the adrenaline was naturally less and less a factor. This had become a matter of mind over matter.

Wish knew that there were stronger painkillers available to him, but he feared that they would have a negative effect on his mind and thus his game. The weekend of the Masters was no time to be experimenting with drugs, no matter how logical it would be to try them under normal circumstances.

At this point, he had only two choices: quit or play through the increasing pain. Anyone who knew Wish knew what his decision would be.

The pain did not diminish once he got home that evening. He could not find a position in bed that was remotely comfortable, so Wish resorted to sleeping in his La-Z-Boy recliner, the one that Donna had been trying unsuccessfully for years to get him to throw out.

No matter how hard he tried, between the pain and his racing mind, there was little sleep to be had that night.

The next day, Wish and Donna were joined for a big breakfast by Jackson, Rachel, and Annie. The kids were still sleeping.

Donna had gone all out with this morning's spread: scrambled eggs, bacon, sausage, pancakes with syrup, and homemade biscuits. As worried as she was about Wish's condition, she wanted him to enter the afternoon's fray with at least a good breakfast. It was all she could do at this point.

With Wish looking like hell, it was left to the now wheelchair-bound Annie to express what was on everyone's mind.

"You don't look so good, son. You sure this is a good idea?"

"Can't say that I ever look good, Momma," Wish said, attempting to fend off the subject.

"Don't patronize me, Aloysius," Annie responded. "There's not a person in this family who's happy about what you're doing to your body right now. It's downright foolish, if you ask me, risking that bad arm of yours for... what? A golf tournament? Just what are you looking for, son?"

Donna and Jackson looked off into the distance.

"Maybe I just want to make you proud of me, Momma."

"Well, if that isn't the biggest load of non-sense I've heard in a while, I don't know what is," Annie retorted, slapping the table for good measure. "I couldn't be more proud of you if you were the president of the United States! You're a wonderful family man and husband, although God knows it took you a while to straighten out in that department. And look what you've done with your business! Who would have dreamed we'd all be living in such grand style?

"No, son, you don't have to win a silly sports event to make me proud of you. No, sir."

"Well, it's just one more day, Momma. I can hold up for that long."

"I surely hope so."

The subject was closed, at least as far as Wish was concerned. Annie, however, continued to shake her head and mutter "Foolish!" every few minutes until Wish and Jackson could make their escape to Jackson's car for the ride to Augusta National.

———

The two friends rode halfway in silence. Jackson didn't want to disturb his player's concentration, but finally, he spoke up.

"They've got a point, you know."

"Who's 'they'?"

"Your mother, Donna, Dr. Jobe," Jackson answered. "And, to a lesser extent, I suppose, me."

"Yeah, but it's my body, right?"

Two more minutes of silence ensued before Jackson again broached the subject.

"So, why exactly are you taking such a risk?"

"You don't know, Jack? I thought you, of all people, would understand."

"Enlighten me."

"I want the jacket."

"Oh, c'mon."

"No, really. I want Tiger to put that green jacket on me, on national television, in the Butler Cabin."

Jackson, nodded, still listening as he tried to concentrate on his driving.

"I've been watching the Masters for at least forty years, Jack. I've seen that stupid ceremony at least forty times now. And yes, I get it, when everyone says, 'It's just a jacket!'

"But that's the point, Jack. It's *not* 'just a jacket.' Not at all. Every golfer who cares about this game at all watches the Masters on Sunday. And I guarantee you, every one of them—*every* one—doesn't turn his TV off until he has watched that innocuous ceremony in the Butler Cabin.

"Why? Because the guy who puts on the green jacket, at that moment, that guy is the best golfer in the world, Jack. I know, maybe not in the world rankings, but in the minds of golfers everywhere—in my mind, for sure—he's it. He's number one."

Jackson found himself nodding again, this time in agreement.

"From the time I was, what, twelve years old? I've dreamed about this. And no matter what happened in all the years since, deep down, I always believed that I could be, or was, or should have been, that guy.

"This is the only shot I'll ever have at this, Jack, and I'll do whatever it takes to win.

"I'm going to be in Butler Cabin tonight, Jack, and Tiger's going to help me on with the green jacket. And I'm going to be number one. Finally."

———

From the opening minutes of the CBS coverage of Sunday's action at the 2003 Masters Golf Tournament:

Jim Nantz: Lanny, as is typical of Sunday at the Masters, it sure looks like we'll be in for a real treat this afternoon. I'm sure none of our viewers is surprised to see the usual cast of the best golfers in the world atop the leader board, especially the hottest figure in sports—Tiger Woods. But I don't think anyone expected to see the guy who is playing with him in today's final pairing, Wish Fitzgerald.

Lanny Wadkins: That's an understatement, Jim. Who would have expected Aloysius "Wish" Fitzgerald, a fifty-three-year-old, former caddie, driving range pro, nonprofessional, with an injured arm that caused him to switch from playing right-handed to left-handed and has him in constant pain, to be neck and neck with Tiger? I sure didn't.

Jim Nantz: So, I'll ask you again. Do you give him a chance to be wearing the green jacket when all is said and done late this afternoon?

Lanny Wadkins: Like I said before, that would make a great story. But I can't help but believe that reality has to set in today. He's old, by golf standards. No one even close to his age has won this tournament.

He's never experienced pressure like this, and there's nothing in golf like the back nine at Augusta National on Sunday of the Masters. He's playing in a twosome with Tiger, who will be followed by a crowd that promises to be loudly behind the superstar and maybe even a little hostile to Wish. He's in a lot of pain from an arm that was so seriously damaged by a gunshot that it's a miracle that he's even playing golf, let alone the Masters. And like you said, there's a bunch of the world's top golfers nipping at his heels, eager to compete with Tiger for the green jacket.

Jim Nantz: Not to mention the fact that when Tiger has the lead on Sunday, he doesn't relinquish it.

Lanny Wadkins: That, too. Bottom line? It's been a great and improbable run for Mr. Wish Fitzgerald, but I have to say, there's virtually no chance that he's going to be wearing the green jacket this evening.

———

Tiger and Wish, along with their caddies, arrived at the first tee on Sunday afternoon, the eyes of hundreds of patrons and millions of television viewers watching their every move. As much as they would have loved to, none of the viewers could hear the brief conversation that took place as they shook hands.

"I hear from some of the older guys that you were kind of a legend back in the day," Tiger said. "I guess if you hadn't had that accident, you might have been me."

"Oh, I wouldn't call it an 'accident,'" Wish responded along with a forced smile of his own. "And if you think about it, it would have been the other way around: you'd be trying to be me.

"But thanks for the memories. And good luck."

As the competitors turned away from other, Jackson handed Wish his driver.

"A not-so-subtle attempt at intimidation," Jackson commented.

Wish merely shrugged, his focus already on his upcoming tee shot.

If it was *a shot at intimidation, sure looks like it backfired on him,* Jackson thought.

———

Once again, Wish and Jackson were oblivious to what the CBS commentators were saying about Wish's chances. What was impossible to ignore, however, was the amazing size and fervor of the gallery following their twosome. The two friends had been pleasantly surprised by the galleries that had cheered Wish on during the first three days of the tournament. Today, Wish's fans were engulfed by the Tiger Woods crowd, growing the size of the gallery perhaps a hundredfold.

Fortunately, Wish had entered his Zen-like, tunnel-vision mentality. Hole after hole, he successfully tuned out the mayhem surrounding him, instead concentrating on his game. His drives were dozens of yards shorter than his playing competitor, but at the same time, they also ended up in the middle of the fairway. Oftentimes, his placement was accurate enough to present Wish with just the right angle from which he could attack the pin.

Wish's approach shots to the extremely challenging Sunday pin placements were as crisp and accurate as ever. Following this up with his uncannily accurate putting on the treacherous greens, Wish was able to produce three birdies and six pars on the front nine.

Wish was not crumbling under the pressure. In fact, he wasn't feeling the pressure at all.

Instead, the golfers who *were* withering under the pressure of Sunday at the Masters were the handful of world-famous professionals who had started the day within a couple of shots of the two leaders, Wish and Tiger. One by one, their aggressive attempts to turn pars into birdies and birdies into eagles failed, causing them to fall out of contention. By the time the final pair had reached the back nine, the only two golfers still realistically in the hunt for the green jacket were Tiger and Wish.

While Wish was shooting -3 on the front nine due to his conservative, yet accurate play, Tiger matched that score with his aggressive, gambling style of play. This resulted in an eagle, three birdies, three pars, and two bogeys. It was great theater, both for the thousands of patrons at Augusta National and the millions of fans watching the action around the world.

So, after nine holes, Wish remained two strokes behind Tiger. Amazingly (to everyone but Wish), he was still within shooting distance.

Adding to the drama was the obvious pain Wish was experiencing (no matter that he was under the impression that he was disguising it well). Shot after shot, the CBS cameras and any nearby patrons could see the pain etched on Wish's face. Jackson, on the other hand, was close enough to hear the grunts of agony that many shots elicited. Even Tiger Woods, well-known for his aloof attitude toward some of those with whom he was playing, was once caught on camera wincing in reaction to Wish's pain.

The group reached the legendary "Amen Corner" area of the course—holes eleven, twelve, and thirteen—still separated by two shots on the scoreboard. So often through the decades, this was where championship dreams were realized or destroyed. Wish was running out of holes to catch Tiger, but his conservative approach was not conducive to coming from behind. He decided to stick with his game plan and hope that Tiger would blink first.

Impressed as he was by his friend's amazing performance against such long odds, Jackson was growing increasingly worried about Wish's health. Wish was handling the stress of the competition admirably. From Jackson's perspective, however, it looked like the pain was at the point where it might overwhelm him.

At several points during the round, Jackson had been able to see Donna and Rachel in the gallery. Where he expected to see joy at how well Wish was competing, instead, Jackson detected nothing but concern for the state of Wish's health.

The competitors arrived at the tee box for the twelfth hole, a short par three named "Golden Bell." This hole is one of the most photographed and painted in the world. Many a golfer's office has a framed representation on his or her wall.

With the traditional Sunday pin placement in the front right portion of the green, the temptation is always to aim for the pin. Leaving such a shot just a little short, or using too much backspin, quite often also results in a visit for the golf ball to Rae's Creek. A longer tee shot that ends in one of the two bunkers behind the green leads to a treacherous and delicate second shot that too often rolls rapidly downhill, right across the slick green and into Rae's Creek. So precision off the tee is a must, and precision is especially difficult given the pressure a golfer is under on Sunday at the Masters.

On the tee, leaning close to his friend, Wish took the opportunity to confide in Jackson. "I'm not sure I'm gonna make it."

"Yeah, I can tell," Jackson answered. "It's getting to be too much, isn't it?"

"Pretty close."

"Seven more holes, Wish."

"We'll see."

Wish's tee shot landed in the white sand of the front bunker, just a few feet from the hole. Not great, but not a bad position to be in on this dangerous hole.

Tiger's shot ended up in the rough just a foot or two from the back left of the green. Again, safe, but a very tricky "up and down" to make par.

The golfers and their caddies crossed the Nelson Bridge, named after another legendary golfer, Byron Nelson, on their way to their balls. Tiger's cautious chip shot curved quickly from left to right down the slippery slope of the green, coming to rest uncomfortably close to the front of the green (and water), five feet below the hole. The many hundreds of spectators had collectively held their breath and now exhaled and applauded in unison.

Wish now swung hard into the sand behind his ball, popping it up through the air to a sure-footed landing just inches from the pin. The audience exploded in applause at this display of dexterity, just as Wish almost collapsed from the agony of his wedge's contact with the sand. Biting his lower lip, Wish handed the club to Jackson in return for his putter.

After the two golfers successfully completed their par putts, the group headed to the next tee. Huffing and puffing, Jackson hustled to catch up with Wish. Jackson had decided that he had to try something—anything—to help his friend through this.

"That was a rough one," Jackson said.

"Yeah, the sand shots. For some reason, those are the ones that hurt the most."

"Well, then don't hit anything in the damn bunkers in the first place, numbskull," Jackson retorted, using his best, high-pitched impersonation of Albert. "That takes care of that!"

Surprised, Wish did a double take.

"Tell me that you didn't say what I thought you said," he responded, laughing.

"Well, damn it, somebody's got to set your ass straight, fool," Jackson continued, throwing in Albert's facial contortions for good measure.

"Stop it, you're killing me," Wish begged, now laughing so hard that it was difficult to catch his breath.

"Whatchyou talkin' 'bout, Willis?" Jackson/Albert's octave was now approaching the soprano range. "I'm the one who's dead. You're just the damn fool who got himself in position to win the freakin' Masters."

Wish loved every bit of this. Gone was his focus on the pain, even if for just these few moments.

"Talkin' 'bout killin' me,'" Jackson continued. "To a damn dead man! Does that make even the slightest bit of sense to you? Does it?"

The long, downhill, par-five thirteenth hole, a dogleg left known as Azalea, was tailor-made for Tiger's length off the tee and gambling style of play. The first to tee off, Tiger crushed his shot down the hill and around the dogleg. A perfect shot—he could now go for the green and an eagle, thus adding to his lead. Tiger was surely confident that with his opponent's relative lack of length off the tee, Wish would be forced to lay up and go for the green in three. The best Wish could hope for would be a birdie, so White Dogwood had the potential to live up to its reputation as a turning point.

Wish was the first to strike his second shot, and, true to form, he did lay up well short of Rae's Creek, which once again guarded the green. All eyes were now on Tiger, who hit a beautifully accurate three iron that zeroed in on the pin like a laser. Tiger's only problem was that shooting at the pin on this green, on this day, was exactly the wrong thing to do.

A loud roar rose from the huge gallery. Tiger's approach shot had actually struck the pin a few inches above the hole, and the ball ricocheted straight back into Rae's Creek. Tiger would now be now forced to drop a new ball on the green side of the creek and, with the penalty, was shooting four. Wish was in the catbird's seat.

Wish first hit his wedge shot to within a few feet of the pin. The group then walked across the picturesque Hogan Bridge, named after the legendary Ben Hogan, to arrive at one of the most beautiful settings in the world of golf. Spectacularly colorful azaleas formed the backdrop for the green, but neither golfer paused to drink in this beauty. Instead, Tiger chipped close to the hole, and each man sank his putt, giving Wish a par and Tiger a bogey. Wish was now within one of tying for the lead.

Through the fourteenth and fifteenth holes, the tension remained unabated. A total of four pars between the two golfers kept Tiger one ahead of Wish on the leader board. Wish continued to grimace with pain on nearly every shot, while Tiger either looked the other way or sometimes winced along with his playing partner. More than once, Tiger actually shook his head in admiration at the fact that the old man was matching him shot for shot, hole after hole. Nevertheless, there was still no discourse between the two.

The television cameras, as well as those patrons fortunate enough to have reserved spots close enough to view the facial expressions of the two warriors, took all of this in. This was certainly owning up to the high drama expected of Sunday afternoon at the Masters.

What the cameras also took in was the fact that Wish and his caddie were often seen laughing. Given the seriousness of the situation and the apparent physical test Wish was experiencing, even the commentators remarked on this turn of events.

Lanny Wadkins: I'm not sure what's going on between the two of them, but they sure seem to be having a good time.

Jim Nantz: If we weren't still witnessing the obvious pain caused by most of Wish's swings, one would have to wonder if he's suddenly found a miracle cure.

Lanny Wadkins: At one point about a half hour ago, I thought he was about to pass out. He certainly has bounced back. This is some show these two guys are putting on.

Jim Nantz: Some show, indeed.

The group now arrived at the tee box for the sixteenth hole, named Redbud. Again, the pin placement on this par three over water was always in the same place on Sunday. Tiger and many of the other golfers in the field had played it a number of times and knew just where to land their shots on the green in order to start the ball on its long, circuitous path down to the hole. Wish had played the hole a grand total of three times, but he, too, was well familiar with where he needed to hit his shot. He had walked and studied this green many more times than any of the other golfers, including Tiger.

Tiger elected the dangerous option of shooting at the pin, applying backspin to stop the ball in the right spot. His gamble backfired, and the ball rolled just off the green, leaving him an exceedingly challenging putt on this famously tricky green.

Wish's tee shot landed exactly on the spot where he had aimed and then began its long, agonizingly slow, semicircular curl toward the hole. The noise from the jam-packed gallery swelled as the ball wound its way on a seemingly crazy path, but it was headed on just the right path. The ball came to rest on the very lip of the hole, almost touching the pin. The audience was initially torn between holding its breath and "oohing," but once it was apparent that the ball wasn't going to drop in, a roar rose up that seemingly created ripples on the glassy surface of the pond. It was hard to tell whether the resultant applause was more a testament to the quality of the shot or relief that their hero Tiger wasn't going to have a hole-in-one thrown at him this late in the round.

Once the group reached the green, Wish looked to Tiger for his OK that he tap his ball into the cup (rather than marking and waiting for Tiger's putt). Tiger quickly indicated his agreement, and the crowd again erupted with approval at the result of Wish's brilliant, pressure-packed shot.

Tiger's putt was not an easy one, but he did succeed in carefully guiding the ball to within a foot of the cup, followed by an easy putt for par.

The score was now tied, with two holes left in the tournament.

Chapter 20

As is so often the case on Sunday at the Masters, it all came down to the 18th hole. If the two golfers remained tied after regulation, they would play as many additional holes as necessary in the fading light to produce a sudden-death winner.

But Wish had already reached the conclusion that this was a moot point. He knew that the tournament would end for him on this hole; there was simply nothing left in the tank. Somehow, some way, he *had* to birdie the hole and pray that Tiger did not do the same. There was no way he could hope that Tiger would slip enough to score a bogey.

Wish knew full well that history was against him. Only four golfers in the long history of the tournament had scored a birdie three on this final hole to win the tournament. In addition, this formerly fairly easy finishing hole had been lengthened just the year before to make it a tougher test of golf for modern golfers and their equipment. In addition to being longer, the fairway was steeply uphill and the elevated green was well-protected by large bunkers.

"Well, no matter what," Wish said to Jackson, "this is it. It's do or die, right here, right now."

Jackson well appreciated the gravity of the moment. In any case, he had run out of material to keep his friend smiling. He, too, had nothing left in the tank.

"Whatever. We're playing the 18th, aren't we?" Jackson said with a smile.

Wish laughed. "Yes, we are."

The tee shot on the 18th was now one of the more demanding shots on the course. A little right, and you'd be in the woods. A little left, and you might end up in a large bunker, not to mention the difficult angle from there to the green.

Apparently, Tiger was also eager to put an end to things on this hole. He wound up on his backswing as far as he could physically take his driver and unleashed a powerfully long drive. Unfortunately for him, it was off-line to the right, flirting with the tree line. He was now facing a real challenge on his second shot.

One more time, Wish stuck to his game plan. His tee shot, while much shorter than Tiger's, was superbly accurate—right in the middle of the fairway. *This damn pain is almost over*, he thought. *Make the next shot great. Just make it great.*

To give himself a chance for a birdie, Wish knew that he had to loft a shot 185 yards up the steep hill and land it softly, just over the deep front bunker. Wish summoned every bit of his knowledge and skill to strike a four iron that looked like it was going to barely clear the front bunker—a perfect shot. Instead, it just caught the top lip of the bunker and rolled back into the middle of the sand.

The sound from the immense gallery, which had been building to an expectant roar of approval, instead died a sudden death.

Wish and Jackson looked at each other with a mixture of disgust and dismay.

"This is gonna hurt," Wish said, handing the four iron to Jackson in exchange for his sand wedge.

"Yeah, but you're a fantastic player out of the sand," Jackson said. "You're gonna hole this one out."

"Sure I am," Wish responded, shaking his head at Jackson's words.

Just then, Tiger hit an eight iron from the edge of the woods. No one was at all surprised that he had salvaged the hole with an excellent, lofted shot to the back of the green. A par looked likely, but with Tiger's uncanny skill and famous flair for the dramatic finish, a birdie was a real possibility.

The two pairs of golfers and caddies began their walk up the steep incline toward the green, one of the most famous walks in golf. Thousands of fans flank the 18th fairway on Sunday. For any golfer still in contention to win the green jacket, the walk is perhaps the most memorable and emotional few minutes of his life.

Fifty yards ahead of Wish and Jackson, Tiger and his caddie approached the green. As expected, Tiger received his usual, well-deserved, loud standing ovation. He tipped his cap to the gallery.

Another ovation began to swell as Wish followed him up the fairway. He suddenly noticed that Jackson was not with him and turned to see his exhausted caddie struggling with the bag as he climbed the sharp incline. Wish waited for his friend to catch up.

The volume of the cheering continued to rise until it seemed like it had the decibel level of a jumbo jet on takeoff. The normally reserved, generally sophisticated patrons were clapping as hard as possible and hollering and whistling as loudly as they could.

"They love this kid," Wish shouted as Jackson caught up with him. "They should. He deserves it."

"You're an idiot," a winded Jackson shouted back. "Don't you realize who they're cheering for? This is for you!"

For the first time in the entire round, Wish looked all around him. *He may be right. Holy cow, I think they're cheering for the old guy!*

And Wish smiled—broadly. Jackson nudged him, indicating that he should acknowledge the ovation by at least tipping his cap. Wish took his cap off, stifling a crazy impulse to take a sweeping bow. The whole scene struck him as other-worldly.

As loud as the ovation had been, the silence as Wish studied his shot shuffled his feet into the sand of the bunker was equally amazing. Although thousands of people surrounded the green, it was as quiet as a library.

As Wish's wedge hit the sand behind his ball, he felt no pain whatsoever. The ball lofted sweetly over the lip of the bunker, bounced twice, rolled four more feet, bumped into the pin, and dropped softly into the cup. Wish had his birdie.

The sound that erupted was the loudest yet. Tiger, who had been studying his putt and not observing Wish's shot, knew immediately what that meant. He nodded almost imperceptibly.

Pros and their caddies avoid most demonstrative celebrations until after a round has concluded. Jackson, however, was not a professional caddie. As soon as Wish emerged from the bunker, his caddie smothered him with a big bear hug, his head on Wish's chest.

"Not yet!" Wish shouted in order to be heard above the roar of the gallery.

"We did it! Just don't expect me to do this again!"

Wish gave up on decorum. As the cheers continued, he hugged Jackson back, the two friends pounding each other on the back.

"Don't worry, I won't be doing this again!"

Finally, the two then stepped to the edge of the green to respectfully watch Tiger's attempt at matching Wish's birdie and forcing a playoff.

Tiger took minutes to study the putt from every angle. Meanwhile, Wish spied Donna, Rachel and the kids, standing with tournament officials a few yards off the green, directly behind Tiger. Wish and Donna locked onto each other.

As Tiger struck his putt, Wish continued to look past his opponent, focusing only on his wife.

———

In the rare event that a Masters champion repeats the accomplishment the next year, the viewing public wonders what will happen during the ensuing ceremony in the Butler Cabin. After all, the champion from the previous year is only present to help the winner don the green jacket of the Masters champion. The former champion is the new champion; he's already wearing the green jacket.

And Tiger Woods was there, wearing his green jacket. However, he had another jacket draped over his arms. Wish's green jacket.

The two men sat patiently through the formalities as Hootie Johnson, chairman of Augusta National, acknowledged the tournament officials and the low-scoring amateur, who was sitting next to Tiger and Wish. He asked a couple of questions of the amateur. Finally, Hootie offered his congratulations to Wish for playing "a courageous round of golf."

Now, it was time for some questions. Jim Nantz began. "First of all, let me add my congratulations, Wish. Hootie said it well. A courageous battle against a formidable foe."

"Tiger is a great competitor," Wish responded. "It took everything I had to beat this young man. He's great for the game of golf and deserves his reputation as the best golfer in the world."

Tiger smiled and nodded in response. Nantz continued. "I know you're a big fan of the Masters and Augusta National. Today's victory means that you can now play this tournament and this storied golf course for the rest of your life. Are you looking forward to that?"

"You have no idea."

Hootie now stood up, followed by the other men in the room. "Wish, it's now time for you to receive the green jacket. Tiger, would you please do the honor?"

Tiger helped Wish on with the jacket, saying that he hoped he wasn't causing any more pain.

"I'm not feeling any pain right now." Wish smiled.

Wish had often wondered what he'd be thinking when this moment finally came. He took a moment to button the jacket.

That's nice. It fits perfectly.

Made in the USA
Charleston, SC
30 March 2014